KU-360-581

Contents

Other books by F. SCOTT FITZGERALD
published by Alma Classics

F. Scott Fitzgerald (1896–1940)

Edward Fitzgerald,
Fitzgerald's father

Mary McQuillan Fitzgerald,
Fitzgerald's mother

Ginevra King

Zelda Fitzgerald

The Fitzgeralds' house in Montgomery, Alabama

The Fitzgeralds' grave in Rockville, Maryland,
inscribed with the closing line from *The Great Gatsby*

The original cover illustration for
Flappers and Philosophers

Flappers and Philosophers

The Offshore Pirate

1

THIS UNLIKELY STORY BEGINS on a sea that was a blue dream, as colourful as blue silk stockings, and beneath a sky as blue as the irises of children's eyes. From the western half of the sky the sun was shying little golden discs at the sea – if you gazed intently enough you could see them skip from wave tip to wave tip until they joined a broad collar of golden coin that was collecting half a mile out and would eventually be a dazzling sunset. About halfway between the Florida shore and the golden collar a white steam yacht, very young and graceful, was riding at anchor and under a blue-and-white awning aft a yellow-haired girl reclined in a wicker settee reading *The Revolt of the Angels*, by Anatole France.*

She was about nineteen, slender and supple, with a spoilt, alluring mouth and quick grey eyes full of a radiant curiosity. Her feet, stockingless and adorned rather than clad in blue satin slippers, which swung nonchalantly from her toes, were perched on the arm of a settee adjoining the one she occupied. And as she read she intermittently regaled herself by a faint application to her tongue of a half-lemon that she held in her hand. The other half, sucked dry, lay on the deck at her feet and rocked very gently to and fro at the almost imperceptible motion of the tide.

The second half-lemon was well-nigh pulpless and the golden collar had grown astonishing in width, when suddenly the drowsy silence which enveloped the yacht was broken by the sound of heavy footsteps and an elderly man topped with orderly grey hair and clad in a white flannel suit appeared at the head of the companionway. There

3

he paused for a moment until his eyes became accustomed to the sun, and then seeing the girl under the awning he uttered a long even grunt of disapproval.

If he had intended thereby to obtain a rise of any sort, he was doomed to disappointment. The girl calmly turned over two pages, turned back one, raised the lemon mechanically to tasting distance, and then very faintly but quite unmistakably yawned.

"Ardita!" said the grey-haired man sternly.

Ardita uttered a small sound indicating nothing.

"Ardita!" he repeated. "Ardita!"

Ardita raised the lemon languidly, allowing three words to slip out before it reached her tongue.

"Oh, shut up."

"Ardita!"

"What?"

"Will you listen to me – or will I have to get a servant to hold you while I talk to you?"

The lemon descended slowly and scornfully.

"Put it in writing."

"Will you have the decency to close that abominable book and discard that damn lemon for two minutes?"

"Oh, can't you lemme alone for a second?"

"Ardita, I have just received a telephone message from the shore—"

"Telephone?" She showed for the first time a faint interest.

"Yes, it was—"

"Do you mean to say," she interrupted wonderingly, "'at they let you run a wire out here?"

"Yes, and just now—"

"Won't other boats bump into it?"

"No. It's run along the bottom. Five min—"

"Well, I'll be darned! Gosh! Science is golden or something – isn't it?"

"Will you let me say what I started to?"

"Shoot!"

"Well, it seems... well, I am up here..." He paused and swallowed several times distractedly. "Oh, yes. Young woman, Colonel Moreland has called up again to ask me to be sure to bring you in to dinner. His son Toby has come all the way from New York to meet you and he's invited several other young people. For the last time, will you—"

"No," said Ardita shortly, "I won't. I came along on this darn cruise with the one idea of going to Palm Beach, and you knew it, and I absolutely refuse to meet any darn old colonel or any darn young Tobey or any darn old young people or to set foot in any other darn old town in this crazy state. So you either take me to Palm Beach or else shut up and go away."

"Very well. This is the last straw. In your infatuation for this man – a man who is notorious for his excesses, a man your father would not have allowed to so much as mention your name – you have reflected the demi-monde rather than the circles in which you have presumably grown up. From now on—"

"I know," interrupted Ardita ironically, "from now on you go your way and I go mine. I've heard that story before. You know I'd like nothing better."

"From now on," he announced grandiloquently, "you are no niece of mine. I—"

"O-o-o-oh!" The cry was wrung from Ardita with the agony of a lost soul. "Will you stop boring me! Will you go 'way! Will you jump overboard and drown! Do you want me to throw this book at you!"

"If you dare do any—"

Smack! *The Revolt of the Angels* sailed through the air, missed its target by the length of a short nose and bumped cheerfully down the companionway.

The grey-haired man made an instinctive step backward and then two cautious steps forward. Ardita jumped to her five feet four and stared at him defiantly, her grey eyes blazing.

"Keep off!"

"How dare you!" he cried.

"Because I darn please!"

"You've grown unbearable! Your disposition—"

"You've made me that way! No child ever has a bad disposition unless it's her family's fault! Whatever I am, you did it."

Muttering something under his breath, her uncle turned and, walking forward, called in a loud voice for the launch. Then he returned to the awning, where Ardita had again seated herself and resumed her attention to the lemon.

"I am going ashore," he said slowly. "I will be out again at nine o'clock tonight. When I return, we will start back to New York, where I shall turn you over to your aunt for the rest of your natural, or rather unnatural, life."

He paused and looked at her, and then all at once something in the utter childishness of her beauty seemed to puncture his anger like an inflated tyre and render him helpless, uncertain, utterly fatuous.

"Ardita," he said not unkindly, "I'm no fool. I've been round. I know men. And, child, confirmed libertines don't reform until they're tired – and then they're not themselves – they're husks of themselves." He looked at her as if expecting agreement, but receiving no sight or sound of it he continued. "Perhaps the man loves you – that's possible. He's loved many women and he'll love many more. Less than a month ago, one month, Ardita, he was involved in a notorious affair with that red-haired woman, Mimi Merril; promised to give her the diamond bracelet that the Tsar of Russia gave his mother. You know – you read the papers."

"Thrilling scandals by an anxious uncle," yawned Ardita. "Have it filmed. Wicked clubman making eyes at virtuous flapper. Virtuous flapper conclusively vamped by his lurid past. Plans to meet him at Palm Beach. Foiled by anxious uncle."

"Will you tell me why the devil you want to marry him?"

"I'm sure I couldn't say," said Ardita shortly. "Maybe because he's the only man I know, good or bad, who has an imagination and the courage of his convictions. Maybe it's to get away from the young fools

6

that spend their vacuous hours pursuing me around the country. But as for the famous Russian bracelet, you can set your mind at rest on that score. He's going to give it to me at Palm Beach – if you'll show a little intelligence."

"How about the... red-haired woman?"

"He hasn't seen her for six months," she said angrily. "Don't you suppose I have enough pride to see to that? Don't you know by this time that I can do any darn thing with any darn man I want to?"

She put her chin in the air like the statue of France Aroused,* and then spoilt the pose somewhat by raising the lemon for action.

"Is it the Russian bracelet that fascinates you?"

"No, I'm merely trying to give you the sort of argument that would appeal to your intelligence. And I wish you'd go 'way," she said, her temper rising again. "You know I never change my mind. You've been boring me for three days until I'm about to go crazy. I won't go ashore! Won't! Do you hear? Won't!"

"Very well," he said, "and you won't go to Palm Beach either. Of all the selfish, spoilt, uncontrolled, disagreeable, impossible girls I have—"

Splush! The half-lemon caught him in the neck. Simultaneously came a hail from over the side.

"The launch is ready, Mr Farnam."

Too full of words and rage to speak, Mr Farnam cast one utterly condemning glance at his niece and, turning, ran swiftly down the ladder.

2

FIVE O'CLOCK ROLLED DOWN from the sun and plumped soundlessly into the sea. The golden collar widened into a glittering island, and a faint breeze that had been playing with the edges of the awning and swaying one of the dangling blue slippers became suddenly freighted with song. It was a chorus of men in close harmony and in perfect rhythm to an accompanying sound of oars cleaving the blue waters. Ardita lifted her head and listened.

"Carrots and peas,
Beans on their knees,
Pigs in the seas,
Lucky fellows!
Blow us a breeze,
Blow us a breeze,
Blow us a breeze,
With your bellows."

Ardita's brow wrinkled in astonishment. Sitting very still, she listened eagerly as the chorus took up a second verse.

"Onions and beans,
Marshalls and Deans,
Goldbergs and Greens
And Costellos.
Blow us a breeze,
Blow us a breeze,
Blow us a breeze,
With your bellows."

With an exclamation she tossed her book to the desk, where it sprawled at a straddle, and hurried to the rail. Fifty feet away a large rowboat was approaching containing seven men, six of them rowing and one standing up in the stern keeping time to their song with an orchestra leader's baton.

"Oysters and rocks,
Sawdust and socks,
Who could make clocks
Out of cellos?..."

The leader's eyes suddenly rested on Ardita, who was leaning over the rail spellbound with curiosity. He made a quick movement with his baton and the singing instantly ceased. She saw that he was the only white man in the boat – the six rowers were Negroes.

"Narcissus ahoy!" he called politely.

"What's the idea of all the discord?" demanded Ardita cheerfully. "Is this the varsity crew from the county nut farm?"

By this time the boat was scraping the side of the yacht and a great hulking Negro in the bow turned round and grasped the ladder. Thereupon the leader left his position in the stern and, before Ardita had realized his intention, he ran up the ladder and stood breathless before her on the deck.

"The women and children will be spared!" he said briskly. "All crying babies will be immediately drowned and all males put in double irons!"

Digging her hands excitedly down into the pockets of her dress, Ardita stared at him, speechless with astonishment.

He was a young man with a scornful mouth and the bright-blue eyes of a healthy baby set in a dark sensitive face. His hair was pitch black, damp and curly – the hair of a Grecian statue gone brunette. He was trimly built, trimly dressed and graceful as an agile quarterback.

"Well, I'll be a son of a gun!" she said dazedly.

They eyed each other coolly.

"Do you surrender the ship?"

"Is this an outburst of wit?" demanded Ardita. "Are you an idiot – or just being initiated to some fraternity?"

"I asked you if you surrendered the ship."

"I thought the country was dry," said Ardita disdainfully. "Have you been drinking fingernail enamel? You better get off this yacht!"

"What?" The young man's voice expressed incredulity.

"Get off the yacht! You heard me!"

He looked at her for a moment as if considering what she had said.

"No," said his scornful mouth slowly, "no, I won't get off the yacht. You can get off if you wish."

Going to the rail, he gave a curt command, and immediately the crew of the rowboat scrambled up the ladder and ranged themselves in line before him, a coal-black and burly darky at one end and a miniature mulatto of four feet nine at the other. They seemed to be uniformly dressed in some sort of blue costume ornamented with dust, mud and tatters; over the shoulder of each was slung a small, heavy-looking white sack, and under their arms they carried large black cases apparently containing musical instruments.

"Ten-*shun*!" commanded the young man, snapping his own heels together crisply. "Right *driss*! Front! Step out here, Babe!"

The smallest Negro took a quick step forward and saluted.

"Yas-suh!"

"Take command, go down below, catch the crew and tie 'em up – all except the engineer. Bring him up to me. Oh, and pile those bags by the rail there."

"Yas-suh!"

Babe saluted again and, wheeling about, motioned for the five others to gather about him. Then after a short whispered consultation they all filed noiselessly down the companionway.

"Now," said the young man cheerfully to Ardita, who had witnessed this last scene in withering silence, "if you will swear on your honour as a flapper – which probably isn't worth much – that you'll keep that spoilt little mouth of yours tight shut for forty-eight hours, you can row yourself ashore in our rowboat."

"Otherwise what?"

"Otherwise you're going to sea in a ship."

With a little sigh as for a crisis well passed, the young man sank into the settee Ardita had lately vacated and stretched his arms lazily. The corners of his mouth relaxed appreciatively as he looked round at the rich striped awning, the polished brass and the luxurious fittings of the deck. His eye fell on the book, and then on the exhausted lemon.

"Hm," he said, "Stonewall Jackson claimed that lemon juice cleared his head.* Your head feel pretty clear?"

Ardita disdained to answer.

"Because inside of five minutes you'll have to make a clear decision whether it's go or stay."

He picked up the book and opened it curiously.

"*The Revolt of the Angels*. Sounds pretty good. French, eh?" He stared at her with new interest. "You French?"

"No."

"What's your name?"

"Farnam."

"Farnam what?"

"Ardita Farnam."

"Well, Ardita, no use standing up there and chewing out the insides of your mouth. You ought to break those nervous habits while you're young. Come over here and sit down."

Ardita took a carved jade case from her pocket, extracted a cigarette and lit it with a conscious coolness, though she knew her hand was trembling a little; then she crossed over with her supple, swinging walk and, sitting down in the other settee, blew a mouthful of smoke at the awning.

"You can't get me off this yacht," she said steadily, "and you haven't got very much sense if you think you'll get far with it. My uncle'll have wirelesses zigzagging all over this ocean by half-past six."

"Hm."

She looked quickly at his face, caught anxiety stamped there plainly in the faintest depression of the mouth's corners.

"It's all the same to me," she said, shrugging her shoulders. "'Tisn't my yacht. I don't mind going for a coupla hours' cruise. I'll even lend you that book so you'll have something to read on the revenue boat that takes you up to Sing Sing."

He laughed scornfully.

"If that's advice, you needn't bother. This is part of a plan arranged before I ever knew this yacht existed. If it hadn't been this one it'd have been the next one we passed anchored along the coast."

"Who are you?'" demanded Ardita suddenly. "And what are you?"

"You've decided not to go ashore?"

"I never even faintly considered it."

"We're generally known," he said, "all seven of us, as Curtis Carlyle and his Six Black Buddies, late of the Winter Garden and the Midnight Frolic."

"You're singers?"

"We were until today. At present, due to those white bags you see there, we're fugitives from justice, and if the reward offered for our capture hasn't by this time reached twenty thousand dollars I miss my guess."

"What's in the bags?" asked Ardita curiously.

"Well," he said, "for the present we'll call it... mud – Florida mud."

3

WITHIN TEN MINUTES after Curtis Carlyle's interview with a very frightened engineer, the yacht Narcissus was under way, steaming south through a balmy tropical twilight. The little mulatto, Babe, who seemed to have Carlyle's implicit confidence, took full command of the situation. Mr Farnam's valet and the chef, the only members of the crew on board except the engineer, having shown fight, were now reconsidering, strapped securely to their bunks below. Trombone Mose, the biggest Negro, was set busy with a can of paint obliterating the name Narcissus from the bow, and substituting the name Hula Hula, and the others congregated aft and became intently involved in a game of craps.

Having given orders for a meal to be prepared and served on deck at seven thirty, Carlyle rejoined Ardita and, sinking back into his settee, half-closed his eyes and fell into a state of profound abstraction.

Ardita scrutinized him carefully – and classed him immediately as a romantic figure. He gave the effect of towering self-confidence erected on a slight foundation – just under the surface of each of his decisions she discerned a hesitancy that was in decided contrast to the arrogant curl of his lips.

"He's not like me," she thought. "There's a difference somewhere."

Being a supreme egotist, Ardita frequently thought about herself; never having had her egotism disputed, she did it entirely naturally and with no detraction from her unquestioned charm. Though she was nineteen she gave the effect of a high-spirited, precocious child, and in the present glow of her youth and beauty all the men and women she had known were but driftwood on the ripples of her temperament. She had met other egotists – in fact she found that selfish people bored her rather less than unselfish people – but as yet there had not been one she had not eventually defeated and brought to her feet.

But though she recognized an egotist in the settee next to her, she felt none of that usual shutting of doors in her mind which meant clearing ship for action; on the contrary her instinct told her that this man was somehow completely pregnable and quite defenceless. When Ardita defied convention – and of late it had been her chief amusement – it was from an intense desire to be herself, and she felt that this man, on the contrary, was preoccupied with his own defiance.

She was much more interested in him than she was in her own situation, which affected her as the prospect of a matinée might affect a ten-year-old child. She had implicit confidence in her ability to take care of herself under any and all circumstances.

The night deepened. A pale new moon smiled misty-eyed upon the sea, and as the shore faded dimly out and dark clouds were blown like leaves along the far horizon a great haze of moonshine suddenly bathed the yacht and spread an avenue of glittering mail in her swift path. From time to time there was the bright flare of a match as one of them lighted a cigarette, but except for the low undertone of the throbbing engines and the even wash of the waves about the stern, the yacht was quiet as a dream boat star-bound through the heavens. Round them flowed the smell of the night sea, bringing with it an infinite languor.

Carlyle broke the silence at last.

"Lucky girl," he sighed, "I've always wanted to be rich – and buy all this beauty."

Ardita yawned.

"I'd rather be you," she said frankly.

"You would – for about a day. But you do seem to possess a lot of nerve for a flapper."

"I wish you wouldn't call me that."

"Beg your pardon."

"As to nerve," she continued slowly, "it's my one redeeming feature. I'm not afraid of anything in heaven or earth."

"Hm, I am."

"To be afraid," said Ardita, "a person has either to be very great and strong – or else a coward. I'm neither." She paused for a moment, and eagerness crept into her tone. "But I want to talk about you. What on earth have you done – and how did you do it?"

"Why?" he demanded cynically. "Going to write a movie about me?"

"Go on," she urged. "Lie to me by the moonlight. Do a fabulous story."

A Negro appeared, switched on a string of small lights under the awning and began setting the wicker table for supper. And while they ate cold sliced chicken, salad, artichokes and strawberry jam from the plentiful larder below, Carlyle began to talk, hesitantly at first, but eagerly as he saw she was interested. Ardita scarcely touched her food as she watched his dark young face – handsome, ironic, faintly ineffectual.

He began life as a poor kid in a Tennessee town, he said, so poor that his people were the only white family in their street. He never remembered any white children – but there were inevitably a dozen piccaninnies streaming in his trail, passionate admirers whom he kept in tow by the vividness of his imagination and the amount of trouble he was always getting them in and out of. And it seemed that this association diverted a rather unusual musical gift into a strange channel.

There had been a coloured woman named Belle Pope Calhoun who played the piano at parties given for white children – nice white children that would have passed Curtis Carlyle with a sniff. But the ragged little "poh white" used to sit beside her piano by the hour and try to get in an alto with one of those kazoos that boys hum through. Before he was thirteen he was picking up a living teasing ragtime out of a battered violin in little cafés round Nashville. Eight years later the ragtime craze hit the country, and he took six darkies on the Orpheum circuit. Five of them were boys he had grown up with; the other was the little mulatto, Babe Divine, who was a wharf nigger round New York, and long before that a plantation hand in Bermuda, until he stuck an eight-inch stiletto in his master's back. Almost before Carlyle realized his good fortune he was on Broadway, with offers of engagements on all sides, and more money than he had ever dreamt of.

It was about then that a change began in his whole attitude, a rather curious, embittering change. It was when he realized that he was spending the golden years of his life gibbering round a stage with a lot of black men. His act was good of its kind – three trombones, three saxophones and Carlyle's flute – and it was his own peculiar sense of rhythm that made all the difference, but he began to grow strangely sensitive about it, began to hate the thought of appearing, dreaded it from day to day.

They were making money – each contract he signed called for more – but when he went to managers and told them that he wanted to separate from his sextet and go on as a regular pianist, they laughed at him and told him he was crazy – it would be an artistic suicide. He used to laugh afterwards at the phrase "artistic suicide". They all used it.

Half a dozen times they played at private dances at three thousand dollars a night, and it seemed as if these crystallized all his distaste for his mode of livelihood. They took place in clubs and houses that he couldn't have gone into in the daytime. After all, he was merely playing the role of the eternal monkey, a sort of sublimated chorus man. He was sick of the very smell of the theatre, of powder and rouge and the chatter of the green room, and the patronizing approval of the boxes. He couldn't put his heart into it any more. The idea of a slow approach to the luxury of leisure drove him wild. He was, of course, progressing towards it, but, like a child, eating his ice cream so slowly that he couldn't taste it at all.

He wanted to have a lot of money and time, and opportunity to read and play, and the sort of men and women round him that he could never have – the kind who, if they thought of him at all, would have considered him rather contemptible; in short he wanted all those things which he was beginning to lump under the general head of aristocracy, an aristocracy which it seemed almost any money could buy except money made as he was making it. He was twenty-five then, without family or education or any promise that he would succeed in a business career. He began speculating wildly, and within three weeks he had lost every cent he had saved.

Then the war came. He went to Plattsburgh, and even there his profession followed him. A brigadier-general called him up to headquarters and told him he could serve the country better as a band leader – so he spent the war entertaining celebrities behind the line with a headquarters band. It was not so bad – except that when the infantry came limping back from the trenches he wanted to be one of them. The sweat and mud they wore seemed only one of those ineffable symbols of aristocracy that were forever eluding him.

"It was the private dances that did it. After I came back from the war the old routine started. We had an offer from a syndicate of Florida hotels. It was only a question of time then."

He broke off and Ardita looked at him expectantly, but he shook his head.

"No," he said, "I'm not going to tell you about it. I'm enjoying it too much, and I'm afraid I'd lose a little of that enjoyment if I shared it with anyone else. I want to hang on to those few breathless, heroic moments when I stood out before them all and let them know I was more than a damn bobbing, squawking clown."

From up forward came suddenly the low sound of singing. The Negroes had gathered together on the deck and their voices rose together in a haunting melody that soared in poignant harmonics towards the moon. And Ardita listened in enchantment.

"Oh down –
Oh down,
Mammy wanna take me downa milky way,
Oh down –
Oh down,
Pappy say to-morra-a-a-ah!
But mammy say today,
Yes – mammy say today!"

Carlyle sighed and was silent for a moment, looking up at the gathered host of stars blinking like arc lights in the warm sky. The Negroes' song had died away to a plaintive humming, and it seemed as if minute by minute the brightness and the great silence were increasing, until he could almost hear the midnight toilet of the mermaids as they combed their silver dripping curls under the moon and gossiped to each other of the fine wrecks they lived in on the green opalescent avenues below.

"You see," said Carlyle softly, "this is the beauty I want. Beauty has got to be astonishing, astounding – it's got to burst in on you like a dream, like the exquisite eyes of a girl."

He turned to her, but she was silent.

"You see, don't you, Anita – I mean, Ardita?"

Again she made no answer. She had been sound asleep for some time.

4

IN THE DENSE SUN-FLOODED NOON of next day a spot in the sea before them resolved casually into a green-and-grey islet, apparently composed of a great granite cliff at its northern end which slanted south through a mile of vivid coppice and grass to a sandy beach melting lazily into the surf. When Ardita, reading in her favourite seat, came to the last page of *The Revolt of the Angels* and, slamming the book shut, looked up and saw it, she gave a little cry of delight and called to Carlyle, who was standing moodily by the rail.

"Is this it? Is this where you're going?"

Carlyle shrugged his shoulders carelessly.

"You've got me." He raised his voice and called up to the acting skipper: "Oh, Babe, is this your island?"

The mulatto's miniature head appeared from round the corner of the deckhouse.

"Yas-suh! This yeah's it."

Carlyle joined Ardita.

"Looks sort of sporting, doesn't it?"

"Yes," she agreed, "but it doesn't look big enough to be much of a hiding place."

"You still putting your faith in those wirelesses your uncle was going to have zigzagging round?"

"No," said Ardita frankly. "I'm all for you. I'd really like to see you make a getaway."

He laughed.

"You're our Lady Luck. Guess we'll have to keep you with us as a mascot – for the present, anyway."

"You couldn't very well ask me to swim back," she said coolly. "If you do, I'm going to start writing dime novels founded on that interminable history of your life you gave me last night."

He flushed and stiffened slightly.

"I'm very sorry I bored you."

"Oh, you didn't – until just at the end with some story about how furious you were because you couldn't dance with the ladies you played music for."

He rose angrily.

"You have got a darn mean little tongue."

"Excuse me," she said, melting into laughter, "but I'm not used to having men regale me with the story of their life ambitions – especially if they've lived such deathly platonic lives."

"Why? What do men usually regale you with?"

"Oh, they talk about me," she yawned. "They tell me I'm the spirit of youth and beauty."

"What do you tell them?"

"Oh, I agree quietly."

"Does every man you meet tell you he loves you?"

Ardita nodded.

"Why shouldn't he? All life is just a progression towards, and then a recession from, one phrase – 'I love you'."

Carlyle laughed and sat down.

"That's very true. That's… that's not bad. Did you make that up?"

"Yes – or rather I found it out. It doesn't mean anything especially. It's just clever."

"It's the sort of remark," he said gravely, "that's typical of your class."

"Oh," she interrupted impatiently, "don't start that lecture on aristocracy again! I distrust people who can be intense at this hour in the morning. It's a mild form of insanity – a sort of breakfast-food jag. Morning's the time to sleep, swim and be careless."

Ten minutes later they had swung round in a wide circle as if to approach the island from the north.

"There's a trick somewhere," commented Ardita thoughtfully. "He can't mean just to anchor up against this cliff."

They were heading straight in now towards the solid rock, which must have been well over a hundred feet tall, and not until they were within fifty yards of it did Ardita see their objective. Then she clapped her hands in delight. There was a break in the cliff entirely hidden by a curious overlapping of rock, and through this break the yacht entered and very slowly traversed a narrow channel of crystal-clear water between high grey walls. Then they were riding at anchor in a miniature world of green and gold, a gilded bay smooth as glass and set round with tiny palms, the whole resembling the mirror lakes and twig trees that children set up in sand piles.

"Not so darned bad!" said Carlyle excitedly. "I guess that little coon knows his way round this corner of the Atlantic."

His exuberance was contagious, and Ardita became quite jubilant.

"It's an absolutely sure-fire hiding place!"

"Lordy, yes! It's the sort of island you read about."

The rowboat was lowered into the golden lake and they pulled ashore.

"Come on," said Carlyle as they landed in the slushy sand, "we'll go exploring."

The fringe of palms was in turn ringed in by a round mile of flat, sandy country. They followed it south and, brushing through a farther rim of tropical vegetation, came out on a pearl-grey virgin beach where Ardita kicked off her brown golf shoes – she seemed to have permanently abandoned stockings – and went wading. Then they sauntered back to the yacht, where the indefatigable Babe had luncheon ready for them. He had posted a lookout on the high cliff to the north to watch the sea on both sides, though he doubted if the entrance to the cliff was generally known – he had never even seen a map on which the island was marked.

"What's its name," asked Ardita – "the island, I mean?"

"No name 'tall," chuckled Babe. "Reckin she jus' island, 'at's all."

In the late afternoon they sat with their backs against great boulders on the highest part of the cliff and Carlyle sketched for her his vague plans. He was sure they were hot after him by this time. The total proceeds of the coup he had pulled off, and concerning which he still refused to enlighten her, he estimated as just under a million dollars. He counted on lying up here several weeks and then setting off southwards, keeping well outside the usual channels of travel, rounding the Horn and heading for Callao, in Peru. The details of coaling and provisioning he was leaving entirely to Babe, who, it seemed, had sailed these seas in every capacity from cabin boy aboard a coffee trader to virtual first mate on a Brazilian pirate craft, whose skipper had long since been hung.

"If he'd been white, he'd have been king of South America long ago," said Carlyle emphatically. "When it comes to intelligence he makes Booker T. Washington* look like a moron. He's got the guile of every race and nationality whose blood is in his veins, and that's half a dozen or I'm a liar. He worships me because I'm the only man in the world who can play better ragtime than he can. We used to sit together on the wharfs down on the New York waterfront, he with a bassoon and me with an oboe, and we'd blend minor keys in African harmonics a thousand years old until the rats would crawl up the posts and sit round groaning and squeaking like dogs will in front of a phonograph."

Ardita roared.

"How you can tell 'em!"

Carlyle grinned.

"I swear that's the gos—"

"What you going to do when you get to Callao?" she interrupted.

"Take ship for India. I want to be a raja. I mean it. My idea is to go up into Afghanistan somewhere, buy up a palace and a reputation, and then after about five years appear in England with a foreign accent and a mysterious past. But India first. Do you know, they say that all the gold in the world drifts very gradually back to India. Something fascinating about that to me. And I want leisure to read – an immense amount."

"How about after that?"

"Then," he answered defiantly, "comes aristocracy. Laugh if you want to – but at least you'll have to admit that I know what I want – which I imagine is more than you do."

"On the contrary," contradicted Ardita, reaching in her pocket for her cigarette case, "when I met you, I was in the midst of a great uproar of all my friends and relatives because I did know what I wanted."

"What was it?"

"A man."

He started.

"You mean you were engaged?"

"After a fashion. If you hadn't come aboard I had every intention of slipping ashore yesterday evening – how long ago it seems – and meeting him in Palm Beach. He's waiting there for me with a bracelet that once belonged to Catherine of Russia. Now don't mutter anything about aristocracy," she put in quickly. "I liked him simply because he had had an imagination and the utter courage of his convictions."

"But your family disapproved, eh?"

"What there is of it – only a silly uncle and a sillier aunt. It seems he got into some scandal with a red-haired woman named Mimi something – it was frightfully exaggerated, he said, and men don't lie to me – and anyway I didn't care what he'd done; it was the future that counted. And I'd see to that. When a man's in love with me, he doesn't care for other amusements. I told him to drop her like a hot cake, and he did."

"I feel rather jealous," said Carlyle, frowning – and then he laughed. "I guess I'll just keep you along with us until we get to Callao. Then I'll lend you enough money to get back to the States. By that time you'll have had a chance to think that gentleman over a little more."

"Don't talk to me like that!" fired up Ardita. "I won't tolerate the parental attitude from anybody! Do you understand me?"

He chuckled and then stopped, rather abashed, as her cold anger seemed to fold him about and chill him.

"I'm sorry," he offered uncertainly.

"Oh, don't apologize! I can't stand men who say 'I'm sorry' in that manly, reserved tone. Just shut up!"

A pause ensued, a pause which Carlyle found rather awkward, but which Ardita seemed not to notice at all as she sat contentedly enjoying her cigarette and gazing out at the shining sea. After a minute she crawled out on the rock and lay with her face over the edge looking down. Carlyle, watching her, reflected how it seemed impossible for her to assume an ungraceful attitude.

"Oh, look!" she cried. "There's a lot of sort of ledges down there. Wide ones of all different heights."

He joined her and together they gazed down the dizzy height.

"We'll go swimming tonight!" she said excitedly. "By moonlight."

"Wouldn't you rather go in at the beach on the other end?"

"Not a chance. I like to dive. You can use my uncle's bathing suit, only it'll fit you like a gunny sack, because he's a very flabby man. I've got a one-piece affair that's shocked the natives all along the Atlantic coast from Biddeford Pool to St Augustine."

"I suppose you're a shark."

"Yes, I'm pretty good. And I look cute too. A sculptor up at Rye last summer told me my calves were worth five hundred dollars."

There didn't seem to be any answer to this, so Carlyle was silent, permitting himself only a discreet interior smile.

5

WHEN THE NIGHT CREPT DOWN in shadowy blue and silver, they threaded the shimmering channel in the rowboat and, tying it to a jutting rock, began climbing the cliff together. The first shelf was ten feet up, wide, and furnishing a natural diving platform. There they sat down in the bright moonlight and watched the faint incessant surge of the waters, almost stilled now as the tide set seaward.

"Are you happy?" he asked suddenly.

She nodded.

"Always happy near the sea. You know," she went on, "I've been thinking all day that you and I are somewhat alike. We're both rebels – only for different reasons. Two years ago, when I was just eighteen, and you were…"

"Twenty-five."

"…well, we were both conventional successes. I was an utterly devastating debutante and you were a prosperous musician just commissioned in the army—"

"Gentleman by act of Congress," he put in ironically.

"Well, at any rate, we both fitted. If our corners were not rubbed off, they were at least pulled in. But deep in us both was something that made us require more for happiness. I didn't know what I wanted. I went from man to man, restless, impatient, month by month getting less acquiescent and more dissatisfied. I used to sit sometimes chewing at the insides of my mouth and thinking I was going crazy – I had a frightful sense of transiency. I wanted things now – now – now! Here I was – beautiful – I am, aren't I?"

"Yes," agreed Carlyle tentatively.

Ardita rose suddenly.

"Wait a second. I want to try this delightful-looking sea."

She walked to the end of the ledge and shot out over the sea, doubling up in mid-air and then straightening out and entering the water straight as a blade in a perfect jack-knife dive.

In a minute her voice floated up to him.

"You see, I used to read all day and most of the night. I began to resent society——"

"Come on up here," he interrupted. "What on earth are you doing?"

"Just floating round on my back. I'll be up in a minute. Let me tell you. The only thing I enjoyed was shocking people; wearing something quite impossible and quite charming to a fancy-dress party, going round with the fastest men in New York and getting into some of the most hellish scrapes imaginable."

The sounds of splashing mingled with her words, and then he heard her hurried breathing as she began climbing up the side of the ledge.

"Go on in!" she called.

Obediently he rose and dived. When he emerged, dripping, and made the climb, he found that she was no longer on the ledge, but after a frightened second he heard her light laughter from another shelf ten feet up. There he joined her and they both sat quietly for a moment, their arms clasped round their knees, panting a little from the climb.

"The family were wild," she said suddenly. "They tried to marry me off. And then when I'd begun to feel that after all life was scarcely worth living, I found something" – her eyes went skywards exultantly – "I found something!"

Carlyle waited and her words came with a rush.

"Courage – just that; courage as a rule of life, and something to cling to always. I began to build up this enormous faith in myself. I began to see that in all my idols in the past some manifestation of courage had unconsciously been the thing that attracted me. I began separating courage from the other things of life. All sorts of courage – the beaten, bloody prizefighter coming up for more – I used to make men take me to prizefights; the déclassée woman sailing through a nest of cats and looking at them as if they were mud under her feet; the liking what you like always; the utter disregard for other people's opinions – just to live as I liked always and to die in my own way – did you bring up the cigarettes?"

He handed one over and held a match for her silently.

"Still," Ardita continued, "the men kept gathering – old men and young men, my mental and physical inferiors, most of them, but all intensely desiring to have me – to own this rather magnificent proud tradition I'd built up round me. Do you see?"

"Sort of. You never were beaten and you never apologized."

"Never!"

She sprang to the edge, poised for a moment like a crucified figure against the sky, then, describing a dark parabola, plunked without a slash between two silver ripples twenty feet below.

Her voice floated up to him again.

"And courage to me meant ploughing through that dull grey mist that comes down on life – not only overriding people and circumstances but overriding the bleakness of living. A sort of insistence on the value of life and the worth of transient things."

She was climbing up now, and at her last words her head, with the damp yellow hair slicked symmetrically back, appeared on his level.

"All very well," objected Carlyle. "You can call it courage, but your courage is really built, after all, on a pride of birth. You were bred to that defiant attitude. On my grey days even courage is one of the things that's grey and lifeless."

She was sitting near the edge, hugging her knees and gazing abstractedly at the white moon; he was farther back, crammed like a grotesque god into a niche in the rock.

"I don't want to sound like Pollyanna,"* she began, "but you haven't grasped me yet. My courage is faith – faith in the eternal resilience of me – that joy'll come back, and hope and spontaneity. And I feel that till it does I've got to keep my lips shut and my chin high, and my eyes wide – not necessarily any silly smiling. Oh, I've been through hell without a whine quite often – and the female hell is deadlier than the male."

"But supposing," suggested Carlyle, "that before joy and hope and all that came back the curtain was drawn on you for good?"

Ardita rose and, going to the wall, climbed with some difficulty to the next ledge, another ten or fifteen feet above.

"Why," she called back, "then I'd have won!"

He edged out till he could see her.

"Better not dive from there! You'll break your back," he said quickly.

She laughed.

"Not I!"

Slowly she spread her arms and stood there swan-like, radiating a pride in her young perfection that lit a warm glow in Carlyle's heart.

"We're going through the black air with our arms wide," she called, "and our feet straight out behind like a dolphin's tail, and we're going to think we'll never hit the silver down there till suddenly it'll be all warm round us and full of little kissing, caressing waves."

Then she was in the air, and Carlyle involuntarily held his breath. He had not realized that the dive was nearly forty feet. It seemed an eternity before he heard the swift compact sound as she reached the sea.

And it was with his glad sigh of relief when her light watery laughter curled up the side of the cliff and into his anxious ears that he knew he loved her.

6

TIME, HAVING NO AXE TO GRIND, showered down upon them three days of afternoons. When the sun cleared the porthole of Ardita's cabin an hour after dawn, she rose cheerily, donned her bathing suit and went up on deck. The Negroes would leave their work when they saw her and crowd, chuckling and chattering, to the rail as she floated, an agile minnow, on and under the surface of the clear water.

Again in the cool of the afternoon she would swim – and loll and smoke with Carlyle upon the cliff; or else they would lie on their sides in the sands of the southern beach, talking little, but watching the day fade colourfully and tragically into the infinite languor of a tropical evening.

And with the long, sunny hours, Ardita's idea of the episode as incidental, madcap, a sprig of romance in a desert of reality, gradually left her. She dreaded the time when he would strike off southward; she dreaded all the eventualities that presented themselves to her; thoughts were suddenly troublesome and decisions odious. Had prayers found place in the pagan rituals of her soul, she would have asked of life only to be unmolested for a while, lazily acquiescent to the ready, naive flow of Carlyle's ideas, his vivid boyish imagination and the vein of monomania that seemed to run crosswise through his temperament and coloured his every action.

But this is not a story of two on an island, nor concerned primarily with love bred of isolation. It is merely the presentation of two personalities, and its idyllic setting among the palms of the Gulf Stream is quite incidental. Most of us are content to exist and breed and fight for the right to do both, and the dominant idea, the foredoomed attempt to control one's destiny, is reserved for the fortunate or unfortunate few. To me the interesting thing about Ardita is the courage that will tarnish with her beauty and youth.

"Take me with you," she said late one night as they sat lazily in the grass under the shadowy spreading palms. The Negroes had brought ashore their musical instruments, and the sound of weird ragtime was drifting softly over on the warm breath of the night. "I'd love to reappear in ten years as a fabulously wealthy high-caste Indian lady," she continued.

Carlyle looked at her quickly.

"You can, you know."

She laughed.

"Is it a proposal of marriage? Extra! Ardita Farnam becomes pirate's bride. Society girl kidnapped by ragtime bank robber."

"It wasn't a bank."

"What was it? Why won't you tell me?"

"I don't want to break down your illusions."

"My dear man, I have no illusions about you."

"I mean your illusions about yourself."

She looked up in surprise.

"About myself! What on earth have I got to do with whatever stray felonies you've committed?"

"That remains to be seen."

She reached over and patted his hand.

"Dear Mr Curtis Carlyle," she said softly, "are you in love with me?"

"As if it mattered."

"But it does – because I think I'm in love with you."

He looked at her ironically.

"Thus swelling your January total to half a dozen," he suggested. "Suppose I call your bluff and ask you to come to India with me?"

"Shall I?"

He shrugged his shoulders.

"We can get married in Callao."

"What sort of life can you offer me? I don't mean that unkindly, but seriously; what would become of me if the people who want that twenty-thousand-dollar reward ever catch up with you?"

"I thought you weren't afraid."

"I never am – but I won't throw my life away just to show one man I'm not."

"I wish you'd been poor. Just a little poor girl dreaming over a fence in a warm cow country."

"Wouldn't it have been nice?"

"I'd have enjoyed astonishing you – watching your eyes open on things. If you only wanted things! Don't you see?"

"I know – like girls who stare into the windows of jewellery stores."

"Yes – and want the big oblong watch that's platinum and has diamonds all round the edge. Only you'd decide it was too expensive and choose one of white gold for a hundred dollars. Then I'd say: 'Expensive? I should say not!' And we'd go into the store and pretty soon the platinum one would be gleaming on your wrist."

"That sounds so nice and vulgar – and fun, doesn't it?" murmured Ardita.

"Doesn't it? Can't you see us travelling round and spending money right and left, and being worshipped by bellboys and waiters? Oh, blessed are the simple rich, for they inherit the earth!"

"I honestly wish we were that way."

"I love you, Ardita," he said gently.

Her face lost its childish look for a moment and became oddly grave.

"I love to be with you," she said, "more than with any man I've ever met. And I like your looks and your dark old hair, and the way you go over the side of the rail when we come ashore. In fact, Curtis Carlyle, I like all the things you do when you're perfectly natural. I think you've got nerve, and you know how I feel about that. Sometimes when you're around I've been tempted to kiss you suddenly and tell you that you were just an idealistic boy with a lot of caste nonsense in his head. Perhaps if I were just a little bit older and a little more bored I'd go with you. As it is, I think I'll go back and marry – that other man."

Over across the silver lake the figures of the Negroes writhed and squirmed in the moonlight, like acrobats who, having been too long inactive, must go through their tricks from sheer surplus energy. In single file they marched, weaving in concentric circles, now with their heads thrown back, now bent over their instruments like piping fauns. And from trombone and saxophone ceaselessly whined a blended melody, sometimes riotous and jubilant, sometimes haunting and plaintive as a death dance from the Congo's heart.

"Let's dance!" cried Ardita. "I can't sit still with that perfect jazz going on."

Taking her hand, he led her out into a broad stretch of hard sandy soil that the moon flooded with great splendour. They floated out like drifting moths under the rich hazy light, and as the fantastic symphony wept and exulted and wavered and despaired, Ardita's last sense of reality dropped away, and she abandoned her imagination to the dreamy summer scents of tropical flowers and the infinite starry spaces overhead, feeling that if she opened her eyes it would be to find herself dancing with a ghost in a land created by her own fancy.

"This is what I should call an exclusive private dance," he whispered.

"I feel quite mad – but delightfully mad!"

"We're enchanted. The shades of unnumbered generations of cannibals are watching us from high up on the side of the cliff there."

"And I'll bet the cannibal women are saying that we dance too close, and that it was immodest of me to come without my nose ring."

They both laughed softly – and then their laughter died as over across the lake they heard the trombone stop in the middle of a bar, and the saxophones give a startled moan and fade out.

"What's the matter?" called Carlyle.

After a moment's silence they made out the dark figure of a man rounding the silver lake at a run. As he came closer, they saw it was Babe in a state of unusual excitement. He drew up before them and gasped out his news in a breath.

"Ship stan'in' off sho' 'bout half a mile, suh. Mose, he uz on watch, he say look's if she's done ancho'd."

"A ship – what kind of a ship?" demanded Carlyle anxiously.

Dismay was in his voice, and Ardita's heart gave a sudden wrench as she saw his whole face suddenly droop.

"He say he don't know, suh."

"Are they landing a boat?"

"No, suh."

"We'll go up," said Carlyle.

They ascended the hill in silence, Ardita's hand still resting in Carlyle's as it had when they finished dancing. She felt it clinch nervously from time to time as though he were unaware of the contact, but though he hurt her, she made no attempt to remove it. It seemed an hour's climb before they reached the top and crept cautiously across the silhouetted plateau to the edge of the cliff. After one short look Carlyle involuntarily gave a little cry. It was a revenue boat with six-inch guns mounted fore and aft.

"They know!" he said with a short intake of breath. "They know! They picked up the trail somewhere."

"Are you sure they know about the channel? They may be only standing by to take a look at the island in the morning. From where they are they couldn't see the opening in the cliff."

"They could with field glasses," he said hopelessly. He looked at his wristwatch. "It's nearly two now. They won't do anything until dawn, that's certain. Of course there's always the faint possibility that they're waiting for some other ship to join – or for a coaler."

"I suppose we may as well stay right here."

The hours passed and they lay there side by side, very silently, their chins in their hands like dreaming children. In back of them squatted the Negroes, patient, resigned, acquiescent, announcing now and then with sonorous snores that not even the presence of danger could subdue their unconquerable African craving for sleep.

Just before five o'clock Babe approached Carlyle. There were half a dozen rifles aboard the Narcissus, he said. Had it been decided to offer no resistance? A pretty good fight might be made, he thought, if they worked out some plan.

Carlyle laughed and shook his head.

"That isn't a spic army out there, Babe. That's a revenue boat. It'd be like a bow and arrow trying to fight a machine gun. If you want to bury those bags somewhere and take a chance on recovering them later, go on and do it. But it won't work – they'd dig this island over from one end to the other. It's a lost battle all round, Babe."

Babe inclined his head silently and turned away, and Carlyle's voice was husky as he turned to Ardita.

"There's the best friend I ever had. He'd die for me, and be proud to, if I'd let him."

"You've given up?"

"I've no choice. Of course there's always one way out – the sure way – but that can wait. I wouldn't miss my trial for anything – it'll be an interesting experiment in notoriety. 'Miss Farnam testifies that the pirate's attitude to her was at all times that of a gentleman.'"

"Don't!" she said. "I'm awfully sorry."

When the colour faded from the sky and lustreless blue changed to leaden grey, a commotion was visible on the ship's deck, and they made out a group of officers clad in white duck, gathered near the rail. They had field glasses in their hands and were attentively examining the islet.

"It's all up," said Carlyle grimly.

"Damn!" whispered Ardita. She felt tears gathering in her eyes.

"We'll go back to the yacht," he said. "I prefer that to being hunted out up here like a 'possum."

Leaving the plateau, they descended the hill and, reaching the lake, were rowed out to the yacht by the silent Negroes. Then, pale and weary, they sank into the settees and waited.

Half an hour later, in the dim grey light, the nose of the revenue boat appeared in the channel and stopped, evidently fearing that the bay might be too shallow. From the peaceful look of the yacht, the man and the girl in the settees, and the Negroes lounging curiously against the rail, they evidently judged that there would be no resistance, for two boats were lowered casually over the side, one containing an officer and six bluejackets, and the other, four rowers and, in the stern, two grey-haired men in yachting flannels. Ardita and Carlyle stood up, and half-unconsciously started towards each other. Then he paused and, putting his hand suddenly into his pocket, he pulled out a round, glittering object and held it out to her.

"What is it?" she asked wonderingly.

"I'm not positive, but I think from the Russian inscription inside that it's your promised bracelet."

"Where... where on earth—"

"It came out of one of those bags. You see, Curtis Carlyle and his Six Black Buddies, in the middle of their performance in the tearoom of the hotel at Palm Beach, suddenly changed their instruments for automatics and held up the crowd. I took this bracelet from a pretty, over-rouged woman with red hair."

Ardita frowned and then smiled.

"So that's what you did! You *have* got nerve!"

He bowed.

"A well-known bourgeois quality," he said.

And then dawn slanted dynamically across the deck and flung the shadows reeling into grey corners. The dew rose and turned to golden mist, thin as a dream, enveloping them until they seemed gossamer relics of the late night, infinitely transient and already fading. For a moment sea and sky were breathless, and dawn held a pink hand over the young mouth of life – then from out in the lake came the complaint of a rowboat and the swish of oars.

Suddenly against the golden furnace low in the east their two graceful figures melted into one, and he was kissing her spoilt young mouth.

"It's a sort of glory," he murmured after a second.

She smiled up at him.

"Happy, are you?"

Her sigh was a benediction – an ecstatic surety that she was youth and beauty now as much as she would ever know. For another instant life was radiant and time a phantom and their strength eternal – then there was a bumping, scraping sound as the rowboat scraped alongside.

Up the ladder scrambled the two grey-haired men, the officer and two of the sailors with their hands on their revolvers. Mr Farnam folded his arms and stood looking at his niece.

"So," he said, nodding his head slowly.

With a sigh her arms unwound from Carlyle's neck, and her eyes, transfigured and far away, fell upon the boarding party. Her uncle saw her upper lip slowly swell into that arrogant pout he knew so well.

"So," he repeated savagely. "So this is your idea of... of romance. A runaway affair, with a high-seas pirate."

Ardita glanced at him carelessly.

"What an old fool you are!" she said quietly.

"Is that the best you can say for yourself?"

"No," she said, as if considering. "No, there's something else. There's that well-known phrase with which I have ended most of our conversations for the past few years – 'Shut up!'"

And with that she turned, included the two old men, the officer and the two sailors in a curt glance of contempt, and walked proudly down the companionway.

But had she waited an instant longer she would have heard a sound from her uncle quite unfamiliar in most of their interviews. He gave vent to a wholehearted amused chuckle, in which the second old man joined.

The latter turned briskly to Carlyle, who had been regarding this scene with an air of cryptic amusement.

"Well, Toby," he said genially, "you incurable, hare-brained, romantic chaser of rainbows, did you find that she was the person you wanted?"

Carlyle smiled confidently.

"Why… naturally," he said. "I've been perfectly sure ever since I first heard tell of her wild career. That's why I had Babe send up the rocket last night."

"I'm glad you did," said Colonel Moreland gravely. "We've been keeping pretty close to you in case you should have trouble with those six strange niggers. And we hoped we'd find you two in some such compromising position," he sighed. "Well, set a crank to catch a crank!"

"Your father and I sat up all night hoping for the best – or perhaps it's the worst. Lord knows you're welcome to her, my boy. She's run me crazy. Did you give her the Russian bracelet my detective got from that Mimi woman?"

Carlyle nodded.

"Sh!" he said. "She's coming on deck."

Ardita appeared at the head of the companionway and gave a quick involuntary glance at Carlyle's wrists. A puzzled look passed across her face. Back aft the Negroes had begun to sing, and the cool lake, fresh with dawn, echoed serenely to their low voices.

"Ardita," said Carlyle unsteadily.

She swayed a step towards him.

"Ardita," he repeated breathlessly, "I've got to tell you the... the truth. It was all a plant, Ardita. My name isn't Carlyle. It's Moreland, Toby Moreland. The story was invented, Ardita, invented out of thin Florida air."

She stared at him, bewildered amazement, disbelief and anger flowing in quick waves across her face. The three men held their breaths. Moreland Senior took a step towards her; Mr Farnam's mouth dropped a little open as he waited, panic-stricken, for the expected crash.

But it did not come. Ardita's face became suddenly radiant, and with a little laugh she went swiftly to young Moreland and looked up at him without a trace of wrath in her grey eyes.

"Will you swear," she said quietly, "that it was entirely a product of your own brain?"

"I swear," said young Moreland eagerly.

She drew his head down and kissed him gently.

"What an imagination!" she said softly and almost enviously. "I want you to lie to me just as sweetly as you know how for the rest of my life."

The Negroes' voices floated drowsily back, mingled in an air that she had heard them sing before.

"Time is a thief;
Gladness and grief
Cling to the leaf
  As it yellows..."

"What was in the bags?" she asked softly.

"Florida mud," he answered. "That was one of the two true things I told you."

"Perhaps I can guess the other one," she said and, reaching up on her tiptoes, she kissed him softly in the illustration.

The Ice Palace

1

THE SUNLIGHT DRIPPED over the house like golden paint over an art jar, and the freckling shadows here and there only intensified the rigour of the bath of light. The Butterworth and Larkin houses flanking were entrenched behind great stodgy trees; only the Happer house took the full sun, and all day long faced the dusty road-street with a tolerant kindly patience. This was the city of Tarleton in southernmost Georgia, September afternoon.

Up in her bedroom window Sally Carrol Happer rested her nineteen-year-old chin on a fifty-two-year-old sill and watched Clark Darrow's ancient Ford turn the corner. The car was hot – being partly metallic, it retained all the heat it absorbed or evolved – and Clark Darrow, sitting bolt upright at the wheel, wore a pained, strained expression as though he considered himself a spare part, and rather likely to break. He laboriously crossed two dust ruts, the wheels squeaking indignantly at the encounter, and then with a terrifying expression he gave the steering gear a final wrench and deposited self and car approximately in front of the Happer steps. There was a plaintive heaving sound, a death rattle, followed by a short silence, and then the air was rent by a startling whistle.

Sally Carrol gazed down sleepily. She started to yawn but, finding this quite impossible unless she raised her chin from the window sill, changed her mind and continued silently to regard the car, whose owner sat brilliantly if perfunctorily at attention as he waited for an answer to his signal. After a moment the whistle once more split the dusty air.

"Good mawnin'."

With difficulty Clark twisted his tall body round and bent a distorted glance on the window.

"'Tain't mawnin', Sally Carrol."

"Isn't it, sure enough?"

"What you doin'?"

"Eatin' 'n apple."

"Come on go swimmin' – want to?"

"Reckon so."

"How 'bout hurrin' up?"

"Sure enough."

Sally Carrol sighed voluminously and raised herself with profound inertia from the floor, where she had been occupied in alternately destroying parts of a green apple and painting paper dolls for her younger sister. She approached a mirror, regarded her expression with a pleased and pleasant languor, dabbed two spots of rouge on her lips and a grain of powder on her nose and covered her bobbed, corn-coloured hair with a rose-littered sun bonnet. Then she kicked over the painting water, said, "Oh, damn!" – but let it lay – and left the room.

"How you, Clark?" she enquired a minute later as she slipped nimbly over the side of the car.

"Mighty fine, Sally Carrol."

"Where we go swimmin'?"

"Out to Walley's Pool. Told Marylyn we'd call by an' get her an' Joe Ewing."

Clark was dark and lean, and when on foot was rather inclined to stoop. His eyes were ominous and his expression somewhat petulant, except when startlingly illuminated by one of his frequent smiles. Clark had "a income" – just enough to keep himself in ease and his car in gasoline – and he had spent the two years since he graduated from Georgia Tech in dozing round the lazy streets of his home town, discussing how he could best invest his capital for an immediate fortune.

Hanging round he found not at all difficult; a crowd of little girls had grown up beautifully, the amazing Sally Carrol foremost among them;

and they enjoyed being swum with and danced with and made love to in the flower-filled summery evenings – and they all liked Clark immensely. When feminine company palled, there were half a dozen other youths who were always just about to do something, and meanwhile were quite willing to join him in a few holes of golf, or a game of billiards, or the consumption of a quart of "hard yella licker". Every once in a while one of these contemporaries made a farewell round of calls before going up to New York or Philadelphia or Pittsburgh to go into business, but mostly they just stayed round in this languid paradise of dreamy skies and firefly evenings and noisy niggery street fairs – and especially of gracious, soft-voiced girls, who were brought up on memories instead of money.

The Ford having been excited into a sort of restless, resentful life, Clark and Sally Carroll rolled and rattled down Valley Avenue into Jefferson Street, where the dust road became a pavement; along opiate Millicent Place, where there were half a dozen prosperous, substantial mansions; and on into the downtown section. Driving was perilous here, for it was shopping time; the population idled casually across the streets and a drove of low-moaning oxen were being urged along in front of a placid streetcar; even the shops seemed only yawning their doors and blinking their windows in the sunshine before retiring into a state of utter and finite coma.

"Sally Carrol," said Clark suddenly, "it a fact that you're engaged?"

She looked at him quickly.

"Where'd you hear that?"

"Sure enough, you engaged?"

"'At's a nice question!"

"Girl told me you were engaged to a Yankee you met up in Asheville last summer."

Sally Carrol sighed.

"Never saw such an old town for rumours."

"Don't marry a Yankee, Sally Carrol. We need you round here."

Sally Carrol was silent a moment.

"Clark," she demanded suddenly, "who on earth shall I marry?"

"I offer my services."

"Honey, you couldn't support a wife," she answered cheerfully. "Anyway, I know you too well to fall in love with you."

"'At doesn't mean you ought to marry a Yankee," he persisted.

"S'pose I love him?"

He shook his head.

"You couldn't. He'd be a lot different from us, every way."

He broke off as he halted the car in front of a rambling, dilapidated house. Marylyn Wade and Joe Ewing appeared in the doorway.

"'Lo, Sally Carrol."

"Hi!"

"How you all?"

"Sally Carrol," demanded Marylyn as they started off again, "you engaged?"

"Lawdy, where'd all this start? Can't I look at a man 'thout everybody in town engagin' me to him?"

Clark stared straight in front of him at a bolt on the clattering windshield.

"Sally Carrol," he said with a curious intensity, "don't you like us?"

"What?"

"Us down here?"

"Why, Clark, you know I do. I adore all you boys."

"Then why you gettin' engaged to a Yankee?"

"Clark, I don't know. I'm not sure what I'll do, but – well, I want to go places and see people. I want my mind to grow. I want to live where things happen on a big scale."

"What you mean?"

"Oh, Clark, I love you, and I love Joe here, and Ben Arrot, and you all, but you'll... you'll—"

"We'll all be failures?"

"Yes. I don't mean only money failures, but just sort of... of ineffectual and sad, and... oh, how can I tell you?"

"You mean because we stay here in Tarleton?"

"Yes, Clark – and because you like it and never want to change things or think or go ahead."

He nodded and she reached over and pressed his hand.

"Clark," she said softly, "I wouldn't change you for the world. You're sweet the way you are. The things that'll make you fail I'll love always – the living in the past, the lazy days and nights you have and all your carelessness and generosity."

"But you're goin' away?"

"Yes – because I couldn't ever marry you. You've a place in my heart no one else ever could have, but tied down here I'd get restless. I'd feel I was… wastin' myself. There's two sides to me, you see. There's the sleepy old side you love; an' there's a sort of energy – the feelin' that makes me do wild things. That's the part of me that may be useful somewhere, that'll last when I'm not beautiful any more."

She broke off with characteristic suddenness and sighed, "Oh, sweet cookie!" as her mood changed.

Half-closing her eyes and tipping back her head till it rested on the seat back, she let the savoury breeze fan her eyes and ripple the fluffy curls of her bobbed hair. They were in the country now, hurrying between tangled growths of bright-green coppice and grass and tall trees that sent sprays of foliage to hang a cool welcome over the road. Here and there they passed a battered Negro cabin, its oldest white-haired inhabitant smoking a corncob pipe beside the door, and half a dozen scantily clothed piccaninnies parading tattered dolls on the wild-grown grass in front. Farther out were lazy cotton fields, where even the workers seemed intangible shadows lent by the sun to the earth, not for toil, but to while away some age-old tradition in the golden September fields. And round the drowsy picturesqueness, over the trees and shacks and muddy rivers, flowed the heat, never hostile, only comforting, like a great warm nourishing bosom for the infant earth.

"Sally Carrol, we're here!"

"Poor chile's soun' asleep."

"Honey, you dead at last outa sheer laziness?"

"Water, Sally Carrol! Cool water waitin' for you!"

Her eyes opened sleepily.

"Hi!" she murmured, smiling.

2

IN NOVEMBER HARRY BELLAMY, tall, broad and brisk, came down from his Northern city to spend four days. His intention was to settle a matter that had been hanging fire since he and Sally Carrol had met in Asheville, North Carolina, in midsummer. The settlement took only a quiet afternoon and an evening in front of a glowing open fire, for Harry Bellamy had everything she wanted; and, besides, she loved him – loved him with that side of her she kept especially for loving. Sally Carrol had several rather clearly defined sides.

On his last afternoon they walked, and she found their steps tending half-unconsciously towards one of her favourite haunts, the cemetery. When it came in sight, grey-white and golden-green under the cheerful late sun, she paused, irresolute, by the iron gate.

"Are you mournful by nature, Harry?" she asked with a faint smile.

"Mournful? Not I."

"Then let's go in here. It depresses some folks, but I like it."

They passed through the gateway and followed a path that led through a wavy valley of graves – dusty-grey and mouldy for the Fifties; quaintly carved with flowers and jars for the Seventies; ornate and hideous for the Nineties, with fat marble cherubs lying in sodden sleep on stone pillows, and great impossible growths of nameless granite flowers. Occasionally they saw a kneeling figure with tributary flowers, but over most of the graves lay silence and withered leaves with only the fragrance that their own shadowy memories could waken in living minds.

They reached the top of a hill where they were fronted by a tall, round headstone, freckled with dark spots of damp and half grown over with vines.

"Margery Lee," she read, "1844–1873. Wasn't she nice? She died when she was twenty-nine. Dear Margery Lee," she added softly. "Can't you see her, Harry?"

"Yes, Sally Carrol."

He felt a little hand insert itself into his.

"She was dark, I think, and she always wore her hair with a ribbon in it, and gorgeous hoop skirts of Alice blue and old rose."

"Yes."

"Oh, she was sweet, Harry! And she was the sort of girl born to stand on a wide, pillared porch and welcome folks in. I think perhaps a lot of men went away to war meanin' to come back to her, but maybe none of 'em ever did."

He stooped down close to the stone, hunting for any record of marriage.

"There's nothing here to show."

"Of course not. How could there be anything there better than just 'Margery Lee' and that eloquent date?"

She drew close to him and an unexpected lump came into his throat as her yellow hair brushed his cheek.

"You see how she was, don't you, Harry?"

"I see," he agreed gently. "I see through your precious eyes. You're beautiful now, so I know she must have been."

Silent and close they stood, and he could feel her shoulders trembling a little. An ambling breeze swept up the hill and stirred the brim of her floppity hat.

"Let's go down there!"

She was pointing to a flat stretch on the other side of the hill, where along the green turf were a thousand greyish-white crosses stretching in endless, ordered rows like the stacked arms of a battalion.

"Those are the Confederate dead," said Sally Carrol simply.

They walked along and read the inscriptions, always only a name and a date, sometimes quite indecipherable.

"The last row is the saddest – see, 'way over there. Every cross has just a date on it, and the word 'Unknown'."

She looked at him and her eyes brimmed with tears.

"I can't tell you how real it is to me, darling – if you don't know."

"How you feel about it is beautiful to me."

"No, no, it's not me, it's them – that old time that I've tried to have live in me. These were just men, unimportant evidently or they wouldn't have been 'unknown', but they died for the most beautiful thing in the world – the dead South. You see," she continued, her voice still husky, her eyes glistening with tears, "people have these dreams they fasten on to things, and I've always grown up with that dream. It was so easy because it was all dead and there weren't any disillusions comin' to me. I've tried in a way to live up to those past standards of *noblesse oblige* – there's just the last remnants of it, you know, like the roses of an old garden dying all round us – streaks of strange courtliness and chivalry in some of these boys an' stories I used to hear from a Confederate soldier who lived next door, and a few old darkies. Oh, Harry, there was something, there was something! I couldn't ever make you understand, but it was there."

"I understand," he assured her again quietly.

Sally Carrol smiled and dried her eyes on the tip of a handkerchief protruding from his breast pocket.

"You don't feel depressed, do you, lover? Even when I cry, I'm happy here, and I get a sort of strength from it."

Hand in hand they turned and walked slowly away. Finding soft grass, she drew him down to a seat beside her with their backs against the remnants of a low broken wall.

"Wish those three old women would clear out," he complained. "I want to kiss you, Sally Carrol."

"Me too."

They waited impatiently for the three bent figures to move off, and then she kissed him until the sky seemed to fade out and all her smiles and tears to vanish in an ecstasy of eternal seconds.

Afterwards they walked slowly back together, while on the corners twilight played at somnolent black-and-white checkers with the end of day.

"You'll be up about mid-January," he said, "and you've got to stay a month at least. It'll be slick. There's a winter carnival on, and if you've never really seen snow it'll be like fairyland to you. There'll be skating and skiing and tobogganing and sleigh-riding, and all sorts of torchlight parades on snowshoes. They haven't had one for years, so they're going to make it a knockout."

"Will I be cold, Harry?" she asked suddenly.

"You certainly won't. You may freeze your nose, but you won't be shivery cold. It's hard and dry, you know."

"I guess I'm a summer child. I don't like any cold I've ever seen."

She broke off, and they were both silent for a minute.

"Sally Carrol," he said very slowly, "what do you say to… March?"

"I say I love you."

"March?"

"March, Harry."

3

ALL NIGHT IN THE PULLMAN it was very cold. She rang for the porter to ask for another blanket, and when he couldn't give her one she tried vainly, by squeezing down into the bottom of her berth and doubling back the bedclothes, to snatch a few hours' sleep. She wanted to look her best in the morning.

She rose at six and, sliding uncomfortably into her clothes, stumbled up to the diner for a cup of coffee. The snow had filtered into the vestibules and covered the floor with a slippery coating. It was intriguing, this cold, it crept in everywhere. Her breath was quite visible and she blew into the air with a naive enjoyment. Seated in the diner, she stared out the window at white hills and valleys and scattered pines whose every branch was a green platter for a cold feast of snow. Sometimes a solitary farmhouse would fly by, ugly and bleak and lone on the white waste, and with each one she had an instant of chill compassion for the souls shut in there waiting for spring.

As she left the diner and swayed back into the Pullman, she experienced a surging rush of energy and wondered if she was feeling the bracing air of which Harry had spoken. This was the North, the North – her land now!

"Then blow, ye winds, heigho!
A-roving I will go,"*

she chanted exultantly to herself.

"What's 'at?" enquired the porter politely.

"I said: 'Brush me off.'"

The long wires of the telegraph poles doubled; two tracks ran up beside the train – three – four; came a succession of white-roofed houses, a glimpse of a trolley car with frosted windows, streets – more streets – the city.

She stood for a dazed moment in the frosty station before she saw three fur-bundled figures descending upon her.

"There she is!"

"Oh, Sally Carrol!"

Sally Carrol dropped her bag.

"Hi!"

A faintly familiar icy-cold face kissed her, and then she was in a group of faces all apparently emitting great clouds of heavy smoke; she was shaking hands. There were Gordon, a short, eager man of thirty who looked like an amateur knocked-about model for Harry, and his wife, Myra, a listless lady with flaxen hair under a fur automobile cap. Almost immediately Sally Carrol thought of her as vaguely Scandinavian. A cheerful chauffeur adopted her bag and, amid ricochets of half-phrases, exclamations and perfunctory listless "my dears" from Myra, they swept each other from the station.

Then they were in a sedan bound through a crooked succession of snowy streets where dozens of little boys were hitching sleds behind grocery wagons and automobiles.

"Oh," cried Sally Carrol, "I want to do that! Can we, Harry?"

"That's for kids. But we might—"

"It looks like such a circus!" she said regretfully.

Home was a rambling frame house set on a white lap of snow, and there she met a big, grey-haired man of whom she approved, and a lady who was like an egg, and who kissed her – these were Harry's parents. There was a breathless, indescribable hour crammed full of half-sentences, hot water, bacon and eggs and confusion, and after that she was alone with Harry in the library, asking him if she dared smoke.

It was a large room with a Madonna over the fireplace and rows upon rows of books in covers of light gold and dark gold and shiny red. All the chairs had little lace squares where one's head should rest, the couch was just comfortable, the books looked as if they had been read – some – and Sally Carrol had an instantaneous vision of the battered old library at home, with her father's huge medical books, and the oil paintings of her three great-uncles, and the old couch that had been mended up for forty-five years and was still luxurious to dream in. This room struck her as being neither attractive nor particularly otherwise. It was simply a room with a lot of fairly expensive things in it that all looked about fifteen years old.

"What do you think of it up here?" demanded Harry eagerly. "Does it surprise you? Is it what you expected, I mean?"

"You are, Harry," she said quietly, and reached out her arms to him. But after a brief kiss he seemed anxious to extort enthusiasm from her.

"The town, I mean. Do you like it? Can you feel the pep in the air?"

"Oh, Harry," she laughed, "you'll have to give me time. You can't just fling questions at me."

She puffed at her cigarette with a sigh of contentment.

"One thing I want to ask you," he began rather apologetically. "You Southerners put quite an emphasis on family, and all that – not that it isn't quite all right, but you'll find it a little different here. I mean... you'll notice a lot of things that'll seem to you sort of vulgar display at first, Sally Carrol, but just remember that this is a three-generation town. Everybody has a father, and about half of us have grandfathers. Back of that we don't go."

"Of course," she murmured.

"Our grandfathers, you see, founded the place, and a lot of them had to take some pretty queer jobs while they were doing the founding. For instance, there's one woman who at present is about the social model for the town; well, her father was the first public ash man – things like that."

"Why," said Sally Carrol, puzzled, "did you s'pose I was goin' to make remarks about people?"

"Not at all," interrupted Harry, "and I'm not apologizing for anyone either. It's just that... well, a Southern girl came up here last summer and said some unfortunate things, and... oh, I just thought I'd tell you."

Sally Carrol felt suddenly indignant – as though she had been unjustly spanked – but Harry evidently considered the subject closed, for he went on with a great surge of enthusiasm.

"It's carnival time, you know. First in ten years. And there's an ice palace they're building now that's the first they've had since Eighty-five. Built out of blocks of the clearest ice they could find – on a tremendous scale."

She rose and, walking to the window, pushed aside the heavy Turkish portières and looked out.

"Oh!" she cried suddenly. "There's two little boys makin' a snowman! Harry, do you reckon I can go out an' help 'em?"

"You dream! Come here and kiss me."

She left the window rather reluctantly.

"I don't guess this is a very kissable climate, is it? I mean, it makes you so you don't want to sit round, doesn't it?"

"We're not going to. I've got a vacation for the first week you're here, and there's a dinner dance tonight."

"Oh, Harry," she confessed, subsiding in a heap, half in his lap, half in the pillows, "I sure do feel confused. I haven't got an idea whether I'll like it or not, an' I don't know what people expect or anythin'. You'll have to tell me, honey."

"I'll tell you," he said softly, "if you'll just tell me you're glad to be here."

"Glad – just awful glad!" she whispered, insinuating herself into his arms in her own peculiar way. "Where you are is home for me, Harry."

And as she said this she had the feeling for almost the first time in her life that she was acting a part.

That night, amid the gleaming candles of a dinner party, where the men seemed to do most of the talking while the girls sat in a haughty and expensive aloofness, even Harry's presence on her left failed to make her feel at home.

"They're a good-looking crowd, don't you think?" he demanded. "Just look round. There's Spud Hubbard, tackle at Princeton last year, and Junie Morton – he and the red-haired fellow next to him were both Yale hockey captains; Junie was in my class. Why, the best athletes in the world come from these states round here. This is a man's country, I tell you. Look at John J. Fishburn!"

"Who's he?" asked Sally Carrol innocently.

"Don't you know?"

"I've heard the name."

"Greatest wheat man in the North-west, and one of the greatest financiers in the country."

She turned suddenly to a voice on her right.

"I guess they forgot to introduce us. My name's Roger Patton."

"My name is Sally Carrol Happer," she said graciously.

"Yes, I know. Harry told me you were coming."

"You a relative?"

"No, I'm a professor."

"Oh," she laughed.

"At the university. You're from the South, aren't you?"

"Yes: Tarleton, Georgia."

She liked him immediately – a reddish-brown moustache under watery-blue eyes that had something in them that these other eyes lacked, some quality of appreciation. They exchanged stray sentences through dinner, and she made up her mind to see him again.

After coffee she was introduced to numerous good-looking young men who danced with conscious precision and seemed to take it for granted that she wanted to talk about nothing except Harry.

"Heavens," she thought, "they talk as if my being engaged made me older than they are – as if I'd tell their mothers on them!"

In the South an engaged girl, even a young married woman, expected the same amount of half-affectionate badinage and flattery that would be accorded a debutante, but here all that seemed banned. One young man, after getting well started on the subject of Sally Carrol's eyes, and how they had allured him ever since she entered the room, went into a violent confusion when he found she was visiting the Bellamys – was Harry's fiancée. He seemed to feel as though he had made some risqué and inexcusable blunder, became immediately formal, and left her at the first opportunity.

She was rather glad when Roger Patton cut in on her and suggested that they sit out a while.

"Well," he enquired, blinking cheerily, "how's Carmen from the South?"

"Mighty fine. How's... how's Dangerous Dan McGrew?* Sorry, but he's the only Northerner I know much about."

He seemed to enjoy that.

"Of course," he confessed, "as a professor of literature I'm not supposed to have read *Dangerous Dan McGrew*."

"Are you a native?"

"No, I'm a Philadelphian. Imported from Harvard to teach French. But I've been here ten years."

"Nine years, three hundred an' sixty-four days longer than me."

"Like it here?"

"Uh-huh. Sure do!"

"Really?"

"Well, why not? Don't I look as if I were havin' a good time?"

"I saw you look out the window a minute ago – and shiver."

"Just my imagination," laughed Sally Carrol. "I'm used to havin' everythin' quiet outside, an' sometimes I look out an' see a flurry of snow, an' it's just as if somethin' dead was movin'."

He nodded appreciatively.

"Ever been North before?"

"Spent two Julys in Asheville, North Carolina."

"Nice-looking crowd, aren't they?" suggested Patton, indicating the swirling floor.

Sally Carrol started. This had been Harry's remark.

"Sure are! They're… canine."

"What?"

She flushed.

"I'm sorry; that sounded worse than I meant it. You see, I always think of people as feline or canine, irrespective of sex."

"Which are you?"

"I'm feline. So are you. So are most Southern men an' most of these girls here."

"What's Harry?"

"Harry's canine distinctly. All the men I've met tonight seem to be canine."

"What does 'canine' imply? A certain conscious masculinity as opposed to subtlety?"

"Reckon so. I never analysed it – only I just look at people an' say 'canine' or 'feline' right off. It's right absurd, I guess."

"Not at all. I'm interested. I used to have a theory about these people. I think they're freezing up."

"What?"

"I think they're growing like Swedes – Ibsenesque, you know. Very gradually getting gloomy and melancholy. It's these long winters. Ever read any Ibsen?"

She shook her head.

"Well, you find in his characters a certain brooding rigidity. They're righteous, narrow and cheerless, without infinite possibilities for great sorrow or joy."

"Without smiles or tears?"

"Exactly. That's my theory. You see there are thousands of Swedes up here. They come, I imagine, because the climate is very much like their own, and there's been a gradual mingling. There're probably not half a dozen here tonight, but – we've had four Swedish governors. Am I boring you?"

"I'm mighty interested."

"Your future sister-in-law is half Swedish. Personally I like her, but my theory is that Swedes react rather badly on us as a whole. Scandinavians, you know, have the largest suicide rate in the world."

"Why do you live here if it's so depressing?"

"Oh, it doesn't get me. I'm pretty well cloistered, and I suppose books mean more than people to me anyway."

"But writers all speak about the South being tragic. You know – Spanish señoritas, black hair and daggers and haunting music."

He shook his head.

"No, the Northern races are the tragic races – they don't indulge in the cheering luxury of tears."

Sally Carrol thought of her graveyard. She supposed that that was vaguely what she had meant when she said it didn't depress her.

"The Italians are about the gayest people in the world – but it's a dull subject," he broke off. "Anyway, I want to tell you you're marrying a pretty fine man."

Sally Carrol was moved by an impulse of confidence.

"I know. I'm the sort of person who wants to be taken care of after a certain point, and I feel sure I will be."

"Shall we dance? You know," he continued as they rose, "it's encouraging to find a girl who knows what she's marrying for. Nine tenths of them think of it as a sort of walking into a moving-picture sunset."

She laughed, and liked him immensely.

Two hours later on the way home she nestled near Harry in the back seat.

"Oh, Harry," she whispered, "it's so co-old!"

"But it's warm in here, darling girl."

"But outside it's cold – and oh, that howling wind!"

She buried her face deep in his fur coat and trembled involuntarily as his cold lips kissed the tip of her ear.

4

THE FIRST WEEK of her visit passed in a whirl. She had her promised toboggan ride at the back of an automobile through a chill January twilight. Swathed in furs, she put in a morning tobogganing on the country-club hill; even tried skiing, to sail through the air for a glorious moment and then land in a tangled laughing bundle on a soft snowdrift. She liked all the winter sports, except an afternoon spent snowshoeing over a glaring plain under pale yellow sunshine, but she soon realized that these things were for children – that she was being humoured and that the enjoyment round her was only a reflection of her own.

At first the Bellamy family puzzled her. The men were reliable and she liked them; to Mr Bellamy especially, with his iron-grey hair and energetic dignity, she took an immediate fancy, once she found that he was born in Kentucky; this made of him a link between the old life and the new. But towards the women she felt a definite hostility. Myra, her future sister-in-law, seemed the essence of spiritless conventionality. Her conversation was so utterly devoid of personality that Sally Carrol, who came from a country where a certain amount of charm and assurance could be taken for granted in the women, was inclined to despise her.

"If those women aren't beautiful," she thought, "they're nothing. They just fade out when you look at them. They're glorified domestics. Men are the centre of every mixed group."

Lastly there was Mrs Bellamy, whom Sally Carrol detested. The first day's impression of an egg had been confirmed – an egg with a cracked, veiny voice and such an ungracious dumpiness of carriage that Sally Carrol felt that if she once fell she would surely scramble. In addition, Mrs Bellamy seemed to typify the town in being innately hostile to strangers. She called Sally Carrol "Sally", and could not be persuaded that the double name was anything more than a tedious, ridiculous nickname. To Sally Carrol this shortening of her name was like presenting her to the public half-clothed. She loved "Sally Carrol";

she loathed "Sally". She knew also that Harry's mother disapproved of her bobbed hair, and she had never dared smoke downstairs after that first day when Mrs Bellamy had come into the library sniffing violently.

Of all the men she met she preferred Roger Patton, who was a frequent visitor at the house. He never again alluded to the Ibsenesque tendency of the populace, but when he came in one day and found her curled upon the sofa bent over *Peer Gynt*,* he laughed and told her to forget what he'd said – that it was all rot.

And then one afternoon in her second week she and Harry hovered on the edge of a dangerously steep quarrel. She considered that he precipitated it entirely, though the Serbia in the case* was an unknown man who had not had his trousers pressed.

They had been walking homeward between mounds of high-piled snow and under a sun which Sally Carrol scarcely recognized. They passed a little girl done up in grey wool until she resembled a small teddy bear, and Sally Carrol could not resist a gasp of maternal appreciation.

"Look! Harry!"

"What?"

"That little girl – did you see her face?"

"Yes, why?"

"It was red as a little strawberry. Oh, she was cute!"

"Why, your own face is almost as red as that already! Everybody's healthy here. We're out in the cold as soon as we're old enough to walk. Wonderful climate!"

She looked at him and had to agree. He was mighty healthy-looking; so was his brother. And she had noticed the new red in her own cheeks that very morning.

Suddenly their glances were caught and held, and they stared for a moment at the street corner ahead of them. A man was standing there, his knees bent, his eyes gazing upward with a tense expression, as though he were about to make a leap towards the chilly sky. And then they both exploded into a shout of laughter, for coming closer they discovered it had been a ludicrous momentary illusion produced by the extreme bagginess of the man's trousers.

"Reckon that's one on us," she laughed.

"He must be a Southerner, judging by those trousers," suggested Harry mischievously.

"Why, Harry!"

Her surprised look must have irritated him.

"Those damn Southerners!"

Sally Carrol's eyes flashed.

"Don't call 'em that!"

"I'm sorry, dear," said Harry, malignantly apologetic, "but you know what I think of them. They're sort of... sort of degenerates – not at all like the old Southerners. They've lived so long down there with all the coloured people that they've gotten lazy and shiftless."

"Hush your mouth, Harry!" she cried angrily. "They're not! They may be lazy – anybody would be in that climate – but they're my best friends, an' I don't want to hear 'em criticized in any such sweepin' way. Some of 'em are the finest men in the world."

"Oh, I know. They're all right when they come North to college, but of all the hangdog, ill-dressed, slovenly lot I ever saw, a bunch of small-town Southerners are the worst!"

Sally Carrol was clenching her gloved hands and biting her lip furiously.

"Why," continued Harry, "there was one in my class at New Haven, and we all thought that at last we'd found the true type of Southern aristocrat, but it turned out that he wasn't an aristocrat at all – just the son of a Northern carpetbagger who owned about all the cotton round Mobile."

"A Southerner wouldn't talk the way you're talking now," she said evenly.

"They haven't the energy!"

"Or the somethin' else."

"I'm sorry, Sally Carrol, but I've heard you say yourself that you'd never marry—"

"That's quite different. I told you I wouldn't want to tie my life to any of the boys that are round Tarleton now, but I never made any sweepin' generalities."

They walked along in silence.

"I probably spread it on a bit thick, Sally Carrol. I'm sorry."

She nodded but made no answer. Five minutes later as they stood in the hallway, she suddenly threw her arms round him.

"Oh, Harry," she cried, her eyes brimming with tears, "let's get married next week. I'm afraid of having fusses like that. I'm afraid, Harry. It wouldn't be that way if we were married."

But Harry, being in the wrong, was still irritated.

"That'd be idiotic. We decided on March."

The tears in Sally Carrol's eyes faded; her expression hardened slightly.

"Very well – I suppose I shouldn't have said that."

Harry melted.

"Dear little nut!" he cried. "Come and kiss me and let's forget."

That very night at the end of a vaudeville performance the orchestra played 'Dixie',* and Sally Carrol felt something stronger and more enduring than her tears and smiles of the day brim up inside her. She leant forward gripping the arms of her chair until her face grew crimson.

"Sort of get you, dear?" whispered Harry.

But she did not hear him. To the spirited throb of the violins and the inspiring beat of the kettledrums her own old ghosts were marching by and on into the darkness, and as fifes whistled and sighed in the low encore they seemed so nearly out of sight that she could have waved goodbye.

"Away, Away,
    Away down South in Dixie!
Away, away,
    Away down South in Dixie!"

5

I T WAS A PARTICULARLY COLD NIGHT. A sudden thaw had nearly cleared the streets the day before, but now they were traversed again with a powdery wraith of loose snow that travelled in wavy lines before the feet of the wind, and filled the lower air with a fine-particled mist. There was no sky – only a dark, ominous tent that draped in the tops of the streets and was in reality a vast approaching army of snowflakes – while over it all, chilling away the comfort from the brown-and-green glow of lighted windows and muffling the steady trot of the horse pulling their sleigh, interminably washed the north wind. It was a dismal town after all, she thought – dismal.

Sometimes at night it had seemed to her as though no one lived here – they had all gone long ago – leaving lighted houses to be covered in time by tombing heaps of sleet. Oh, if there should be snow on her grave! To be beneath great piles of it all winter long, where even her headstone would be a light shadow against light shadows. Her grave – a grave that should be flower-strewn and washed with sun and rain.

She thought again of those isolated country houses that her train had passed, and of the life there the long winter through – the ceaseless glare through the windows, the crust forming on the soft drifts of snow, finally the slow, cheerless melting, and the harsh spring of which Roger Patton had told her. Her spring – to lose it for ever – with its lilacs and the lazy sweetness it stirred in her heart. She was laying away that spring – afterwards she would lay away that sweetness.

With a gradual insistence the storm broke. Sally Carrol felt a film of flakes melt quickly on her eyelashes, and Harry reached over a furry arm and drew down her complicated flannel cap. Then the small flakes came in skirmish line, and the horse bent his neck patiently as a transparency of white appeared momentarily on his coat.

"Oh, he's cold, Harry," she said quickly.

"Who? The horse? Oh, no, he isn't. He likes it!"

After another ten minutes they turned a corner and came in sight of their destination. On a tall hill, outlined in vivid glaring green against the wintry sky, stood the ice palace. It was three storeys in the air, with battlements and embrasures and narrow icicled windows, and the innumerable electric lights inside made a gorgeous transparency of the great central hall. Sally Carrol clutched Harry's hand under the fur robe.

"It's beautiful!" he cried excitedly. "My golly, it's beautiful, isn't it! They haven't had one here since Eighty-five!"

Somehow the notion of there not having been one since Eighty-five oppressed her. Ice was a ghost, and this mansion of it was surely peopled by those shades of the Eighties, with pale faces and blurred, snow-filled hair.

"Come on, dear," said Harry.

She followed him out of the sleigh and waited while he hitched the horse. A party of four – Gordon, Myra, Roger Patton and another girl – drew up beside them with a mighty jingle of bells. There was quite a crowd already, bundled in fur or sheepskin, shouting and calling to each other as they moved through the snow, which was now so thick that people could scarcely be distinguished a few yards away.

"It's a hundred and seventy feet tall," Harry was saying to a muffled figure beside him as they trudged towards the entrance, "covers six thousand square yards."

She caught snatches of conversation: "One main hall"… "walls twenty to forty inches thick"… "and the ice cave has almost a mile of"… "this Canuck who built it…"

They found their way inside and, dazed by the magic of the great crystal walls, Sally Carrol found herself repeating over and over two lines from 'Kubla Khan':

"It was a miracle of rare device,
A sunny pleasure-dome with caves of ice!"*

In the great glittering cavern with the dark shut out she took a seat on a wooden bench, and the evening's oppression lifted. Harry was right – it was beautiful – and her gaze travelled the smooth surface of the walls, the blocks for which had been selected for their purity and clearness to obtain this opalescent, translucent effect.

"Look! Here we go – oh, boy!" cried Harry.

A band in a far corner struck up 'Hail, Hail, the Gang's All Here!'* which echoed over to them in wild muddled acoustics, and then the lights suddenly went out; silence seemed to flow down the icy sides and sweep over them. Sally Carrol could still see her white breath in the darkness, and a dim row of pale faces over on the other side.

The music eased to a sighing complaint, and from outside drifted in the full-throated resonant chant of the marching clubs. It grew louder like some paean of a Viking tribe traversing an ancient wild; it swelled – they were coming nearer; then a row of torches appeared, and another and another, and keeping time with their moccasined feet a long column of grey-mackinawed figures swept in, snowshoes slung at their shoulders, torches soaring and flickering as their voices rose along the great walls.

The grey column ended and another followed, the light streaming luridly this time over red toboggan caps and flaming crimson mackinaws, and as they entered they took up the refrain; then came a long platoon of blue and white, of green, of white, of brown and yellow.

"Those white ones are the Wacouta Club," whispered Harry eagerly. "Those are the men you've met round at dances."

The volume of the voices grew; the great cavern was a phantasmagoria of torches waving in great banks of fire, of colours and the rhythm of soft-leather steps. The leading column turned and halted, platoon deployed in front of platoon until the whole procession made a solid flag of flame, and then from thousands of voices burst a mighty shout that filled the air like a crash of thunder and sent the torches wavering. It was magnificent, it was tremendous! To Sally Carrol it was the North offering sacrifice on some mighty altar to the grey pagan God of Snow. As the shout died, the band struck up again and there came more singing, and then long reverberating cheers by each club. She sat very quiet, listening while the staccato cries rent the stillness, and then she started, for there was a volley of explosion, and great clouds of smoke went up here and there through the cavern – the flashlight photographers at work – and the council was over. With the band at their head the clubs formed in column once more, took up their chant and began to march out.

"Come on!" shouted Harry. "We want to see the labyrinths downstairs before they turn the lights off!"

They all rose and started towards the chute – Harry and Sally Carrol in the lead, her little mitten buried in his big fur gantlet. At the bottom of the chute was a long empty room of ice, with the ceiling so low that they had to stoop – and their hands were parted. Before she realized what he intended, Harry had darted down one of the half-dozen glittering passages that opened into the room, and was only a vague receding blot against the green shimmer.

"Harry!" she called.

"Come on!" he cried back.

She looked round the empty chamber; the rest of the party had evidently decided to go home, were already outside somewhere in the blundering snow. She hesitated and then darted in after Harry.

"Harry!" she shouted.

She had reached a turning point thirty feet down; she heard a faint muffled answer far to the left, and with a touch of panic fled towards it. She passed another turning, two more yawning alleys.

"Harry!"

No answer. She started to run straight forward, and then turned like lightning and sped back the way she had come, enveloped in a sudden icy terror.

She reached a turn – was it here? – took the left and came to what should have been the outlet into the long, low room, but it was only another glittering passage with darkness at the end. She called again, but the walls gave back a flat, lifeless echo with no reverberations. Retracing her steps, she turned another corner, this time following a wide passage. It was like the green lane between the parted waters of the Red Sea, like a damp vault connecting empty tombs.

She slipped a little now as she walked, for ice had formed on bottom of her overshoes; she had to run her gloves along the half-slippery, half-sticky walls to keep her balance.

"Harry!"

Still no answer. The sound she made bounced mockingly down to the end of the passage.

Then on an instant the lights went out, and she was in complete darkness. She gave a small, frightened cry, and sank down into a cold little heap on the ice. She felt her left knee do something as she fell, but she scarcely noticed it as some deep terror far greater than any fear of being lost settled upon her. She was alone with this presence that came out of the North, the dreary loneliness that rose from ice-bound whalers in the Arctic seas, from smokeless, trackless wastes where were strewn the whitened bones of adventure. It was an icy breath of death; it was rolling down low across the land to clutch at her.

With a furious, despairing energy she rose again and started blindly down the darkness. She must get out. She might be lost in here for days, freeze to death and lie embedded in the ice like corpses she had read of, kept perfectly preserved until the melting of a glacier. Harry probably thought she had left with the others – he had gone by now; no one would know until late next day. She reached pitifully for the wall. Forty inches thick, they had said – forty inches thick!

"Oh!"

On both sides of her along the walls she felt things creeping, damp souls that haunted this palace, this town, this North.

"Oh, send somebody – send somebody!" she cried aloud.

Clark Darrow – he would understand – or Joe Ewing; she couldn't be left here to wander for ever – to be frozen, heart, body and soul. This her – this Sally Carrol! Why, she was a happy thing. She was a happy little girl. She liked warmth and summer and Dixie. These things were foreign – foreign.

"You're not crying," something said aloud. "You'll never cry any more. Your tears would just freeze; all tears freeze up here!"

She sprawled full length on the ice.

"Oh, God!" she faltered.

A long single file of minutes went by, and with a great weariness she felt her eyes closing. Then someone seemed to sit down near her and take her face in warm, soft hands. She looked up gratefully.

"Why, it's Margery Lee," she crooned softly to herself. "I knew you'd come." It really was Margery Lee, and she was just as Sally Carrol had known she would be, with a young, white brow and wide, welcoming eyes, and a hoop skirt of some soft material that was quite comforting to rest on.

"Margery Lee."

It was getting darker now and darker – all those tombstones ought to be repainted, sure enough, only that would spoil 'em, of course. Still, you ought to be able to see 'em.

Then, after a succession of moments that went fast and then slow, but seemed to be ultimately resolving themselves into a multitude of blurred rays converging toward a pale-yellow sun, she heard a great cracking noise break her new-found stillness.

It was the sun, it was a light; a torch, and a torch beyond that, and another one, and voices; a face took flesh below the torch, heavy arms raised her, and she felt something on her cheek – it felt wet. Someone had seized her and was rubbing her face with snow. How ridiculous – with snow!

"Sally Carrol! Sally Carrol!"

It was Dangerous Dan McGrew – and two other faces she didn't know.

"Child, child! We've been looking for you two hours! Harry's half-crazy!"

Things came rushing back into place – the singing, the torches, the great shout of the marching clubs. She squirmed in Patton's arms and gave a long, low cry.

"Oh, I want to get out of here! I'm going back home. Take me home" – her voice rose to a scream that sent a chill to Harry's heart as he came racing down the next passage – "tomorrow!" she cried with delirious, unrestrained passion. "Tomorrow! Tomorrow! Tomorrow!"

6

THE WEALTH OF GOLDEN SUNLIGHT poured a quite enervating yet oddly comforting heat over the house where day-long it faced the dusty stretch of road. Two birds were making a great to-do in a cool spot found among the branches of a tree next door, and down the street a coloured woman was announcing herself melodiously as a purveyor of strawberries. It was April afternoon.

Sally Carrol Happer, resting her chin on her arm, and her arm on an old window seat, gazed sleepily down over the spangled dust whence the heatwaves were rising for the first time this spring. She was watching a very ancient Ford turn a perilous corner and rattle and groan to a jolting stop at the end of the walk. She made no sound, and in a minute a strident familiar whistle rent the air. Sally Carrol smiled and blinked.

"Good mawnin'."

A head appeared tortuously from under the car top below.

"'Tain't mawnin', Sally Carrol."

"Sure enough!" she said in affected surprise. "I guess maybe not."

"What you doin'?"

"Eatin' green peach. 'Spect to die any minute."

Clark twisted himself a last impossible notch to get a view of her face. "Water's warm as a kettle steam, Sally Carrol. Wanta go swimmin'?"

"Hate to move," sighed Sally Carrol lazily, "but I reckon so."

Head and Shoulders

1

I N 1915 HORACE TARBOX was thirteen years old. In that year he took the examinations for entrance to Princeton University and received the Grade A – excellent – in Caesar, Cicero, Virgil, Xenophon, Homer, Algebra, Plane Geometry, Solid Geometry and Chemistry.

Two years later, while George M. Cohan was composing 'Over There',* Horace was leading the sophomore class by several lengths and digging out theses on "The Syllogism as an Obsolete Scholastic Form", and during the battle of Château-Thierry* he was sitting at his desk deciding whether or not to wait until his seventeenth birthday before beginning his series of essays on "The Pragmatic Bias of the New Realists".

After a while some newsboy told him that the War was over, and he was glad, because it meant that Peat Brothers, publishers, would get out their new edition of *Spinoza's Improvement of the Understanding*. Wars were all very well in their way, made young men self-reliant or something, but Horace felt that he could never forgive the President for allowing a brass band to play under his window on the night of the false armistice, causing him to leave three important sentences out of his thesis on "German Idealism".

The next year he went up to Yale to take his degree as Master of Arts.

He was seventeen then, tall and slender, with near-sighted grey eyes and an air of keeping himself utterly detached from the mere words he let drop.

"I never feel as though I'm talking to him," expostulated Professor Dillinger to a sympathetic colleague. "He makes me feel as though I were talking to his representative. I always expect him to say: 'Well, I'll ask myself and find out.'"

And then, just as nonchalantly as though Horace Tarbox had been Mr Beef the butcher or Mr Hat the haberdasher, life reached in, seized him, handled him, stretched him and unrolled him like a piece of Irish lace on a Saturday-afternoon bargain counter.

To move in the literary fashion I should say that this was all because when way back in colonial days the hardy pioneers had come to a bald place in Connecticut and asked of each other, "Now, what shall we build here?" the hardiest one among 'em had answered: "Let's build a town where theatrical managers can try out musical comedies!" How afterwards they founded Yale College there, to try the musical comedies on, is a story everyone knows. At any rate one December, *Home James* opened at the Shubert, and all the students encored Marcia Meadow, who sang a song about the Blundering Blimp in the first act and did a shaky, shivery, celebrated dance in the last.

Marcia was nineteen. She didn't have wings, but audiences agreed generally that she didn't need them. She was a blonde by natural pigment, and she wore no paint on the streets at high noon. Outside of that she was no better than most women.

It was Charlie Moon who promised her five thousand Pall Malls if she would pay a call on Horace Tarbox, prodigy extraordinary. Charlie was a senior in Sheffield, and he and Horace were first cousins. They liked and pitied each other.

Horace had been particularly busy that night. The failure of the Frenchman Laurier to appreciate the significance of the new realists was preying on his mind. In fact, his only reaction to a low, clear-cut rap at his study was to make him speculate as to whether any rap would have actual existence without an ear there to hear it. He fancied he was verging more and more towards pragmatism. But at that moment, though he did not know it, he was verging with astounding rapidity towards something quite different.

The rap sounded – three seconds leaked by – the rap sounded.

"Come in," muttered Horace automatically.

He heard the door open and then close, but, bent over his book in the big armchair before the fire, he did not look up.

"Leave it on the bed in the other room," he said absently.

"Leave what on the bed in the other room?"

Marcia Meadow had to talk her songs, but her speaking voice was like byplay on a harp.

"The laundry."

"I can't."

Horace stirred impatiently in his chair.

"Why can't you?"

"Why because I haven't got it."

"Hm!" he replied testily. "Suppose you go back and get it."

Across the fire from Horace was another easy chair. He was accustomed to change to it in the course of an evening by way of exercise and variety. One chair he called Berkeley, the other he called Hume. He suddenly heard a sound as of a rustling, diaphanous form sinking into Hume. He glanced up.

"Well," said Marcia with the sweet smile she used in Act Two ("Oh, so the Duke liked my dancing!"). "Well, Omar Khayyam,* here I am beside you singing in the wilderness."

Horace stared at her dazedly. The momentary suspicion came to him that she existed there only as a phantom of his imagination. Women didn't come into men's rooms and sink into men's Humes. Women brought laundry and took your seat in the streetcar and married you later on when you were old enough to know fetters.

This woman had clearly materialized out of Hume. The very froth of her brown gauzy dress was an emanation from Hume's leather arm there! If he looked long enough he would see Hume right through her and then he would be alone again in the room. He passed his fist across his eyes. He really must take up those trapeze exercises again.

"For Pete's sake, don't look so critical!" objected the emanation pleasantly. "I feel as if you were going to wish me away with that patent dome of yours. And then there wouldn't be anything left of me except my shadow in your eyes."

Horace coughed. Coughing was one of his two gestures. When he talked, you forgot he had a body at all. It was like hearing a phonograph record by a singer who had been dead a long time.

"What do you want?" he asked.

"I want them letters," whined Marcia melodramatically – "them letters of mine you bought from my grandsire in 1881."

Horace considered.

"I haven't got your letters," he said evenly. "I am only seventeen years old. My father was not born until March 3rd, 1879. You evidently have me confused with some one else."

"You're only seventeen?" repeated Marcia suspiciously.

"Only seventeen."

"I knew a girl," said Marcia reminiscently, "who went on the ten-twenty-thirty* when she was sixteen. She was so stuck on herself that she could never say 'sixteen' without putting the 'only' before it. We got to calling her 'Only Jessie'. And she's just where she was when she started – only worse. 'Only' is a bad habit, Omar – it sounds like an alibi."

"My name is not Omar."

"I know," agreed Marcia, nodding – "your name's Horace. I just call you Omar because you remind me of a smoked cigarette."*

"And I haven't your letters. I doubt if I've ever met your grandfather. In fact, I think it very improbable that you yourself were alive in 1881."

Marcia stared at him in wonder.

"Me – 1881? Why sure! I was second-line stuff when the *Florodora* Sextet* was still in the convent. I was the original nurse to Mrs Sol Smith's Juliet.* Why, Omar, I was a canteen singer during the war of 1812."

Horace's mind made a sudden successful leap, and he grinned.

"Did Charlie Moon put you up to this?"

Marcia regarded him inscrutably.

"Who's Charlie Moon?"

"Small – wide nostrils – big ears."

She grew several inches and sniffed.

"I'm not in the habit of noticing my friends' nostrils."

"Then it was Charlie?"

Marcia bit her lip – and then yawned.

"Oh, let's change the subject, Omar. I'll pull a snore in this chair in a minute."

"Yes," relied Horace gravely, "Hume has often been considered soporific."

"Who's your friend – and will he die?"

Then of a sudden Horace Tarbox rose slenderly and began to pace the room with his hands in his pockets. This was his other gesture.

"I don't care for this," he said, as if he were talking to himself – "at all. Not that I mind your being here – I don't. You're quite a pretty little thing, but I don't like Charlie Moon's sending you up here. Am I a laboratory experiment on which the janitors as well as the chemists can make experiments? Is my intellectual development humorous in any way? Do I look like the pictures of the little Boston boy in the comic magazines? Has that callow ass, Moon, with eternal tales about his week in Paris, any right to—"

"No," interrupted Marcia emphatically. "And you're a sweet boy. Come here and kiss me."

Horace stopped quickly in front of her.

"Why do you want me to kiss you?" he asked intently. "Do you just go round kissing people?"

"Why, yes," admitted Marcia, unruffled. "'At's all life is. Just going round kissing people."

"Well," replied Horace emphatically, "I must say your ideas are horribly garbled! In the first place life isn't just that, and in the second place I won't kiss you. It might get to be a habit and I can't get rid of habits. This year I've got in the habit of lolling in bed until seven thirty."

Marcia nodded understandingly.

"Do you ever have any fun?" she asked.

"What do you mean by fun?"

"See here," said Marcia sternly, "I like you, Omar, but I wish you'd talk as if you had a line on what you were saying. You sound as if you were gargling a lot of words in your mouth and lost a bet every time you spilt a few. I asked you if you ever had any fun."

Horace shook his head.

"Later, perhaps," he answered. "You see, I'm a plan. I'm an experiment. I don't say that I don't get tired of it sometimes – I do. Yet… oh, I can't explain! But what you and Charlie Moon call fun wouldn't be fun to me."

"Please explain."

Horace stared at her, started to speak and then, changing his mind, resumed his walk. After an unsuccessful attempt to determine whether or not he was looking at her, Marcia smiled at him.

"Please explain."

Horace turned.

"If I do, will you promise to tell Charlie Moon that I wasn't in?"

"Uh-uh."

"Very well, then. Here's my history: I was a 'why' child. I wanted to see the wheels go round. My father was a young economics professor at Princeton. He brought me up on the system of answering every question I asked him to the best of his ability. My response to that gave him the idea of making an experiment in precocity. To aid in the massacre I had ear trouble – seven operations between the ages of nine and twelve. Of course this kept me apart from other boys and made me ripe for forcing. Anyway, while my generation was labouring through Uncle Remus* I was honestly enjoying Catullus in the original.

"I passed off my college examinations when I was thirteen because I couldn't help it. My chief associates were professors, and I took a tremendous pride in knowing that I had a fine intelligence, for though I was unusually gifted I was not abnormal in other ways. When I was sixteen I got tired of being a freak; I decided that someone had made a bad mistake. Still, as I'd gone that far, I concluded to finish it up by taking my degree of Master of Arts. My chief interest in life is the study of modern philosophy. I am a realist of the School of Anton Laurier

– with Bergsonian* trimmings – and I'll be eighteen years old in two months. That's all."

"Whew!" exclaimed Marcia. "That's enough! You do a neat job with the parts of speech."

"Satisfied?"

"No, you haven't kissed me."

"It's not in my programme," demurred Horace. "Understand that I don't pretend to be above physical things. They have their place, but—"

"Oh, don't be so darned reasonable!"

"I can't help it."

"I hate these slot-machine people."

"I assure you I—" began Horace.

"Oh, shut up!"

"My own rationality—"

"I didn't say anything about your nationality. You're an Amuricun, ar'n't you?"

"Yes."

"Well, that's OK with me. I got a notion I want to see you do something that isn't in your highbrow programme. I want to see if a what-ch-call-em with Brazilian trimmings – that thing you said you were – can be a little human."

Horace shook his head again.

"I won't kiss you."

"My life is blighted," muttered Marcia tragically. "I'm a beaten woman. I'll go through life without ever having a kiss with Brazilian trimmings." She sighed. "Anyways, Omar, will you come and see my show?"

"What show?"

"I'm a wicked actress from *Home James*!"

"Light opera?"

"Yes – at a stretch. One of the characters is a Brazilian rice-planter. That might interest you."

"I saw *The Bohemian Girl** once," reflected Horace aloud. "I enjoyed it – to some extent."

"Then you'll come?"

"Well, I'm…I'm—"

"Oh, I know – you've got to run down to Brazil for the weekend."

"Not at all. I'd be delighted to come."

Marcia clapped her hands.

"Goodyforyou! I'll mail you a ticket – Thursday night?"

"Why, I—"

"Good! Thursday night it is."

She stood up and, walking close to him, laid both hands on his shoulders.

"I like you, Omar. I'm sorry I tried to kid you. I thought you'd be sort of frozen, but you're a nice boy."

He eyed her sardonically.

"I'm several thousand generations older than you are."

"You carry your age well."

They shook hands gravely.

"My name's Marcia Meadow," she said emphatically. "'Member it – Marcia Meadow. And I won't tell Charlie Moon you were in."

An instant later, as she was skimming down the last flight of stairs three at a time, she heard a voice call over the upper banister: "Oh, say…"

She stopped and looked up – made out a vague form leaning over.

"Oh, say!" called the prodigy again. "Can you hear me?"

"Here's your connection, Omar."

"I hope I haven't given you the impression that I consider kissing intrinsically irrational."

"Impression? Why, you didn't even give me the kiss… Never fret – so long."

Two doors near her opened curiously at the sound of a feminine voice. A tentative cough sounded from above. Gathering her skirts, Marcia dived wildly down the last flight and was swallowed up in the murky Connecticut air outside.

Upstairs Horace paced the floor of his study. From time to time he glanced towards Berkeley waiting there in suave dark-red respectability, an open book lying suggestively on his cushions. And then he found that his circuit of the floor was bringing him each time nearer to Hume. There was something about Hume that was strangely and inexpressibly different. The diaphanous form still seemed hovering near, and had Horace sat there he would have felt as if he were sitting on a lady's lap. And though Horace couldn't have named the quality of difference, there was such a quality – quite intangible to the speculative mind, but real nevertheless. Hume was radiating something that in all the two hundred years of his influence he had never radiated before.

Hume was radiating attar of roses.

2

ON THURSDAY NIGHT Horace Tarbox sat in an aisle seat in the fifth row and witnessed *Home James*. Oddly enough he found that he was enjoying himself. The cynical students near him were annoyed at his audible appreciation of time-honoured jokes in the Hammerstein tradition. But Horace was waiting with anxiety for Marcia Meadow singing her song about a Jazz-bound Blundering Blimp. When she did appear, radiant under a floppity flower-faced hat, a warm glow settled over him, and when the song was over he did not join in the storm of applause. He felt somewhat numb.

In the intermission after the second act, an usher materialized beside him, demanded to know if he were Mr Tarbox, and then handed him a note written in a round adolescent hand. Horace read it in some confusion, while the usher lingered with withering patience in the aisle.

DEAR OMAR: After the show I always grow an awful hunger. If you want to satisfy it for me in the Taft Grill just communicate your answer to the big-timber guide that brought this and oblige.
   Your friend,
      MARCIA MEADOW

"Tell her" – he coughed – "tell her that it will be quite all right. I'll meet her in front of the theatre."

The big-timber guide smiled arrogantly.

"I giss she meant for you to come roun' t' the stage door."

"Where... where is it?"

"Ou'side. Tunayulef. Down ee alley."

"What?"

"Ou'side. Turn to y' left! Down ee alley!"

The arrogant person withdrew. A freshman behind Horace snickered.

Then half an hour later, sitting in the Taft Grill opposite the hair that was yellow by natural pigment, the prodigy was saying an odd thing.

"Do you have to do that dance in the last act?" he was asking earnestly. "I mean, would they dismiss you if you refused to do it?"

Marcia grinned.

"It's fun to do it. I like to do it."

And then Horace came out with a faux pas.

"I should think you'd detest it," he remarked succinctly. "The people behind me were making remarks about your bosom."

Marcia blushed fiery red.

"I can't help that," she said quickly. "The dance to me is only a sort of acrobatic stunt. Lord, it's hard enough to do! I rub liniment into my shoulders for an hour every night."

"Do you have... fun while you're on the stage?"

"Uh-huh – sure! I got in the habit of having people look at me, Omar, and I like it."

"Hm!" Horace sank into a brownish study.

"How's the Brazilian trimmings?"

"Hm!" repeated Horace, and then after a pause: "Where does the play go from here?"

"New York."

"For how long?"

"All depends. Winter – maybe."

"Oh!"

"Coming up to lay eyes on me, Omar, or aren't you int'rested? Not as nice here, is it, as it was up in your room? I wish we was there now."

"I feel idiotic in this place," confessed Horace, looking around him nervously.

"Too bad! We got along pretty well."

At this he looked suddenly so melancholy that she changed her tone, and reaching over patted his hand.

"Ever take an actress out to supper before?"

"No," said Horace miserably, "and I never will again. I don't know why I came tonight. Here under all these lights and with all these people laughing and chattering I feel completely out of my sphere. I don't know what to talk to you about."

"We'll talk about me. We talked about you last time."

"Very well."

"Well, my name really is Meadow, but my first name isn't Marcia – it's Veronica. I'm nineteen. Question – how did the girl make her leap to the footlights? Answer – she was born in Passaic, New Jersey, and up to a year ago she got the right to breathe by pushing Nabiscoes in Marcel's tearoom in Trenton. She started going with a guy named Robbins, a singer in the Trent House cabaret, and he got her to try a song and dance with him one evening. In a month we were filling the supper room every night. Then we went to New York with meet-my-friend letters thick as a pile of napkins.

"In two days we'd landed a job at Divinerries', and I learnt to shimmy from a kid at the Palais Royal. We stayed at Divinerries' six months until one night Peter Boyce Wendell, the columnist, ate his milk toast there. Next morning a poem about Marvellous Marcia came out in his newspaper, and within two days I had three vaudeville offers and a chance at the Midnight Frolic. I wrote Wendell a thank-you letter, and he printed it in his column – said that the style was like Carlyle's, only more rugged, and that I ought to quit dancing and do North American literature. This got me a coupla more vaudeville offers and a chance as an ingénue in a regular show. I took it – and here I am, Omar."

When she finished, they sat for a moment in silence, she draping the last skeins of a Welsh rabbit on her fork and waiting for him to speak.

"Let's get out of here," he said suddenly.

Marcia's eyes hardened.

"What's the idea? Am I making you sick?"

"No, but I don t like it here. I don't like to be sitting here with you."

Without another word Marcia signalled for the waiter.

"What's the cheque?" she demanded briskly. "My part – the rabbit and the ginger ale."

Horace watched blankly as the waiter figured it.

"See here," he began, "I intended to pay for yours too. You're my guest."

With a half-sigh Marcia rose from the table and walked from the room. Horace, his face a document in bewilderment, laid a bill down and followed her out, up the stairs and into the lobby. He overtook her in front of the elevator and they faced each other.

"See here," he repeated, "you're my guest. Have I said something to offend you?"

After an instant of wonder Marcia's eyes softened.

"You're a rude fella," she said slowly. "Don't you know you're rude?"

"I can't help it," said Horace with a directness she found quite disarming. "You know I like you."

"You said you didn't like being with me."

"I didn't like it."

"Why not?"

Fire blazed suddenly from the grey forests of his eyes.

"Because I didn't. I've formed the habit of liking you. I've been thinking of nothing much else for two days."

"Well, if you—"

"Wait a minute," he interrupted. "I've got something to say. It's this: in six weeks I'll be eighteen years old. When I'm eighteen years old I'm coming up to New York to see you. Is there some place in New York where we can go and not have a lot of people in the room?"

"Sure!" smiled Marcia. "You can come up to my 'partment. Sleep on the couch, if you want to."

"I can't sleep on couches," he said shortly. "But I want to talk to you."

"Why, sure," repeated Marcia – "in my 'partment."

In his excitement Horace put his hands in his pockets.

"All right – just so I can see you alone. I want to talk to you as we talked up in my room."

"Honey boy," cried Marcia, laughing, "is it that you want to kiss me?"

"Yes," Horace almost shouted. "I'll kiss you if you want me to."

The elevator man was looking at them reproachfully. Marcia edged towards the grated door.

"I'll drop you a postcard," she said.

Horace's eyes were quite wild.

"Send me a postcard! I'll come up any time after January first. I'll be eighteen then."

And as she stepped into the elevator he coughed enigmatically with a vague challenge, at the ceiling, and walked quickly away.

3

H E WAS THERE AGAIN. She saw him when she took her first glance at the restless Manhattan audience – down in the front row with his head bent a bit forward and his grey eyes fixed on her. And she knew that to him they were alone together in a world where the high-rouged row of ballet faces and the massed whines of the violins were as imperceivable as powder on a marble Venus. An instinctive defiance rose within her.

"Silly boy!" she said to herself hurriedly, and she didn't take her encore.

"What do they expect for a hundred a week – perpetual motion?" she grumbled to herself in the wings.

"What's the trouble, Marcia?"

"Guy I don't like down in front."

During the last act, as she waited for her specialty, she had an odd attack of stage fright. She had never sent Horace the promised postcard.

Last night she had pretended not to see him – had hurried from the theatre immediately after her dance to pass a sleepless night in her apartment, thinking – as she had so often in the last month – of his pale, rather intent face, his slim, boyish figure, the merciless, unworldly abstraction that made him charming to her.

And now that he had come she felt vaguely sorry – as though an unwonted responsibility was being forced on her.

"Infant prodigy!" she said aloud.

"What?" demanded the Negro comedian standing beside her.

"Nothing – just talking about myself."

On the stage she felt better. This was her dance – and she always felt that the way she did it wasn't suggestive any more than to some men every pretty girl is suggestive. She made it a stunt.

"Uptown, downtown, jelly on a spoon,
After sundown shiver by the moon."

He was not watching her now. She saw that clearly. He was looking very deliberately at a castle on the backdrop, wearing that expression he had worn in the Taft Grill. A wave of exasperation swept over her – he was criticizing her.

"That's the vibration that thr-ills me,
Funny how affection fi-lls me,
Uptown, downtown..."

Unconquerable revulsion seized her. She was suddenly and horribly conscious of her audience as she had never been since her first appearance. Was that a leer on a pallid face in the front row, droop of disgust on one young girl's mouth? These shoulders of hers – these shoulders shaking – were they hers? Were they real? Surely shoulders weren't made for this!

"Then – you'll see at a glance
I'll need some funeral ushers with St Vitus dance
At the end of the world I'll…"

The bassoon and two cellos crashed into a final chord. She paused and poised a moment on her toes with every muscle tense, her young face looking out dully at the audience in what one young girl afterward called "such a curious, puzzled look", and then without bowing rushed from the stage. Into the dressing room she sped, kicked out of one dress and into another, and caught a taxi outside.

Her apartment was very warm – small, it was, with a row of professional pictures and sets of Kipling and O. Henry which she had bought once from a blue-eyed agent and read occasionally. And there were several chairs which matched, but were none of them comfortable, and a pink-shaded lamp with blackbirds painted on it and an atmosphere of rather stifled pink throughout. There were nice things in it – nice things unrelentingly hostile to each other, offsprings of a vicarious, impatient taste acting in stray moments. The worst was typified by a great picture framed in oak bark of Passaic as seen from the Erie Railroad – altogether a frantic, oddly extravagant, oddly penurious attempt to make a cheerful room. Marcia knew it was a failure.

Into this room came the prodigy and took her two hands awkwardly.

"I followed you this time," he said.

"Oh!"

"I want you to marry me," he said.

Her arms went out to him. She kissed his mouth with a sort of passionate wholesomeness.

"There!"

"I love you," he said.

She kissed him again, and then with a little sigh flung herself into an armchair and half-lay there, shaken with absurd laughter.

"Why, you infant prodigy!" she cried.

"Very well, call me that if you want to. I once told you that I was ten thousand years older than you – I am."

She laughed again.

"I don't like to be disapproved of."

"No one's ever going to disapprove of you again."

"Omar," she asked, "why do you want to marry me?"

The prodigy rose and put his hands in his pockets.

"Because I love you, Marcia Meadow."

And then she stopped calling him Omar.

"Dear boy," she said, "you know I sort of love you. There's something about you – I can't tell what – that just puts my heart through the wringer every time I'm round you. But, honey…" She paused.

"But what?"

"But lots of things. But you're only just eighteen, and I'm nearly twenty."

"Nonsense!" he interrupted. "Put it this way – that I'm in my nine-teenth year and you're nineteen. That makes us pretty close – without counting that other ten thousand years I mentioned."

Marcia laughed.

"But there are some more 'buts'. Your people—"

"My people!" exclaimed the prodigy ferociously. "My people tried to make a monstrosity out of me." His face grew quite crimson at the enormity of what he was going to say. "My people can go way back and sit down!"

"My Heavens!" cried Marcia in alarm. "All that? On tacks, I suppose."

"Tacks – yes," he agreed wildly – "on anything. The more I think of how they allowed me to become a little dried-up mummy—"

"What makes you think you're that?" asked Marcia quietly. "Me?"

"Yes. Every person I've met on the streets since I met you has made me jealous, because they knew what love was before I did. I used to call it the 'sex impulse'. Heavens!"

"There's more 'buts'," said Marcia.

"What are they?"

"How could we live?"

"I'll make a living."

"You're in college."

"Do you think I care anything about taking a Master of Arts degree?"

"You want to be Master of Me, hey?"

"Yes! What? I mean, no!"

Marcia laughed and, crossing swiftly over, sat in his lap. He put his arm round her wildly and implanted the vestige of a kiss somewhere near her neck.

"There's something white about you," mused Marcia, "but it doesn't sound very logical."

"Oh, don't be so darned reasonable!"

"I can't help it," said Marcia.

"I hate these slot-machine people!"

"But we—"

"Oh, shut up!"

And as Marcia couldn't talk through her ears she had to.

4

H ORACE AND MARCIA WERE MARRIED early in February. The sensation in academic circles both at Yale and Princeton was tremendous. Horace Tarbox, who at fourteen had been played up in the Sunday-magazine sections of metropolitan newspapers, was throwing over his career, his chance of being a world authority on American philosophy, by marrying a chorus girl – they made Marcia a chorus girl. But like all modern stories it was a four-and-a-half-day wonder.

They took a flat in Harlem. After two weeks' search, during which his idea of the value of academic knowledge faded unmercifully, Horace took a position as clerk with a South American export company – someone had told him that exporting was the coming thing. Marcia was to stay in her show for a few months – anyway until he got on his feet. He was getting a hundred and twenty-five to start with, and though of course they told him it was only a question of months until he would be earning double that, Marcia refused even to consider giving up the hundred and fifty a week she was getting at the time.

"We'll call ourselves Head and Shoulders, dear," she said softly, "and the shoulders'll have to keep shaking a little longer until the old head gets started."

"I hate it," he objected gloomily.

"Well," she replied emphatically, "your salary wouldn't keep us in a tenement. Don't think I want to be public – I don't. I want to be yours. But I'd be a halfwit to sit in one room and count the sunflowers on the wallpaper while I waited for you. When you pull down three hundred a month I'll quit."

And much as it hurt his pride, Horace had to admit that hers was the wiser course.

March mellowed into April. May read a gorgeous riot act to the parks and waters of Manhattan, and they were very happy. Horace, who had no habits whatsoever – he had never had time to form any – proved the most adaptable of husbands, and as Marcia entirely lacked opinions on the subjects that engrossed him there were very few joltings and bumpings. Their minds moved in different spheres. Marcia acted as practical factotum, and Horace lived either in his old world of abstract ideas or in a sort of triumphantly earthy worship and adoration of his wife. She was a continual source of astonishment to him – the freshness and originality of her mind, her dynamic, clear-headed energy and her unfailing good humour.

And Marcia's co-workers in the nine-o'clock show, whither she had transferred her talents, were impressed with her tremendous pride in her husband's mental powers. Horace they knew only as a very slim, tight-lipped and immature-looking young man, who waited every night to take her home.

"Horace," said Marcia one evening when she met him as usual at eleven, "you looked like a ghost standing there against the streetlights. You losing weight?"

He shook his head vaguely.

"I don't know. They raised me to a hundred and thirty-five dollars today, and—"

"I don't care," said Marcia severely. "You're killing yourself working at night. You read those big books on economy—"

"Economics," corrected Horace.

"Well, you read 'em every night long after I'm asleep. And you're getting all stooped over like you were before we were married."

"But, Marcia, I've got to—"

"No, you haven't, dear. I guess I'm running this shop for the present, and I won't let my fella ruin his health and eyes. You got to get some exercise."

"I do. Every morning I—"

"Oh, I know! But those dumbbells of yours wouldn't give a consumptive two degrees of fever. I mean real exercise. You've got to join a gymnasium. 'Member you told me you were such a trick gymnast once that they tried to get you out for the team in college and they couldn't, because you had a standing date with Herb Spencer?"

"I used to enjoy it," mused Horace, "but it would take up too much time now."

"All right," said Marcia. "I'll make a bargain with you. You join a gym and I'll read one of those books from the brown row of 'em."

"*Pepys's Diary*? Why, that ought to be enjoyable. He's very light."

"Not for me – he isn't. It'll be like digesting plate glass. But you been telling me how much it'd broaden my lookout. Well, you go to a gym three nights a week and I'll take one big dose of Sammy."

Horace hesitated.

"Well—"

"Come on, now! You do some giant swings for me and I'll chase some culture for you."

So Horace finally consented, and all through a baking summer he spent three and sometimes four evenings a week experimenting on the trapeze in Skipper's Gymnasium. And in August he admitted to Marcia that it made him capable of more mental work during the day.

"*Mens sana in corpore sano*,"* he said.

"Don't believe in it," replied Marcia. "I tried one of those patent medicines once and they're all bunk. You stick to gymnastics."

One night in early September, while he was going through one of his contortions on the rings in the nearly deserted room, he was addressed by a meditative fat man whom he had noticed watching him for several nights.

"Say, lad, do that stunt you were doin' last night."

Horace grinned at him from his perch.

"I invented it," he said. "I got the idea from the fourth proposition of Euclid."

"What circus he with?"

"He's dead."

"Well, he must of broke his neck doin' that stunt. I set here last night thinkin' sure you was goin' to break yours."

"Like this!" said Horace, and swinging onto the trapeze he did his stunt.

"Don't it kill your neck an' shoulder muscles?"

"It did at first, but inside of a week I wrote the *quod erat demonstrandum** on it."

"Hm!"

Horace swung idly on the trapeze.

"Ever think of takin' it up professionally?" asked the fat man.

"Not I."

"Good money in it if you're willin' to do stunts like 'at an' can get away with it."

"Here's another," chirped Horace eagerly, and the fat man's mouth dropped suddenly agape as he watched this pink-jerseyed Prometheus again defy the gods and Isaac Newton.

The night following this encounter, Horace got home from work to find a rather pale Marcia stretched out on the sofa waiting for him.

"I fainted twice today," she began without preliminaries.

"What?"

"Yep. You see baby's due in four months now. Doctor says I ought to have quit dancing two weeks ago."

Horace sat down and thought it over.

"I'm glad, of course," he said pensively. "I mean glad that we're going to have a baby. But this means a lot of expense."

"I've got two hundred and fifty in the bank," said Marcia hopefully, "and two weeks' pay coming."

Horace computed quickly.

"Including my salary, that'll give us nearly fourteen hundred for the next six months."

Marcia looked blue.

"That all? Course I can get a job singing somewhere this month. And I can go to work again in March."

"Of course nothing!" said Horace gruffly. "You'll stay right here. Let's see now – there'll be doctor's bills and a nurse, besides the maid. We've got to have some more money."

"Well," said Marcia wearily, "I don't know where it's coming from. It's up to the old head now. Shoulders is out of business."

Horace rose and pulled on his coat.

"Where are you going?"

"I've got an idea," he answered. "I'll be right back."

Ten minutes later, as he headed down the street toward Skipper's Gymnasium, he felt a placid wonder, quite unmixed with humour, at what he was going to do. How he would have gaped at himself a year before! How everyone would have gaped! But when you opened your door at the rap of life you let in many things.

The gymnasium was brightly lit, and when his eyes became accustomed to the glare he found the meditative fat man seated on a pile of canvas mats smoking a big cigar.

"Say," began Horace directly, "were you in earnest last night when you said I could make money on my trapeze stunts?"

"Why, yes," said the fat man in surprise.

"Well, I've been thinking it over, and I believe I'd like to try it. I could work at night and on Saturday afternoons – and regularly if the pay is high enough."

The fat man looked at his watch.

"Well," he said. "Charlie Paulson's the man to see. He'll book you inside of four days, once he sees you work out. He won't be in now, but I'll get hold of him for tomorrow night."

The fat man was as good as his word. Charlie Paulson arrived next night and put in a wondrous hour watching the prodigy swoop through the air in amazing parabolas, and on the night following he brought two large men with him who looked as though they had been born smoking black cigars and talking about money in low, passionate voices. Then on the succeeding Saturday Horace Tarbox's torso made its first professional appearance in a gymnastic exhibition at the Coleman Street Gardens. But though the audience numbered nearly five thousand people, Horace felt no nervousness. From his childhood he had read papers to audiences – learnt that trick of detaching himself.

"Marcia," he said cheerfully later that same night, "I think we're out of the woods. Paulson thinks he can get me an opening at the Hippodrome, and that means an all-winter engagement. The Hippodrome, you know, is a big—"

"Yes, I believe I've heard of it," interrupted Marcia, "but I want to know about this stunt you're doing. It isn't any spectacular suicide, is it?"

"It's nothing," said Horace quietly. "But if you can think of any nicer way of a man killing himself than taking a risk for you, why that's the way I want to die."

Marcia reached up and wound both arms tightly round his neck.

"Kiss me," she whispered, "and call me 'dear heart'. I love to hear you say 'dear heart'. And bring me a book to read tomorrow. No more Sam Pepys, but something trick and trashy. I've been wild for something to do all day. I felt like writing letters, but I didn't have anybody to write to."

"Write to me," said Horace. "I'll read them."

"I wish I could," breathed Marcia. "If I knew words enough I could write you the longest love letter in the world – and never get tired."

But after two more months Marcia grew very tired indeed, and for a row of nights it was a very anxious, weary-looking young athlete who walked out before the Hippodrome crowd. Then there were two days when his place was taken by a young man who wore pale blue instead of white, and got very little applause. But after the two days Horace appeared again, and those who sat close to the stage remarked an expression of beatific happiness on that young acrobat's face, even when he was twisting breathlessly in the air in the middle of his amazing and original shoulder swing. After that performance he laughed at the elevator man and dashed up the stairs to the flat five steps at a time – and then tiptoed very carefully into a quiet room.

"Marcia," he whispered.

"Hello!" She smiled up at him wanly. "Horace, there's something I want you to do. Look in my top bureau drawer and you'll find a big stack of paper. It's a book – sort of – Horace. I wrote it down in these last three months while I've been laid up. I wish you'd take it to that Peter Boyce Wendell who put my letter in his paper. He could tell you whether it'd be a good book. I wrote it just the way I talk, just the way I wrote that letter to him. It's just a story about a lot of things that happened to me. Will you take it to him, Horace?"

"Yes, darling."

He leant over the bed until his head was beside her on the pillow, and began stroking back her yellow hair.

"Dearest Marcia," he said softly.

"No," she murmured, "call me what I told you to call me."

"Dear heart," he whispered passionately – "dearest, dearest heart."

"What'll we call her?"

They rested a minute in happy, drowsy content, while Horace considered.

"We'll call her Marcia Hume Tarbox," he said at length.

"Why the Hume?"

"Because he's the fellow who first introduced us."

"That so?" she murmured, sleepily surprised. "I thought his name was Moon."

Her eyes closed, and after a moment the slow, lengthening surge of the bedclothes over her breast showed that she was asleep.

Horace tiptoed over to the bureau and, opening the top drawer, found a heap of closely scrawled, lead-smeared pages. He looked at the first sheet:

SANDRA PEPYS, SYNCOPATED
BY MARCIA TARBOX

He smiled. So Samuel Pepys had made an impression on her after all. He turned a page and began to read. His smile deepened – he read on. Half an hour passed and he became aware that Marcia had waked and was watching him from the bed.

"Honey," came in a whisper.

"What, Marcia?"

"Do you like it?"

Horace coughed.

"I seem to be reading on. It's bright."

"Take it to Peter Boyce Wendell. Tell him you got the highest marks in Princeton once and that you ought to know when a book's good. Tell him this one's a world-beater."

"All right, Marcia," said Horace gently.

Her eyes closed again and Horace crossing over kissed her forehead – stood there for a moment with a look of tender pity. Then he left the room.

All that night the sprawly writing on the pages, the constant mistakes in spelling and grammar and the weird punctuation danced before his eyes. He woke several times in the night, each time full of a welling chaotic sympathy for this desire of Marcia's soul to express itself in words. To him there was something infinitely pathetic about it, and for the first time in months he began to turn over in his mind his own half-forgotten dreams.

He had meant to write a series of books, to popularize the new realism as Schopenhauer had popularized pessimism and William James pragmatism.*

But life hadn't come that way. Life took hold of people and forced them into flying rings. He laughed to think of that rap at his door, the diaphanous shadow in Hume, Marcia's threatened kiss.

"And it's still me," he said aloud in wonder as he lay awake in the darkness. "I'm the man who sat in Berkeley with temerity to wonder if that rap would have had actual existence had my ear not been there to hear it. I'm still that man. I could be electrocuted for the crimes he committed.

"Poor gauzy souls trying to express ourselves in something tangible. Marcia with her written book; I with my unwritten ones. Trying to choose our mediums and then taking what we get – and being glad."

5

S ANDRA PEPYS, SYNCOPATED, with an introduction by Peter Boyce Wendell, the columnist, appeared serially in *Jordan's Magazine,* and came out in book form in March. From its first published instalment it attracted attention far and wide. A trite enough subject – a girl from a small New Jersey town coming to New York to go on the stage – treated simply, with a peculiar vividness of phrasing and a haunting undertone of sadness in the very inadequacy of its vocabulary, it made an irresistible appeal.

Peter Boyce Wendell, who happened at that time to be advocating the enrichment of the American language by the immediate adoption of expressive vernacular words, stood as its sponsor and thundered his endorsement over the placid bromides of the conventional reviewers.

Marcia received three hundred dollars an instalment for the serial publication, which came at an opportune time, for though Horace's monthly salary at the Hippodrome was now more than Marcia's had ever been, young Marcia was emitting shrill cries which they interpreted as a demand for country air. So early April found them installed in a bungalow in Westchester County, with a place for a lawn, a place for a garage and a place for everything, including a soundproof impregnable study, in which Marcia faithfully promised Mr Jordan she would shut herself up when her daughter's demands began to be abated, and compose immortally illiterate literature.

"It's not half bad," thought Horace one night as he was on his way from the station to his house. He was considering several prospects that had opened up, a four months' vaudeville offer in five figures, a chance to go back to Princeton in charge of all gymnasium work. Odd! He had once intended to go back there in charge of all philosophic work, and now he had not even been stirred by the arrival in New York of Anton Laurier, his old idol.

The gravel crunched raucously under his heel. He saw the lights of his sitting room gleaming and noticed a big car standing in the drive. Probably Mr Jordan again, come to persuade Marcia to settle down to work.

She had heard the sound of his approach and her form was silhouetted against the lighted door as she came out to meet him.

"There's some Frenchman here," she whispered nervously. "I can't pronounce his name, but he sounds awful deep. You'll have to jaw with him."

"What Frenchman?"

"You can't prove it by me. He drove up an hour ago with Mr Jordan and said he wanted to meet Sandra Pepys, and all that sort of thing."

Two men rose from chairs as they went inside.

"Hello, Tarbox," said Jordan. "I've just been bringing together two celebrities. I've brought M'sieur Laurier out with me. M'sieur Laurier, let me present Mr Tarbox, Mrs Tarbox's husband."

"Not Anton Laurier!" exclaimed Horace.

"But, yes. I must come. I have to come. I have read the book of Madame, and I have been charmed" – he fumbled in his pocket – "ah, I have read of you too. In this newspaper which I read today it has your name."

He finally produced a clipping from a magazine.

"Read it!" he said eagerly. "It has about you too."

Horace's eye skipped down the page.

"A distinct contribution to American dialect literature," it said. "No attempt at literary tone; the book derives its very quality from this fact, as did *Huckleberry Finn*."

Horace's eyes caught a passage lower down; he became suddenly aghast – read on hurriedly:

"Marcia Tarbox's connection with the stage is not only as a spectator but as the wife of a performer. She was married last year to Horace Tarbox, who every evening delights the children at the Hippodrome with his wondrous flying-ring performance. It is said that the young couple have dubbed themselves Head and Shoulders, referring doubtless to the fact that Mrs Tarbox supplies the literary and mental qualities, while the supple and agile shoulders of her husband contribute their share to the family fortunes.

"Mrs Tarbox seems to merit that much abused title – 'prodigy'. Only twenty…"

Horace stopped reading, and with a very odd expression in his eyes gazed intently at Anton Laurier.

"I want to advise you…" he began hoarsely.

"What?"

"About raps. Don't answer them! Let them alone – have a padded door."

The Cut-Glass Bowl

1

THERE WAS A ROUGH-STONE AGE and a smooth-stone age and a bronze age, and many years afterwards a cut-glass age. In the cut-glass age, when young ladies had persuaded young men with long, curly moustaches to marry them, they sat down several months afterwards and wrote thank-you notes for all sorts of cut-glass presents – punchbowls, finger bowls, dinner glasses, wineglasses, ice-cream dishes, bonbon dishes, decanters and vases – for, though cut glass was nothing new in the Nineties, it was then especially busy reflecting the dazzling light of fashion from the Back Bay to the fastnesses of the Middle West.

After the wedding the punchbowls were arranged on the sideboard with the big bowl in the centre; the glasses were set up in the china closet; the candlesticks were put at both ends of things – and then the struggle for existence began. The bonbon dish lost its little handle and became a pin tray upstairs; a promenading cat knocked the little bowl off the sideboard, and the hired girl chipped the middle-sized one with the sugar dish; then the wineglasses succumbed to leg fractures, and even the dinner glasses disappeared one by one like the ten little niggers, the last one ending up, scarred and maimed, as toothbrush holder among other shabby genteels on the bathroom shelf. But by the time all this had happened, the cut-glass age was over anyway.

It was well past its first glory on the day the curious Mrs Roger Fairboalt came to see the beautiful Mrs Harold Piper.

"My *dear*," said the curious Mrs Roger Fairboalt, "I *love* your house. I think it's *quite* artistic."

"I'm *so* glad," said the beautiful Mrs Harold Piper, lights appearing in her young, dark eyes, "and you *must* come often. I'm almost *always* alone in the afternoon."

Mrs Fairboalt would have liked to remark that she didn't believe this at all and couldn't see how she'd be expected to – it was all over town that Mr Freddy Gedney had been dropping in on Mrs Piper five afternoons a week for the past six months. Mrs Fairboalt was at that ripe age where she distrusted all beautiful women...

"I love the dining room *most*," she said, "all that *marvellous* china, and that *huge* cut-glass bowl."

Mrs Piper laughed, so prettily that Mrs Fairboalt's lingering reservations about the Freddy Gedney story quite vanished.

"Oh, that big bowl!" Mrs Piper's mouth forming the words was a vivid rose petal. "There's a story about that bowl..."

"Oh..."

"You remember young Carleton Canby? Well, he was very attentive at one time, and the night I told him I was going to marry Harold, seven years ago, in Ninety-two, he drew himself way up and said: 'Evylyn, I'm going to give a present that's as hard as you are and as beautiful and as empty and as easy to see through.' He frightened me a little – his eyes were so black. I thought he was going to deed me a haunted house or something that would explode when you opened it. That bowl came, and of course it's beautiful. Its diameter or circumference or something is two and a half feet – or perhaps it's three and a half. Anyway, the sideboard is really too small for it: it sticks way out."

"My *dear*, wasn't that *odd*! And he left town about then, didn't he?" Mrs Fairboalt was scribbling italicized notes on her memory: "Hard, beautiful, empty and easy to see through."

"Yes, he went West... or South... or somewhere," answered Mrs Piper, radiating that divine vagueness that helps to lift beauty out of time.

Mrs Fairboalt drew on her gloves, approving the effect of largeness given by the open sweep from the spacious music room through the library, disclosing a part of the dining room beyond. It was really the nicest smaller house in town, and Mrs Piper had talked of moving to a larger one on Devereaux Avenue. Harold Piper must be *coining* money.

As she turned into the sidewalk under the gathering autumn dusk, she assumed that disapproving, faintly unpleasant expression that almost all successful women of forty wear on the street.

If *I* were Harold Piper, she thought, I'd spend a *little* less time on business and a *little* more time at home. Some *friend* should speak to him.

But if Mrs Fairboalt had considered it a successful afternoon, she would have named it a triumph had she waited two minutes longer. For while she was still a black receding figure a hundred yards down the street, a very good-looking distraught young man turned up the walk to the Piper house. Mrs Piper answered the doorbell herself, and with a rather dismayed expression led him quickly into the library.

"I had to see you," he began wildly. "Your note played the devil with me. Did Harold frighten you into this?"

She shook her head.

"I'm through, Fred," she said slowly, and her lips had never looked to him so much like tearings from a rose. "He came home last night sick with it. Jessie Piper's sense of duty was too much for her, so she went down to his office and told him. He was hurt and... oh, I can't help seeing it his way, Fred. He says we've been club gossip all summer and he didn't know it, and now he understands snatches of conversation he's caught and veiled hints people have dropped about me. He's mighty angry, Fred, and he loves me and I love him – rather."

Gedney nodded slowly and half-closed his eyes.

"Yes," he said, "yes, my trouble's like yours. I can see other people's points of view too plainly." His grey eyes met her dark ones frankly. "The blessed thing's over. My God, Evylyn, I've been sitting down at the office all day looking at the outside of your letter, and looking at it and looking at it—"

"You've got to go, Fred," she said steadily, and the slight emphasis of hurry in her voice was a new thrust for him. "I gave him my word of honour I wouldn't see you. I know just how far I can go with

Harold, and being here with you this evening is one of the things I can't do."

They were still standing, and as she spoke she made a little movement towards the door. Gedney looked at her miserably, trying, here at the end, to treasure up a last picture of her – and then suddenly both of them were stiffened into marble at the sound of steps on the walk outside. Instantly her arm reached out grasping the lapel of his coat – half urged, half swung him through the big door into the dark dining room.

"I'll make him go upstairs," she whispered close to his ear. "Don't move till you hear him on the stairs. Then go out the front way."

Then he was alone listening as she greeted her husband in the hall.

Harold Piper was thirty-six, nine years older than his wife. He was handsome – with marginal notes: these being eyes that were too close together and a certain woodenness when his face was in repose. His attitude towards this Gedney matter was typical of all his attitudes. He had told Evylyn that he considered the subject closed and would never reproach her nor allude to it in any form, and he told himself that this was rather a big way of looking at it – that she was not a little impressed. Yet, like all men who are preoccupied with their own broadness, he was exceptionally narrow.

He greeted Evylyn with emphasized cordiality this evening.

"You'll have to hurry and dress, Harold," she said eagerly. "We're going to the Bronsons'."

He nodded.

"It doesn't take me long to dress, dear," and, his words trailing off, he walked on into the library. Evylyn's heart clattered loudly.

"Harold…" she began, with a little catch in her voice, and followed him in. He was lighting a cigarette. "You'll have to hurry, Harold," she finished, standing in the doorway.

"Why?" he asked, a trifle impatiently. "You're not dressed yourself yet, Evie."

He stretched out in a Morris chair and unfolded a newspaper. With a sinking sensation Evylyn saw that this meant at least ten minutes – and

Gedney was standing breathless in the next room. Supposing Harold decided that before he went upstairs he wanted a drink from the decanter on the sideboard. Then it occurred to her to forestall this contingency by bringing him the decanter and a glass. She dreaded calling his attention to the dining room in any way, but she couldn't risk the other chance.

But at the same moment Harold rose and, throwing his paper down, came towards her.

"Evie, dear," he said, bending and putting his arms about her, "I hope you're not thinking about last night..." She moved close to him, trembling. "I know," he continued, "it was just an imprudent friendship on your part. We all make mistakes."

Evylyn hardly heard him. She was wondering if by sheer clinging to him she could draw him out and up the stairs. She thought of playing sick, asking to be carried up – unfortunately, she knew he would lay her on the couch and bring her whiskey.

Suddenly her nervous tension moved up a last impossible notch. She had heard a very faint but quite unmistakable creak from the floor of the dining room. Fred was trying to get out the back way.

Then her heart took a flying leap as a hollow ringing note like a gong echoed and re-echoed through the house. Gedney's arm had struck the big cut-glass bowl.

"What's that!" cried Harold. "Who's there?"

She clung to him but he broke away, and the room seemed to crash about her ears. She heard the pantry door swing open, a scuffle, the rattle of a tin pan, and in wild despair she rushed into the kitchen and pulled up the gas. Her husband's arm slowly unwound from Gedney's neck, and he stood there very still, first in amazement, then with pain dawning in his face.

"My golly!" he said in bewilderment, and then repeated: "My *golly*!"

He turned as if to jump again at Gedney, stopped, his muscles visibly relaxed, and he gave a bitter little laugh.

"You people... you people..." Evylyn's arms were around him and her eyes were pleading with him frantically, but he pushed her away and sank dazed into a kitchen chair, his face like porcelain. "You've been doing things to me, Evylyn. Why, you little devil! You little *devil*!"

She had never felt so sorry for him; she had never loved him so much.

"It wasn't her fault," said Gedney rather humbly. "I just came." But Piper shook his head, and his expression when he stared up was as if some physical accident had jarred his mind into a temporary inability to function. His eyes, grown suddenly pitiful, struck a deep, unsounded chord in Evylyn – and simultaneously a furious anger surged in her. She felt her eyelids burning; she stamped her foot violently; her hands scurried nervously over the table as if searching for a weapon, and then she flung herself wildly at Gedney.

"Get out!" she screamed, dark eyes blazing, little fists beating help-lessly on his outstretched arm. "You did this! Get out of here – get out – get *out*! *Get out!*"

2

CONCERNING MRS HAROLD PIPER at thirty-five, opinion was divided – women said she was still handsome; men said she was pretty no longer. And this was probably because the qualities in her beauty that women had feared and men had followed had vanished. Her eyes were still as large and as dark and as sad, but the mystery had departed; their sadness was no longer eternal, only human, and she had developed a habit, when she was startled or annoyed, of twitching her brows together and blinking several times. Her mouth also had lost: the red had receded and the faint down-turning of its corners when she smiled, that had added to the sadness of the eyes and been vaguely mock-ing and beautiful, was quite gone. When she smiled now the corners of her lips turned up. Back in the days when she revelled in her own beauty Evylyn had enjoyed that smile of hers – she had accentuated it. When she stopped accentuating it, it faded out and the last of her mystery with it.

Evylyn had ceased accentuating her smile within a month after the Freddy Gedney affair. Externally things had gone on very much as they had before. But in those few minutes during which she had discovered how much she loved her husband, Evylyn had realized how indelibly she had hurt him. For a month she struggled against aching silences, wild reproaches and accusations – she pled with him, made quiet, pitiful little love to him, and he laughed at her bitterly – and then she too slipped gradually into silence and a shadowy, unpenetrable barrier dropped between them. The surge of love that had risen in her she lavished on Donald, her little boy, realizing him almost wonderingly as a part of her life.

The next year a piling-up of mutual interests and responsibilities and some stray flicker from the past brought husband and wife together again – but after a rather pathetic flood of passion Evylyn realized that her great opportunity was gone. There simply wasn't anything left. She might have been youth and love for both – but that time of silence had slowly dried up the springs of affection and her own desire to drink again of them was dead.

She began for the first time to seek women friends, to prefer books she had read before, to sew a little where she could watch her two children to whom she was devoted. She worried about little things – if she saw crumbs on the dinner table her mind drifted off the conversation: she was receding gradually into middle age.

Her thirty-fifth birthday had been an exceptionally busy one, for they were entertaining on short notice that night, and as she stood in her bedroom window in the late afternoon she discovered that she was quite tired. Ten years before she would have lain down and slept, but now she had a feeling that things needed watching: maids were cleaning downstairs, bric-a-brac was all over the floor, and there were sure to be grocery men that had to be talked to imperatively – and then there was a letter to write Donald, who was fourteen and in his first year away at school.

She had nearly decided to lie down, nevertheless, when she heard a sudden familiar signal from little Julie downstairs. She compressed her lips, her brows twitched together, and she blinked.

"Julie!" she called.

"Ah-h-h-ow!" prolonged Julie plaintively. Then the voice of Hilda, the second maid, floated up the stairs.

"She cut herself a little, Mis' Piper."

Evylyn flew to her sewing basket, rummaged until she found a torn handkerchief, and hurried downstairs. In a moment Julie was crying in her arms as she searched for the cut, faint, disparaging evidences of which appeared on Julie's dress!

"My *thu*-mb!" explained Julie. "Oh-h-h-h, t'urts."

"It was the bowl here, the he one," said Hilda apologetically. "It was waitin' on the floor while I polished the sideboard, and Julie come along an' went to foolin' with it. She yust scratch herself."

Evylyn frowned heavily at Hilda and, twisting Julie decisively in her lap, began tearing strips off the handkerchief.

"Now – let's see it, dear."

Julie held it up, and Evylyn pounced.

"There!"

Julie surveyed her swatched thumb doubtfully. She crooked it; it waggled. A pleased, interested look appeared in her tear-stained face. She sniffled and waggled it again.

"You *precious*!" cried Evylyn and kissed her, but before she left the room she levelled another frown at Hilda. Careless! Servants all that way nowadays. If she could get a good Irishwoman... but you couldn't any more – and these Swedes...

At five o'clock Harold arrived and, coming up to her room, threatened in a suspiciously jovial tone to kiss her thirty-five times for her birthday. Evylyn resisted.

"You've been drinking," she said shortly, and then added qualitatively, "a little. You know I loathe the smell of it."

"Evie," he said, after a pause, seating himself in a chair by the window, "I can tell you something now. I guess you've known things haven't been going quite right downtown."

She was standing at the window combing her hair, but at these words she turned and looked at him.

"How do you mean? You've always said there was room for more than one wholesale hardware house in town." Her voice expressed some alarm.

"There *was*," said Harold significantly, "but this Clarence Ahearn is a smart man."

"I was surprised when you said he was coming to dinner."

"Evie," he went on, with another slap at his knee, "after January first 'The Clarence Ahearn Company' becomes 'The Ahearn, Piper Company' – and 'Piper Brothers' as a company ceases to exist."

Evylyn was startled. The sound of his name in second place was somehow hostile to her; still he appeared jubilant.

"I don't understand, Harold."

"Well, Evie, Ahearn had been fooling around with Marx. If those two had combined we'd have been the little fellow, struggling along, picking up smaller orders, hanging back on risks. It's a question of capital, Evie, and 'Ahearn and Marx' would have had the business just like 'Ahearn and Piper' is going to now." He paused and coughed and a little cloud of whiskey floated up to her nostrils. "Tell you the truth, Evie, I've suspected that Ahearn's wife had something to do with it. Ambitious little lady, I'm told. Guess she knew the Marxes couldn't help her much here."

"Is she... common?" asked Evie.

"Never met her, I'm sure – but I don't doubt it. Clarence Ahearn's name's been up at the Country Club five months – no action taken." He waved his hand disparagingly. "Ahearn and I had lunch together today and just about clinched it, so I thought it'd be nice to have him and his wife up tonight – just have nine, mostly family. After all, it's a big thing for me, and of course we'll have to see something of them, Evie."

"Yes," said Evie thoughtfully, "I suppose we will."

Evylyn was not disturbed over the social end of it – but the idea of "Piper Brothers" becoming "The Ahearn, Piper Company" startled her. It seemed like going down in the world.

Half an hour later, as she began to dress for dinner, she heard his voice from downstairs.

"Oh, Evie, come down!"

She went out into the hall and called over the banister: "What is it?"

"I want you to help me make some of that punch before dinner."

Hurriedly rehooking her dress, she descended the stairs and found him grouping the essentials on the dining-room table. She went to the sideboard and, lifting one of the bowls, carried it over.

"Oh, no," he protested, "let's use the big one. There'll be Ahearn and his wife and you and I and Milton – that's five – and Tom and Jessie – that's seven – and your sister and Joe Ambler – that's nine. You don't know how quick that stuff goes when *you* make it."

"We'll use this bowl," she insisted. "It'll hold plenty. You know how Tom is."

Tom Lowrie, husband to Jessie, Harold's first cousin, was rather inclined to finish anything in a liquid way that he began.

Harold shook his head.

"Don't be foolish. That one holds only about three quarts and there's nine of us, and the servants'll want some – and it isn't very strong punch. It's so much more cheerful to have a lot, Evie; we don't have to drink all of it."

"I say the small one."

Again he shook his head obstinately.

"No, be reasonable."

"I *am* reasonable," she said shortly. "I don't want any drunken men in the house."

"Who said you did?"

"Then use the small bowl."

"Now, Evie…"

He grasped the smaller bowl to lift it back. Instantly her hands were on it, holding it down. There was a momentary struggle, and then, with a little exasperated grunt, he raised his side, slipped it from her fingers and carried it to the sideboard.

She looked at him and tried to make her expression contemptuous, but he only laughed. Acknowledging her defeat but disclaiming all future interest in the punch, she left the room.

3

A T SEVEN THIRTY, HER CHEEKS GLOWING and her high-piled hair gleaming with a suspicion of brilliantine, Evylyn descended the stairs. Mrs Ahearn, a little woman concealing a slight nervousness under red hair and an extreme Empire gown, greeted her volubly. Evylyn disliked her on the spot, but the husband she rather approved of. He had keen blue eyes and a natural gift of pleasing people that might have made him, socially, had he not so obviously committed the blunder of marrying too early in his career.

"I'm glad to know Piper's wife," he said simply. "It looks as though your husband and I are going to see a lot of each other in the future."

She bowed, smiled graciously and turned to greet the others: Milton Piper, Harold's quiet, unassertive younger brother; the two Lowries, Jessie and Tom; Irene, her own unmarried sister; and finally Joe Ambler, a confirmed bachelor and Irene's perennial beau.

Harold led the way into dinner.

"We're having a punch evening," he announced jovially – Evylyn saw that he had already sampled his concoction – "so there won't be any cocktails except the punch. It's m' wife's greatest achievement, Mrs Ahearn; she'll give you the recipe if you want it; but owing to a slight" – he caught his wife's eye and paused – "to a slight indisposition, I'm responsible for this batch. Here's how!"

All through dinner there was punch, and Evylyn, noticing that Ahearn and Milton Piper and all the women were shaking their heads negatively at the maid, knew she had been right about the bowl; it was still half full. She resolved to caution Harold directly afterwards, but when the women left the table Mrs Ahearn cornered her, and she found herself talking cities and dressmakers with a polite show of interest.

"We've moved around a lot," chattered Mrs Ahearn, her red hair nodding violently. "Oh, yes, we've never stayed so long in a town before – but I do hope we're here for good. I like it here – don't you?"

"Well, you see, I've always lived here, so, naturally—"

"Oh, that's true," said Mrs Ahearn and laughed. "Clarence always used to tell me he had to have a wife he could come home to and say: 'Well, we're going to Chicago tomorrow to live, so pack up.' I got so I never expected to live *any*where." She laughed her little laugh again; Evylyn suspected that it was her society laugh.

"Your husband is a very able man, I imagine."

"Oh, yes," Mrs Ahearn assured her eagerly. "He's brainy, Clarence is. Ideas and enthusiasm, you know. Finds out what he wants and then goes and gets it."

Evylyn nodded. She was wondering if the men were still drinking punch back in the dining room. Mrs Ahearn's history kept unfolding jerkily, but Evylyn had ceased to listen. The first odour of massed cigars began to drift in. It wasn't really a large house, she reflected; on an evening like this the library sometimes grew blue with smoke, and next day one had to leave the windows open for hours to air the heavy staleness out of the curtains. Perhaps this partnership might... she began to speculate on a new house...

Mrs Ahearn's voice drifted in on her:

"I really would like the recipe if you have it written down somewhere..."

Then there was a sound of chairs in the dining room and the men strolled in. Evylyn saw at once that her worst fears were realized. Harold's face was flushed and his words ran together at the ends of sentences, while Tom Lowrie lurched when he walked and narrowly missed Irene's lap when he tried to sink onto the couch beside her. He sat there blinking dazedly at the company. Evylyn found herself blinking back at him, but she saw no humour in it. Joe Ambler was smiling contentedly and purring on his cigar. Only Ahearn and Milton Piper seemed unaffected.

"It's a pretty fine town, Ahearn," said Ambler, "you'll find that."

"I've found it so," said Ahearn pleasantly.

"You find it more, Ahearn," said Harold, nodding emphatically, "'f I've an'thin' do 'th it."

He soared into a eulogy of the city, and Evylyn wondered uncomfortably if it bored everyone as it bored her. Apparently not. They were all listening attentively. Evylyn broke in at the first gap.

"Where've you been living, Mr Ahearn?" she asked interestedly. Then she remembered that Mrs Ahearn had told her, but it didn't matter. Harold mustn't talk so much. He was such an *ass* when he'd been drinking. But he plopped directly back in.

"Tell you, Ahearn. Firs' you wanna get a house up here on the hill. Get Stearne house or Ridgeway house. Wanna have it so people say: 'There's Ahearn house.' Solid, you know, tha's effec' it gives."

Evylyn flushed. This didn't sound right at all. Still Ahearn didn't seem to notice anything amiss, only nodded gravely.

"Have you been looking..." But her words trailed off unheard as Harold's voice boomed on.

"Get house – tha's start. Then you get know people. Snobbish town first towards outsider, but not long – not after know you. People like you" – he indicated Ahearn and his wife with a sweeping gesture – "all right. Cordial as an'thin' once get by first barrer-bar-barrer..." He swallowed, and then said "barrier", repeated it masterfully.

Evylyn looked appealingly at her brother-in-law, but before he could intercede a thick mumble had come crowding out of Tom Lowrie, hindered by the dead cigar which he gripped firmly with his teeth.

"Huma uma ho huma ahdy um—"

"What?" demanded Harold earnestly.

Resignedly and with difficulty Tom removed the cigar – that is, he removed part of it, and then blew the remainder with a *whut* sound across the room, where it landed liquidly and limply in Mrs Ahearn's lap.

"Beg pardon," he mumbled, and rose with the vague intention of going after it. Milton's hand on his coat collapsed him in time, and Mrs Ahearn not ungracefully flounced the tobacco from her skirt to the floor, never once looking at it.

"I was sayin'," continued Tom thickly, "'fore 'at happened" – he waved his hand apologetically towards Mrs Ahearn – "I was sayin' I heard all truth that Country Club matter."

Milton leant and whispered something to him.

"Lemme 'lone," he said petulantly, "know what I'm doin'. 'At's what they came for."

Evylyn sat there in a panic, trying to make her mouth form words. She saw her sister's sardonic expression and Mrs Ahearn's face turning a vivid red. Ahearn was looking down at his watch chain, fingering it.

"I heard who's been keepin' y' out, an' he's not a bit better'n you. I can fix whole damn thing up. Would've before, but I didn't know you. Harol' tol' me you felt bad about the thing..."

Milton Piper rose suddenly and awkwardly to his feet. In a second everyone was standing tensely and Milton was saying something very hurriedly about having to go early, and the Ahearns were listening with eager intentness. Then Mrs Ahearn swallowed and turned with a forced smile towards Jessie. Evylyn saw Tom lurch forward and put his hand on Ahearn's shoulder – and suddenly she was listening to a new, anxious voice at her elbow and, turning, found Hilda, the second maid.

"Please, Mis' Piper, I tank Yulie got her hand poisoned. It's all swole up and her cheeks is hot and she's moanin' an' groanin'—"

"Julie is?" Evylyn asked sharply. The party suddenly receded. She turned quickly, sought with her eyes for Mrs Ahearn, slipped towards her.

"If you'll excuse me, Mrs..." She had momentarily forgotten the name, but she went right on: "My little girl's been taken sick. I'll be down when I can." She turned and ran quickly up the stairs, retaining a confused picture of rays of cigar smoke and a loud discussion in the centre of the room that seemed to be developing into an argument.

Switching on the light in the nursery, she found Julie tossing feverishly and giving out odd little cries. She put her hand against the cheeks. They were burning. With an exclamation she followed the arm down under the cover until she found the hand. Hilda was right. The whole thumb was swollen to the wrist and in the centre was a little inflamed sore.

Blood poisoning! her mind cried in terror. The bandage had come off the cut and she'd gotten something in it. She'd cut it at three o'clock – it was now nearly eleven. Eight hours. Blood poisoning couldn't possibly develop so soon. She rushed to the 'phone.

Doctor Martin across the street was out. Doctor Foulke, their family physician, didn't answer. She racked her brains and in desperation called her throat specialist, and bit her lip furiously while he looked up the numbers of two physicians. During that interminable moment she thought she heard loud voices downstairs – but she seemed to be in another world now. After fifteen minutes she located a physician who sounded angry and sulky at being called out of bed. She ran back to the nursery and, looking at the hand, found it was somewhat more swollen.

"Oh, God!" she cried and, kneeling beside the bed, began smoothing back Julie's hair over and over. With a vague idea of getting some hot water, she rose and started towards the door, but the lace of her dress caught in the bed rail and she fell forward on her hands and knees. She struggled up and jerked frantically at the lace. The bed moved and Julie groaned. Then more quietly but with suddenly fumbling fingers she found the pleat in front, tore the whole pannier completely off and rushed from the room.

Out in the hall she heard a single loud, insistent voice, but as she reached the head of the stairs it ceased and an outer door banged.

The music room came into view. Only Harold and Milton were there, the former leaning against a chair, his face very pale, his collar open and his mouth moving loosely.

"What's the matter?"

Milton looked at her anxiously.

"There was a little trouble…"

Then Harold saw her and, straightening up with an effort, began to speak.

"'Sult m'own cousin m'own house. God damn common nouveau rish. 'Sult m'own cousin—"

"Tom had trouble with Ahearn and Harold interfered," said Milton.

"My Lord, Milton," cried Evylyn, "couldn't you have done something?"

"I tried; I—"

"Julie's sick," she interrupted. "She's poisoned herself. Get him to bed if you can."

Harold looked up.

"Julie sick?"

Paying no attention, Evylyn brushed by through the dining room, catching sight, with a burst of horror, of the big punchbowl still on the table, the liquid from melted ice in its bottom. She heard steps on the front stairs – it was Milton helping Harold up – and then a mumble: "Why, Julie's a'righ'."

"Don't let him go into the nursery!" she shouted.

The hours blurred into a nightmare. The doctor arrived just before midnight and within a half-hour had lanced the wound. He left at two, after giving her the addresses of two nurses to call up and promising to return at half-past six. It was blood poisoning.

At four, leaving Hilda by the bedside, she went to her room and, slipping with a shudder out of her evening dress, kicked it into a corner. She put on a house dress and returned to the nursery while Hilda went to make coffee.

Not until noon could she bring herself to look into Harold's room, but when she did, it was to find him awake and staring very miserably at the ceiling. He turned bloodshot hollow eyes upon her. For a minute she hated him, couldn't speak. A husky voice came from the bed.

"What time is it?"

"Noon."

"I made a damn fool—"

"It doesn't matter," she said sharply, "Julie's got blood poisoning. They may" – she choked over the words – "they think she'll have to lose her hand."

"What?"

"She cut herself on that... that bowl."

"Last night?"

"Oh, what does it matter?" she cried. "She's got blood poisoning. Can't you hear?"

He looked at her bewildered – sat halfway up in bed.

"I'll get dressed," he said.

Her anger subsided and a great wave of weariness and pity for him rolled over her. After all, it was his trouble too.

"Yes," she answered listlessly, "I suppose you'd better."

4

IF EVYLYN'S BEAUTY HAD HESITATED in her early thirties, it came to an abrupt decision just afterwards and completely left her. A tentative outlay of wrinkles on her face suddenly deepened, and flesh collected rapidly on her legs and hips and arms. Her mannerism of drawing her brows together had become an expression – it was habitual when she was reading or speaking and even while she slept. She was forty-six.

As in most families whose fortunes have gone down rather than up, she and Harold had drifted into a colourless antagonism. In repose they looked at each other with the toleration they might have felt for broken old chairs; Evylyn worried a little when he was sick and did her best to be cheerful under the wearying depression of living with a disappointed man.

Family bridge was over for the evening and she sighed with relief. She had made more mistakes than usual this evening and she didn't care. Irene shouldn't have made that remark about the infantry being particularly dangerous. There had been no letter for three weeks now, and while this was nothing out of the ordinary, it never failed to make her nervous; naturally she hadn't known how many clubs were out.

Harold had gone upstairs, so she stepped out on the porch for a breath of fresh air. There was a bright glamour of moonlight diffusing on the sidewalks and lawns, and with a little half yawn, half laugh, she remembered one long moonlight affair of her youth. It was astonishing to think that life had once been the sum of her current love affairs. It was now the sum of her current problems.

There was the problem of Julie – Julie was thirteen, and lately she was growing more and more sensitive about her deformity and preferred to stay always in her room reading. A few years before she had been frightened at the idea of going to school, and Evylyn could not bring herself to send her, so she grew up in her mother's shadow, a pitiful little figure with the artificial hand that she made no attempt to use, but kept forlornly in her pocket. Lately she had been taking lessons in using it, because Evylyn had feared she would cease to lift the arm altogether, but after the lessons, unless she made a move with it in listless obedience to her mother, the little hand would creep back to the pocket of her dress. For a while her dresses were made without pockets, but Julie had moped around the house so miserably at a loss all one month that Evylyn weakened and never tried the experiment again.

The problem of Donald had been different from the start. She had attempted vainly to keep him near her as she had tried to teach Julie to lean less on her – lately the problem of Donald had been snatched out of her hands; his division had been abroad for three months.

She yawned again – life was a thing for youth. What a happy youth she must have had! She remembered her pony, Bijou, and the trip to Europe with her mother when she was eighteen...

"Very, very complicated," she said aloud and severely to the moon, and, stepping inside, was about to close the door when she heard a noise in the library and started.

It was Martha, the middle-aged servant: they kept only one now.

"Why, Martha!" she said in surprise.

Martha turned quickly.

"Oh, I thought you was upstairs. I was jist—"

"Is anything the matter?"

Martha hesitated.

"No, I..." She stood there fidgeting. "It was a letter, Mrs Piper, that I put somewhere."

"A letter? Your own letter?" asked Evylyn, switching on the light.

"No, it was to you. 'Twas this afternoon, Mrs Piper, in the last mail. The postman give it to me and then the back doorbell rang. I had it in my hand, so I must have stuck it somewhere. I thought I'd just slip in now and find it."

"What sort of a letter? From Mr Donald?"

"No, it was an advertisement, maybe, or a business letter. It was a long, narrow one, I remember."

They began a search through the music room, looking on trays and mantelpieces, and then through the library, feeling on the tops of rows of books. Martha paused in despair.

"I can't think where. I went straight to the kitchen. The dining room, maybe." She started hopefully for the dining room, but turned suddenly at the sound of a gasp behind her. Evylyn had sat down heavily in a Morris chair, her brows drawn very close together, eyes blinking furiously.

"Are you sick?"

For a minute there was no answer. Evylyn sat there very still, and Martha could see the very quick rise and fall of her bosom.

"Are you sick?" she repeated.

"No," said Evylyn slowly, "but I know where the letter is. Go 'way, Martha. I know."

Wonderingly, Martha withdrew, and still Evylyn sat there, only the muscles around her eyes moving – contracting and relaxing and contracting again. She knew now where the letter was – she knew as well as if she had put it there herself. And she felt instinctively and unquestionably what the letter was. It was long and narrow like an advertisement, but up in the corner in large letters it said "War Department" and, in smaller letters below, "Official Business". She knew it lay there in the big bowl with her name in ink on the outside and her soul's death within.

Rising uncertainly, she walked toward the dining room, feeling her way along the bookcases and through the doorway. After a moment she found the light and switched it on.

There was the bowl, reflecting the electric light in crimson squares edged with black and yellow squares edged with blue, ponderous and glittering, grotesquely and triumphantly ominous. She took a step forward and paused again; another step and she would see over the top and into the inside – another step and she would see an edge of white – another step – her hands fell on the rough, cold surface...

In a moment she was tearing it open, fumbling with an obstinate fold, holding it before her while the typewritten page glared out and struck at her. Then it fluttered like a bird to the floor. The house that had seemed whirring, buzzing a moment since, was suddenly very quiet; a breath of air crept in through the open front door carrying the noise of a passing motor; she heard faint sounds from upstairs and then a grinding racket in the pipe behind the bookcases – her husband turning off a water-tap...

And in that instant it was as if this were not, after all, Donald's hour, except in so far as he was a marker in the insidious contest that had gone on in sudden surges and long, listless interludes between Evylyn and this cold, malignant thing of beauty, a gift of enmity from a man whose face she had long since forgotten. With its massive, brooding passivity, it lay there in the centre of her house as it had lain for years, throwing out the ice-like beams of a thousand eyes, perverse glitterings merging each into each, never ageing, never changing.

Evylyn sat down on the edge of the table and stared at it fascinated. It seemed to be smiling now, a very cruel smile, as if to say:

"You see, this time I didn't have to hurt you directly. I didn't bother. You know it was I who took your son away. You know how cold I am and how hard and how beautiful, because once you were just as cold and hard and beautiful."

The bowl seemed suddenly to turn itself over and then to distend and swell until it became a great canopy that glittered and trembled over the room, over the house, and as the walls melted slowly into mist Evylyn saw that it was still moving out, out and far away from her, shutting off far horizons and suns and moons and stars, except as inky blots seen faintly through it. And under it walked all the people, and the light that came through to them was refracted and twisted until shadow seemed light and light seemed shadow – until the whole panorama of the world became changed and distorted under the twinkling heaven of the bowl.

Then there came a faraway, booming voice like a low clear bell. It came from the centre of the bowl and down the great sides to the ground and then bounced towards her eagerly.

"You see, I am fate," it shouted, "and stronger than your puny plans; and I am how-things-turn-out and I am different from your little dreams and I am the flight of time and the end of beauty and unfulfilled desire; all the accidents and imperceptions and the little minutes that shape the crucial hours are mine. I am the exception that proves no rules, the limits of your control, the condiment in the dish of life."

The booming sound stopped; the echoes rolled away over the wide land to the edge of the bowl that bounded the world and up the great sides and back to the centre, where they hummed for a moment and died. Then the great walls began slowly to bear down upon her, growing smaller and smaller, coming closer and closer as if to crush her; and as she clinched her hands and waited for the swift bruise of the cold glass, the bowl gave a sudden wrench and turned over – and lay there on the sideboard, shining and inscrutable, reflecting in a hundred prisms myriad, many-coloured glints and gleams and crossings and interlacings of light.

The cold wind blew in again through the front door, and with a desperate, frantic energy Evylyn stretched both her arms around the bowl. She must be quick – she must be strong. She tightened her arms until they ached, tauted the thin strips of muscle under her soft flesh, and with a mighty effort raised it and held it. She felt the wind blow cold on her back, where her dress had come apart from the strain of her effort, and as she felt it she turned towards it and staggered under the great weight out through the library and on towards the front door. She must be quick – she must be strong. The blood in her arms throbbed dully and her knees kept giving way under her, but the feel of the cool glass was good.

Out the front door she tottered and over to the stone steps, and there, summoning every fibre of her soul and body for a last effort, swung herself half around – for a second, as she tried to loose her hold, her numb fingers clung to the rough surface, and in that second she slipped and, losing balance, toppled forward with a despairing cry, her arms still around the bowl... down...

Over the way lights went on; far down the block the crash was heard, and pedestrians rushed up wonderingly; upstairs a tired man awoke from the edge of sleep and a little girl whimpered in a haunted doze. And all over the moonlit sidewalk around the still, black form, hundreds of prisms and cubes and splinters of glass reflected the light in little gleams of blue, and black edged with yellow, and yellow, and crimson edged with black.

Bernice Bobs Her Hair

1

AFTER DARK ON SATURDAY NIGHT one could stand on the first tee of the golf course and see the country-club windows as a yellow expanse over a very black and wavy ocean. The waves of this ocean, so to speak, were the heads of many curious caddies, a few of the more ingenious chauffeurs, the golf professional's deaf sister – and there were usually several stray, diffident waves who might have rolled inside had they so desired. This was the gallery.

The balcony was inside. It consisted of the circle of wicker chairs that lined the wall of the combination clubroom and ballroom. At these Saturday-night dances it was largely feminine; a great babble of middle-aged ladies with sharp eyes and icy hearts behind lorgnettes and large bosoms. The main function of the balcony was critical. It occasionally showed grudging admiration, but never approval, for it is well known among ladies over thirty-five that when the younger set dance in the summertime it is with the very worst intentions in the world, and if they are not bombarded with stony eyes, stray couples will dance weird barbaric interludes in the corners, and the more popular, more dangerous girls will sometimes be kissed in the parked limousines of unsuspecting dowagers.

But, after all, this critical circle is not close enough to the stage to see the actors' faces and catch the subtler byplay. It can only frown and lean, ask questions and make satisfactory deductions from its set of postulates, such as the one which states that every young man with a large income leads the life of a hunted partridge. It never really appreciates the drama of the shifting, semi-cruel world of adolescence. No: boxes, orchestra circle, principals and chorus are represented by the medley of faces and voices that sway to the plaintive African rhythm of Dyer's dance orchestra.

From sixteen-year-old Otis Ormonde, who has two more years at Hill School, to G. Reese Stoddard, over whose bureau at home hangs a Harvard law diploma; from little Madeleine Hogue, whose hair still feels strange and uncomfortable on top of her head, to Bessie MacRae, who has been the life of the party a little too long – more than ten years – the medley is not only the centre of the stage, but contains the only people capable of getting an unobstructed view of it.

With a flourish and a bang the music stops. The couples exchange artificial, effortless smiles, facetiously repeat "*la*-de-*dad-da* dum-*dum*", and then the clatter of young feminine voices soars over the burst of clapping.

A few disappointed stags, caught in mid-floor as they had been about to cut in, subsided listlessly back to the walls, because this was not like the riotous Christmas dances – these summer hops were considered just pleasantly warm and exciting, where even the younger marrieds rose and performed ancient waltzes and terrifying foxtrots to the tolerant amusement of their younger brothers and sisters.

Warren McIntyre, who casually attended Yale, being one of the unfortunate stags, felt in his dinner-coat pocket for a cigarette and strolled out onto the wide, semi-dark veranda, where couples were scattered at tables, filling the lantern-hung night with vague words and hazy laughter. He nodded here and there at the less absorbed, and as he passed each couple some half-forgotten fragment of a story played in his mind, for it was not a large city and everyone was Who's Who to everyone else's past. There, for example, were Jim Strain and Ethel Demorest, who had been privately engaged for three years. Everyone knew that as soon as Jim managed to hold a job for more than two months she would marry him. Yet how bored they both looked, and how wearily Ethel regarded Jim sometimes, as if she wondered why she had trained the vines of her affection on such a wind-shaken poplar.

Warren was nineteen and rather pitying with those of his friends who had gone East to college. But, like most boys, he bragged tremendously about the girls of his city when he was away from it. There was Genevieve Ormonde, who regularly made the rounds of dances, house parties and football games at Princeton, Yale, Williams and Cornell; there was black-eyed Roberta Dillon, who was quite as famous to her own generation as Hiram Johnson or Ty Cobb;* and, of course, there was Marjorie Harvey who, besides having a fairy-like face and a dazzling, bewildering tongue, was already justly celebrated for having turned five cartwheels in succession during the last pump-and-slipper dance at New Haven.

Warren, who had grown up across the street from Marjorie, had long been "crazy about her". Sometimes she seemed to reciprocate his feeling with a faint gratitude, but she had tried him by her infallible test and informed him gravely that she did not love him. Her test was that when she was away from him she forgot him and had affairs with other boys. Warren found this discouraging, especially as Marjorie had been making little trips all summer, and for the first two or three days after each arrival home he saw great heaps of mail on the Harveys' hall table addressed to her in various masculine handwritings. To make matters worse, all during the month of August she had been visited by her cousin Bernice from Eau Claire, and it seemed impossible to see her alone. It was always necessary to hunt round and find someone to take care of Bernice. As August waned, this was becoming more and more difficult.

Much as Warren worshipped Marjorie, he had to admit that Cousin Bernice was sorta dopeless. She was pretty, with dark hair and high colour, but she was no fun on a party. Every Saturday night he danced a long arduous duty dance with her to please Marjorie, but he had never been anything but bored in her company.

"Warren" – a soft voice at his elbow broke in upon his thoughts, and he turned to see Marjorie, flushed and radiant as usual. She laid a hand on his shoulder and a glow settled almost imperceptibly over him.

"Warren," she whispered, "do something for me – dance with Bernice. She's been stuck with little Otis Ormonde for almost an hour."

Warren's glow faded.

"Why... sure," he answered half-heartedly.

"You don't mind, do you? I'll see that you don't get stuck."

"'Sall right."

Marjorie smiled – that smile that was thanks enough.

"You're an angel, and I'm obliged loads."

With a sigh the angel glanced round the veranda, but Bernice and Otis were not in sight. He wandered back inside, and there in front of the women's dressing room he found Otis in the centre of a group of young men who were convulsed with laughter. Otis was brandishing a piece of timber he had picked up, and discoursing volubly.

"She's gone in to fix her hair," he announced wildly. "I'm waiting to dance another hour with her."

Their laughter was renewed.

"Why don't some of you cut in?" cried Otis resentfully. "She likes more variety."

"Why, Otis," suggested a friend, "you've just barely got used to her."

"Why the two-by-four, Otis?" enquired Warren, smiling.

"The two-by-four? Oh, this? This is a club. When she comes out, I'll hit her on the head and knock her in again."

Warren collapsed on a settee and howled with glee.

"Never mind, Otis," he articulated finally. "I'm relieving you this time."

Otis simulated a sudden fainting attack and handed the stick to Warren.

"If you need it, old man," he said hoarsely.

No matter how beautiful or brilliant a girl may be, the reputation of not being frequently cut in on makes her position at a dance unfortunate. Perhaps boys prefer her company to that of the butterflies with whom they dance a dozen times an evening, but youth in this jazz-nourished generation is temperamentally restless, and the idea of foxtrotting more than one full foxtrot with the same girl is distasteful, not to say odious.

When it comes to several dances and the intermissions between, she ca
be quite sure that a young man, once relieved, will never tread on he
wayward toes again.

Warren danced the next full dance with Bernice, and finally, thankful
for the intermission, he led her to a table on the veranda. There was a
moment's silence while she did unimpressive things with her fan.

"It's hotter here than in Eau Claire," she said.

Warren stifled a sigh and nodded. It might be for all he knew or
cared. He wondered idly whether she was a poor conversationalist
because she got no attention or got no attention because she was a poor
conversationalist.

"You going to be here much longer?" he asked, and then turned rather
red. She might suspect his reasons for asking.

"Another week," she answered, and stared at him as if to lunge at his
next remark when it left his lips.

Warren fidgeted. Then with a sudden charitable impulse he decided
to try part of his line on her. He turned and looked at her eyes.

"You've got an awfully kissable mouth," he began quietly.

This was a remark that he sometimes made to girls at college proms
when they were talking in just such half-dark as this. Bernice distinctly
jumped. She turned an ungraceful red and became clumsy with her fan.
No one had ever made such a remark to her before.

"Fresh!" – the word had slipped out before she realized it, and she bit
her lip. Too late she decided to be amused, and offered him a flustered
smile.

Warren was annoyed. Though not accustomed to have that remark
taken seriously, still it usually provoked a laugh or a paragraph of sentimental banter. And he hated to be called fresh, except in a joking way.
His charitable impulse died and he switched the topic.

"Jim Strain and Ethel Demorest sitting out as usual," he commented.

This was more in Bernice's line, but a faint regret mingled with her
relief as the subject changed. Men did not talk to her about kissable
mouths, but she knew that they talked in some such way to other girls.

'Oh, yes," she said, and laughed. "I hear they've been mooning round
r years without a red penny. Isn't it silly?"

Warren's disgust increased. Jim Strain was a close friend of his broth-
r's, and anyway he considered it bad form to sneer at people for not
laving money. But Bernice had had no intention of sneering. She was
merely nervous.

2

WHEN MARJORIE AND BERNICE reached home at half after
midnight they said goodnight at the top of the stairs. Though
cousins, they were not intimates. As a matter of fact Marjorie had no
female intimates – she considered girls stupid. Bernice on the contrary
all through this parent-arranged visit had rather longed to exchange
those confidences flavoured with giggles and tears that she considered
an indispensable factor in all feminine intercourse. But in this respect
she found Marjorie rather cold; felt somehow the same difficulty in talking to her that she had in talking to men. Marjorie never giggled, was
never frightened, seldom embarrassed, and in fact had very few of the
qualities which Bernice considered appropriately and blessedly feminine.

As Bernice busied herself with toothbrush and paste this night, she
wondered for the hundredth time why she never had any attention when
she was away from home. That her family were the wealthiest in Eau
Claire, that her mother entertained tremendously, gave little dinners
for her daughter before all dances and bought her a car of her own
to drive round in, never occurred to her as factors in her home-town
social success. Like most girls she had been brought up on the warm
milk prepared by Annie Fellows Johnston* and on novels in which the
female was beloved because of certain mysterious womanly qualities,
always mentioned but never displayed.

Bernice felt a vague pain that she was not at present engaged in
being popular. She did not know that had it not been for Marjorie's
campaigning she would have danced the entire evening with one man,

but she knew that even in Eau Claire other girls with less positi
and less pulchritude were given a much bigger rush. She attribut
this to something subtly unscrupulous in those girls. It had nev
worried her, and if it had her mother would have assured her tha
the other girls cheapened themselves and that men really respecte
girls like Bernice.

She turned out the light in her bathroom, and on an impulse decided
to go in and chat for a moment with her aunt Josephine, whose light
was still on. Her soft slippers bore her noiselessly down the carpeted
hall but, hearing voices inside, she stopped near the partly opened door.
Then she caught her own name and, without any definite intention of
eavesdropping, lingered – and the thread of the conversation going on
inside pierced her consciousness sharply as if it had been drawn through
with a needle.

"She's absolutely hopeless!" It was Marjorie's voice. "Oh, I know
what you're going to say! So many people have told you how pretty
sweet she is, and how she can cook! What of it? She has a bum time.
Men don't like her."

"What's a little cheap popularity?"

Mrs Harvey sounded annoyed.

"It's everything when you're eighteen," said Marjorie emphatically.
"I've done my best. I've been polite and I've made men dance with her,
but they just won't stand being bored. When I think of that gorgeous
colouring wasted on such a ninny, and think what Martha Carey could
do with it – oh!"

"There's no courtesy these days."

Mrs Harvey's voice implied that modern situations were too much for
her. When she was a girl, all young ladies who belonged to nice families
had glorious times.

"Well," said Marjorie, "no girl can permanently bolster up a lame-
duck visitor, because these days it's every girl for herself. I've even tried
to drop her hints about clothes and things, and she's been furious – given
me the funniest looks. She's sensitive enough to know she's not getting

away with much, but I'll bet she consoles herself by thinking that she's very virtuous and that I'm too gay and fickle and will come to a bad end. All unpopular girls think that way. Sour grapes! Sarah Hopkins refers to Genevieve and Roberta and me as gardenia girls! I'll bet she'd give ten years of her life and her European education to be a gardenia girl and have three or four men in love with her and be cut in on every few feet at dances."

"It seems to me," interrupted Mrs Harvey rather wearily, "that you ought to be able to do something for Bernice. I know she's not very vivacious."

Marjorie groaned.

"Vivacious! Good grief! I've never heard her say anything to a boy except that it's hot or the floor's crowded or that she's going to school in New York next year. Sometimes she asks them what kind of car they have and tells them the kind she has. Thrilling!"

There was a short silence, and then Mrs Harvey took up her refrain: "All I know is that other girls not half so sweet and attractive get partners. Martha Carey, for instance, is stout and loud, and her mother is distinctly common. Roberta Dillon is so thin this year that she looks as though Arizona were the place for her. She's dancing herself to death."

"But, Mother," objected Marjorie impatiently, "Martha is cheerful and awfully witty and an awfully slick girl, and Roberta's a marvellous dancer. She's been popular for ages!"

Mrs Harvey yawned.

"I think it's that crazy Indian blood in Bernice," continued Marjorie. "Maybe she's a reversion to type. Indian women all just sat round and never said anything."

"Go to bed, you silly child," laughed Mrs Harvey. "I wouldn't have told you that if I'd thought you were going to remember it. And I think most of your ideas are perfectly idiotic," she finished sleepily.

There was another silence, while Marjorie considered whether or not convincing her mother was worth the trouble. People over forty can seldom be permanently convinced of anything. At eighteen our convictions are hills from which we look; at forty-five they are caves in which we hide.

Having decided this, Marjorie said goodnight. When she came out into the hall it was quite empty.

3

WHILE MARJORIE WAS BREAKFASTING late next day, Bernice came into the room with a rather formal good morning, sat down opposite, stared intently over and slightly moistened her lips.

"What's on your mind?" enquired Marjorie, rather puzzled.

Bernice paused before she threw her hand grenade.

"I heard what you said about me to your mother last night."

Marjorie was startled, but she showed only a faintly heightened colour and her voice was quite even when she spoke.

"Where were you?"

"In the hall. I didn't mean to listen – at first."

After an involuntary look of contempt, Marjorie dropped her eyes and became very interested in balancing a stray corn flake on her finger.

"I guess I'd better go back to Eau Claire – if I'm such a nuisance." Bernice's lower lip was trembling violently and she continued on a wavering note: "I've tried to be nice, and... and I've been first neglected and then insulted. No one ever visited me and got such treatment."

Marjorie was silent.

"But I'm in the way, I see. I'm a drag on you. Your friends don't like me." She paused, and then remembered another one of her grievances. "Of course I was furious last week when you tried to hint to me that that dress was unbecoming. Don't you think I know how to dress myself?"

"No," murmured Marjorie less than half-aloud.

"What?"

"I didn't hint anything," said Marjorie succinctly. "I said, as I remember, that it was better to wear a becoming dress three times straight than to alternate it with two frights."

"Do you think that was a very nice thing to say?"

"I wasn't trying to be nice." Then after a pause: "When do you want to go?"

Bernice drew in her breath sharply.

"Oh!" It was a little half-cry.

Marjorie looked up in surprise.

"Didn't you say you were going?"

"Yes, but—"

"Oh, you were only bluffing!"

They stared at each other across the breakfast table for a moment. Misty waves were passing before Bernice's eyes, while Marjorie's face wore that rather hard expression that she used when slightly intoxicated undergraduates were making love to her.

"So you were bluffing," she repeated, as if it were what she might have expected.

Bernice admitted it by bursting into tears. Marjorie's eyes showed boredom.

"You're my cousin," sobbed Bernice. "I'm v-v-visiting you. I was to stay a month, and if I go home my mother will know and she'll wah-wonder…"

Marjorie waited until the shower of broken words collapsed into little sniffles.

"I'll give you my month's allowance," she said coldly, "and you can spend this last week anywhere you want. There's a very nice hotel—"

Bernice's sobs rose to a flute note, and rising of a sudden she fled from the room.

An hour later, while Marjorie was in the library absorbed in composing one of those non-committal, marvellously elusive letters that only a young girl can write, Bernice reappeared, very red-eyed and consciously calm. She cast no glance at Marjorie but took a book at random from the shelf and sat down as if to read. Marjorie seemed absorbed in her letter and continued writing. When the clock showed noon, Bernice closed her book with a snap.

"I suppose I'd better get my railroad ticket."

This was not the beginning of the speech she had rehearsed upstairs, but as Marjorie was not getting her cues – wasn't urging her to be reasonable; it's all a mistake – it was the best opening she could muster.

"Just wait till I finish this letter," said Marjorie without looking round. "I want to get it off in the next mail."

After another minute, during which her pen scratched busily, she turned round and relaxed with an air of "at your service". Again Bernice had to speak.

"Do you want me to go home?"

"Well," said Marjorie, considering, "I suppose if you're not having a good time you'd better go. No use being miserable."

"Don't you think common kindness—"

"Oh, please don't quote *Little Women*!"* cried Marjorie impatiently. "That's out of style."

"You think so?"

"Heavens, yes! What modern girl could live like those inane females?"

"They were the models for our mothers."

Marjorie laughed.

"Yes, they were – not! Besides, our mothers were all very well in their way, but they know very little about their daughters' problems."

Bernice drew herself up.

"Please don't talk about my mother."

Marjorie laughed.

"I don't think I mentioned her."

Bernice felt that she was being led away from her subject.

"Do you think you've treated me very well?"

"I've done my best. You're rather hard material to work with."

The lids of Bernice's eyes reddened.

"I think you're hard and selfish, and you haven't a feminine quality in you."

"Oh, my Lord!" cried Marjorie in desperation. "You little nut! Girls like you are responsible for all the tiresome colourless marriages; all those ghastly inefficiencies that pass as feminine qualities. What a blow it must be when a man with imagination marries the beautiful bundle of clothes that he's been building ideals around, and finds that she's just a weak, whining, cowardly mass of affectations!"

Bernice's mouth had slipped half open.

"The womanly woman!" continued Marjorie. "Her whole early life is occupied in whining criticisms of girls like me who really do have a good time."

Bernice's jaw descended farther as Marjorie's voice rose.

"There's some excuse for an ugly girl whining. If I'd been irretrievably ugly I'd never have forgiven my parents for bringing me into the world. But you're starting life without any handicap" – Marjorie's little fist clenched. "If you expect me to weep with you, you'll be disappointed. Go or stay, just as you like." And picking up her letters, she left the room.

Bernice claimed a headache and failed to appear at luncheon. They had a matinée date for the afternoon but, the headache persisting, Marjorie made explanation to a not very downcast boy. But when she returned late in the afternoon, she found Bernice with a strangely set face waiting for her in her bedroom.

"I've decided," began Bernice without preliminaries, "that maybe you're right about things – possibly not. But if you'll tell me why your friends aren't... aren't interested in me, I'll see if I can do what you want me to."

Marjorie was at the mirror shaking down her hair.

"Do you mean it?"

"Yes."

"Without reservations? Will you do exactly what I say?"

"Well, I—"

"Well nothing! Will you do exactly as I say?"

"If they're sensible things."

"They're not! You're no case for sensible things."

"Are you going to make... to recommend—"

"Yes, everything. If I tell you to take boxing lessons, you'll have to do it. Write home and tell your mother you're going to stay another two weeks."

"If you'll tell me—"

"All right – I'll just give you a few examples now. First, you have no ease of manner. Why? Because you're never sure about your personal appearance. When a girl feels that she's perfectly groomed and dressed, she can forget that part of her. That's charm. The more parts of yourself you can afford to forget, the more charm you have."

"Don't I look all right?"

"No – for instance, you never take care of your eyebrows. They're black and lustrous, but by leaving them straggly they're a blemish. They'd be beautiful if you'd take care of them in one tenth the time you take doing nothing. You're going to brush them so that they'll grow straight."

Bernice raised the brows in question.

"Do you mean to say that men notice eyebrows?"

"Yes – subconsciously. And when you go home you ought to have your teeth straightened a little. It's almost imperceptible, still—"

"But I thought," interrupted Bernice in bewilderment, "that you despised little dainty feminine things like that."

"I hate dainty minds," answered Marjorie. "But a girl has to be dainty in person. If she looks like a million dollars, she can talk about Russia, ping-pong or the League of Nations and get away with it."

"What else?"

"Oh, I'm just beginning! There's your dancing."

"Don't I dance all right?"

"No, you don't: you lean on a man – yes, you do – ever so slightly. I noticed it when we were dancing together yesterday. And you dance standing up straight instead of bending over a little. Probably some old lady on the sideline once told you that you looked so dignified that way. But except with a very small girl it's much harder on the man, and he's the one that counts."

"Go on." Bernice's brain was reeling.

"Well, you've got to learn to be nice to men who are sad birds. You look as if you'd been insulted whenever you're thrown with any except the most popular boys. Why, Bernice, I'm cut in on every few feet – and who does most of it? Why, those very sad birds. No girl can afford to neglect them. They're the big part of any crowd. Young boys too shy to talk are the very best conversational practice. Clumsy boys are the best dancing practice. If you can follow them and yet look graceful, you can follow a baby tank across a barb-wire skyscraper."

Bernice sighed profoundly, but Marjorie was not through.

"If you go to a dance and really amuse, say, three sad birds that dance with you; if you talk so well to them that they forget they're stuck with you, you've done something. They'll come back next time, and gradually so many sad birds will dance with you that the attractive boys will see there's no danger of being stuck – then they'll dance with you."

"Yes," agreed Bernice faintly. "I think I begin to see."

"And finally," concluded Marjorie, "poise and charm will just come. You'll wake up some morning knowing you've attained it, and men will know it too."

Bernice rose.

"It's been awfully kind of you – but nobody's ever talked to me like this before, and I feel sort of startled."

Marjorie made no answer, but gazed pensively at her own image in the mirror.

"You're a peach to help me," continued Bernice.

Still Marjorie did not answer, and Bernice thought she had seemed too grateful.

"I know you don't like sentiment," she said timidly.

Marjorie turned to her quickly.

"Oh, I wasn't thinking about that. I was considering whether we hadn't better bob your hair."

Bernice collapsed backwards upon the bed.

4

O N THE FOLLOWING Wednesday evening there was a dinner dance at the country club. When the guests strolled in, Bernice found her place card with a slight feeling of irritation. Though at her right sat G. Reece Stoddard, a most desirable and distinguished young bachelor, the all-important left held only Charley Paulson. Charley lacked height, beauty and social shrewdness, and in her new enlightenment Bernice decided that his only qualification to be her partner was that he had never been stuck with her. But this feeling of irritation left with the last of the soup plates, and Marjorie's specific instruction came to her. Swallowing her pride, she turned to Charley Paulson and plunged.

"Do you think I ought to bob my hair, Mr Charley Paulson?"

Charley looked up in surprise.

"Why?"

"Because I'm considering it. It's such a sure and easy way of attracting attention."

Charley smiled pleasantly. He could not know this had been rehearsed. He replied that he didn't know much about bobbed hair. But Bernice was there to tell him.

"I want to be a society vampire, you see," she announced coolly, and went on to inform him that bobbed hair was the necessary prelude. She added that she wanted to ask his advice, because she had heard he was so critical about girls.

Charley, who knew as much about the psychology of women as he did of the mental states of Buddhist contemplatives, felt vaguely flattered.

"So I've decided," she continued, her voice rising slightly, "that early next week I'm going down to the Sevier Hotel barber shop, sit in the first chair and get my hair bobbed." She faltered, noticing that the people near her had paused in their conversation and were listening, but after a confused second Marjorie's coaching told, and she finished her paragraph to the vicinity at large. "Of course I'm charging admission, but if you'll all come down and encourage me I'll issue passes for the inside seats."

There was a ripple of appreciative laughter, and under cover of it G. Reece Stoddard leant over quickly and said close to her ear: "I'll take a box right now."

She met his eyes and smiled as if he had said something surpassingly brilliant.

"Do you believe in bobbed hair?" asked G. Reece in the same undertone.

"I think it's unmoral," affirmed Bernice gravely. "But, of course, you've either got to amuse people or feed 'em or shock 'em." Marjorie had culled this from Oscar Wilde. It was greeted with a ripple of laughter from the men and a series of quick, intent looks from the girls. And then, as though she had said nothing of wit or moment, Bernice turned again to Charley and spoke confidentially in his ear.

"I want to ask you your opinion of several people. I imagine you're a wonderful judge of character."

Charley thrilled faintly – paid her a subtle compliment by overturning her water.

Two hours later, while Warren McIntyre was standing passively in the stag line abstractedly watching the dancers and wondering whither and with whom Marjorie had disappeared, an unrelated perception began to creep slowly upon him – a perception that Bernice, cousin to Marjorie, had been cut in on several times in the past five minutes. He closed his eyes, opened them and looked again. Several minutes back she had been dancing with a visiting boy, a matter easily accounted for: a visiting boy would know no better. But now she was dancing with someone else, and there was Charley Paulson headed for her with enthusiastic determination in his eye. Funny – Charley seldom danced with more than three girls an evening.

Warren was distinctly surprised when – the exchange having been effected – the man relieved proved to be none other than G. Reece Stoddard himself. And G. Reece seemed not at all jubilant at being relieved. Next time Bernice danced near, Warren regarded her intently.

Yes, she was pretty, distinctly pretty, and tonight her face seemed really vivacious. She had that look that no woman, however histrionically proficient, can successfully counterfeit – she looked as if she were having a good time. He liked the way she had her hair arranged, wondered if it was brilliantine that made it glisten so. And that dress was becoming – a dark red that set off her shadowy eyes and high colouring. He remembered that he had thought her pretty when she first came to town, before he had realized that she was dull. Too bad she was dull – dull girls unbearable – certainly pretty though.

His thoughts zigzagged back to Marjorie. This disappearance would be like other disappearances. When she reappeared he would demand where she had been – would be told emphatically that it was none of his business. What a pity she was so sure of him! She basked in the knowledge that no other girl in town interested him; she defied him to fall in love with Genevieve or Roberta.

Warren sighed. The way to Marjorie's affections was a labyrinth indeed. He looked up. Bernice was again dancing with the visiting boy. Half-unconsciously he took a step out from the stag line in her direction, and hesitated. Then he said to himself that it was charity. He walked towards her – collided suddenly with G. Reece Stoddard.

"Pardon me," said Warren.

But G. Reece had not stopped to apologize. He had again cut in on Bernice.

That night at one o'clock, Marjorie, with one hand on the electric-light switch in the hall, turned to take a last look at Bernice's sparkling eyes.

"So it worked?"

"Oh, Marjorie, yes!" cried Bernice.

"I saw you were having a gay time."

"I did! The only trouble was that about midnight I ran short of talk. I had to repeat myself – with different men of course. I hope they won't compare notes."

"Men don't," said Marjorie, yawning, "and it wouldn't matter if they did – they'd think you were even trickier."

She snapped out the light and, as they started up the stairs, Bernice grasped the banister thankfully. For the first time in her life she had been danced tired.

"You see," said Marjorie at the top of the stairs, "one man sees another man cut in and he thinks there must be something there. Well, we'll fix up some new stuff tomorrow. Goodnight."

"Goodnight."

As Bernice took down her hair, she passed the evening before her in review. She had followed instructions exactly. Even when Charley Paulson cut in for the eighth time, she had simulated delight and had apparently been both interested and flattered. She had not talked about the weather or Eau Claire or automobiles or her school, but had confined her conversation to me, you and us.

But a few minutes before she fell asleep, a rebellious thought was churning drowsily in her brain – after all, it was she who had done it. Marjorie, to be sure, had given her her conversation, but then Marjorie got much of her conversation out of things she read. Bernice had bought the red dress, though she had never valued it highly before Marjorie dug it out of her trunk – and her own voice had said the words, her own lips had smiled, her own feet had danced. Marjorie nice girl… vain, though… nice evening… nice boys… like Warren… Warren… Warren… what's-his-name… Warren…

She fell asleep.

5

To BERNICE THE NEXT WEEK was a revelation. With the feeling that people really enjoyed looking at her and listening to her came the foundation of self-confidence. Of course there were numerous mistakes at first. She did not know, for instance, that Draycott Deyo was studying for the ministry; she was unaware that he had cut in on her because he thought she was a quiet, reserved girl. Had she known these things she would not have treated him to the line which began "Hello, Shell Shock!" and continued with the bathtub story – "It takes a frightful lot of energy to fix my hair in the summer – there's so much of it – so I always fix it first and powder my face and put on my hat; then I get into the bathtub, and dress afterwards. Don't you think that's the best plan?"

Though Draycott Deyo was in the throes of difficulties concerning baptism by immersion and might possibly have seen a connection, it must be admitted that he did not. He considered feminine bathing an immoral subject, and gave her some of his ideas on the depravity of modern society.

But to offset that unfortunate occurrence Bernice had several signal successes to her credit. Little Otis Ormonde pleaded off from a trip East and elected instead to follow her with a puppy-like devotion, to the amusement of his crowd and to the irritation of G. Reece Stoddard, several of whose afternoon calls Otis completely ruined by the disgusting tenderness of the glances he bent on Bernice. He even told her the story of the two-by-four and the dressing room to show her how frightfully mistaken he and everyone else had been in their first judgement of her. Bernice laughed off that incident with a slight sinking sensation.

Of all Bernice's conversation perhaps the best known and most universally approved was the line about the bobbing of her hair.

"Oh, Bernice, when you goin' to get the hair bobbed?"

"Day after tomorrow maybe," she would reply, laughing. "Will you come and see me? Because I'm counting on you, you know."

"Will we? You know! But you better hurry up."

Bernice, whose tonsorial intentions were strictly dishonourable, would laugh again.

"Pretty soon now. You'd be surprised."

But perhaps the most significant symbol of her success was the grey car of the hypercritical Warren McIntyre, parked daily in front of the Harvey house. At first the parlourmaid was distinctly startled when he asked for Bernice instead of Marjorie; after a week of it she told the cook that Miss Bernice had gotta holda Miss Marjorie's best fella.

And Miss Bernice had. Perhaps it began with Warren's desire to rouse jealousy in Marjorie; perhaps it was the familiar though unrecognized strain of Marjorie in Bernice's conversation; perhaps it was both of these and something of sincere attraction besides. But somehow the collective mind of the younger set knew within a week that Marjorie's most reliable beau had made an amazing face-about and was giving an indisputable rush to Marjorie's guest. The question of the moment was how Marjorie would take it. Warren called Bernice on the phone twice a day, sent her notes, and they were frequently seen together in his roadster, obviously engrossed in one of those tense, significant conversations as to whether or not he was sincere.

Marjorie on being twitted only laughed. She said she was mighty glad that Warren had at last found someone who appreciated him. So the younger set laughed too, and guessed that Marjorie didn't care and let it go at that.

One afternoon, when there were only three days left of her visit, Bernice was waiting in the hall for Warren, with whom she was going to a bridge party. She was in rather a blissful mood, and when Marjorie – also bound for the party – appeared beside her and began casually to adjust her hat in the mirror, Bernice was utterly unprepared for anything in the nature of a clash. Marjorie did her work very coldly and succinctly in three sentences.

"You may as well get Warren out of your head," she said coldly.

"What?" Bernice was utterly astounded.

"You may as well stop making a fool of yourself over Warren McIntyre. He doesn't care a snap of his fingers about you."

For a tense moment they regarded each other – Marjorie scornful, aloof; Bernice astounded, half-angry, half-afraid. Then two cars drove up in front of the house and there was a riotous honking. Both of them gasped faintly, turned, and side by side hurried out.

All through the bridge party Bernice strove in vain to master a rising uneasiness. She had offended Marjorie, the sphinx of sphinxes. With the most wholesome and innocent intentions in the world she had stolen Marjorie's property. She felt suddenly and horribly guilty. After the bridge game, when they sat in an informal circle and the conversation became general, the storm gradually broke. Little Otis Ormonde inadvertently precipitated it.

"When you going back to kindergarten, Otis?" someone had asked.

"Me? Day Bernice gets her hair bobbed."

"Then your education's over," said Marjorie quickly. "That's only a bluff of hers. I should think you'd have realized."

"That a fact?" demanded Otis, giving Bernice a reproachful glance.

Bernice's ears burned as she tried to think up an effectual comeback. In the face of this direct attack her imagination was paralysed.

"There's a lot of bluffs in the world," continued Marjorie quite pleasantly. "I should think you'd be young enough to know that, Otis."

"Well," said Otis, "maybe so. But gee! With a line like Bernice's—"

"Really?" yawned Marjorie. "What's her latest bon mot?"

No one seemed to know. In fact, Bernice, having trifled with her muse's beau, had said nothing memorable of late.

"Was that really all a line?" asked Roberta curiously.

Bernice hesitated. She felt that wit in some form was demanded of her, but under her cousin's suddenly frigid eyes she was completely incapacitated.

"I don't know," she stalled.

"Splush!" said Marjorie. "Admit it!"

Bernice saw that Warren's eyes had left a ukulele he had been tinkering with and were fixed on her questioningly.

"Oh, I don't know!" she repeated steadily. Her cheeks were glowing.

"Splush!" remarked Marjorie again.

"Come through, Bernice," urged Otis. "Tell her where to get off,"

Bernice looked round again – she seemed unable to get away from Warren's eyes.

"I like bobbed hair," she said hurriedly, as if he had asked her a question, "and I intend to bob mine."

"When?" demanded Marjorie.

"Any time."

"No time like the present," suggested Roberta.

Otis jumped to his feet.

"Good stuff!" he cried. "We'll have a summer bobbing party. Sevier Hotel barber shop, I think you said."

In an instant all were on their feet. Bernice's heart throbbed violently.

"What?" she gasped.

Out of the group came Marjorie's voice, very clear and contemptuous. "Don't worry – she'll back out!"

"Come on, Bernice!" cried Otis, starting towards the door.

Four eyes – Warren's and Marjorie's – stared at her, challenged her, defied her. For another second she wavered wildly.

"All right," she said swiftly, "I don't care if I do."

An eternity of minutes later, riding downtown through the late afternoon beside Warren, the others following in Roberta's car close behind, Bernice had all the sensations of Marie Antoinette bound for the guillotine in a tumbrel. Vaguely she wondered why she did not cry out that it was all a mistake. It was all she could do to keep from clutching her hair with both hands to protect it from the suddenly hostile world. Yet she did neither. Even the thought of her mother was no deterrent now. This was the test supreme of her sportsmanship, her right to walk unchallenged in the starry heaven of popular girls.

Warren was moodily silent, and when they came to the hotel he drew up at the kerb and nodded to Bernice to precede him out. Roberta's car emptied a laughing crowd into the shop, which presented two bold plate-glass windows to the street.

Bernice stood on the kerb and looked at the sign, Sevier Barber Shop. It was a guillotine indeed, and the hangman was the first barber, who, attired in a white coat and smoking a cigarette, leant nonchalantly against the first chair. He must have heard of her; he must have been waiting all week, smoking eternal cigarettes beside that portentous, too often mentioned first chair. Would they blindfold her? No, but they would tie a white cloth round her neck lest any of her blood – nonsense: hair – should get on her clothes.

"All right, Bernice," said Warren quickly.

With her chin in the air she crossed the sidewalk, pushed open the swinging screen door and, giving not a glance to the uproarious, riotous row that occupied the waiting bench, went up to the first barber.

"I want you to bob my hair."

The first barber's mouth slid somewhat open. His cigarette dropped to the floor.

"Huh?"

"My hair – bob it!"

Refusing further preliminaries, Bernice took her seat on high. A man in the chair next to her turned on his side and gave her a glance, half lather, half amazement. One barber started and spoilt little Willy Schuneman's monthly haircut. Mr O'Reilly in the last chair grunted and swore musically in ancient Gaelic as a razor bit into his cheek. Two bootblacks became wide-eyed and rushed for her feet. No, Bernice didn't care for a shine.

Outside a passer-by stopped and stared; a couple joined him; half a dozen small boys' noses sprang into life, flattened against the glass; and snatches of conversation borne on the summer breeze drifted in through the screen door.

"Lookada long hair on a kid!"

"Where'd yuh get 'at stuff? 'At's a bearded lady he just finished shavin'."

But Bernice saw nothing, heard nothing. Her only living sense told her that this man in the white coat had removed one tortoiseshell comb and then another; that his fingers were fumbling clumsily with unfamiliar hairpins; that this hair, this wonderful hair of hers, was going – she would never again feel its long voluptuous pull as it hung in a dark-brown glory down her back. For a second she was near breaking down, and then the picture before her swam mechanically into her vision – Marjorie's mouth curling in a faint ironic smile as if to say: "Give up and get down! You tried to buck me and I called your bluff. You see you haven't got a prayer."

And some last energy rose up in Bernice, for she clenched her hands under the white cloth, and there was a curious narrowing of her eyes that Marjorie remarked on to someone long afterwards.

Twenty minutes later the barber swung her round to face the mirror, and she flinched at the full extent of the damage that had been wrought. Her hair was not curly, and now it lay in lank lifeless blocks on both sides of her suddenly pale face. It was ugly as sin – she had known it would be ugly as sin. Her face's chief charm had been a Madonna-like simplicity. Now that was gone and she was – well, frightfully mediocre – not stagy, only ridiculous, like a Greenwich Villager who had left her spectacles at home.

As she climbed down from the chair, she tried to smile – failed miserably. She saw two of the girls exchange glances; noticed Marjorie's mouth curved in attenuated mockery – and that Warren's eyes were suddenly very cold.

"You see" – her words fell into an awkward pause – "I've done it."

"Yes, you've... done it," admitted Warren.

"Do you like it?"

There was a half-hearted "Sure" from two or three voices, another awkward pause, and then Marjorie turned swiftly and with serpent-like intensity to Warren.

"Would you mind running me down to the cleaners?" she asked. "I've simply got to get a dress there before supper. Roberta's driving right home and she can take the others."

Warren stared abstractedly at some infinite speck out the window. Then for an instant his eyes rested coldly on Bernice before they turned to Marjorie.

"Be glad to," he said slowly.

6

BERNICE DID NOT FULLY REALIZE the outrageous trap that had been set for her until she met her aunt's amazed glance just before dinner.

"Why, Bernice!"

"I've bobbed it, Aunt Josephine."

"Why, child!"

"Do you like it?"

"Why, Ber-nice!"

"I suppose I've shocked you."

"No, but what'll Mrs Deyo think tomorrow night? Bernice, you should have waited until after the Deyos' dance – you should have waited if you wanted to do that."

"It was sudden, Aunt Josephine. Anyway, why does it matter to Mrs Deyo particularly?"

"Why, child," cried Mrs Harvey, "in her paper on 'The Foibles of the Younger Generation' that she read at the last meeting of the Thursday Club she devoted fifteen minutes to bobbed hair. It's her pet abomination. And the dance is for you and Marjorie!"

"I'm sorry."

"Oh, Bernice, what'll your mother say? She'll think I let you do it."

"I'm sorry."

Dinner was an agony. She had made a hasty attempt with a curling iron, and burned her finger and much hair. She could see that her aunt was both worried and grieved, and her uncle kept saying, "Well, I'll be darned!" over and over in a hurt and faintly hostile tone. And Marjorie sat very quietly, entrenched behind a faint smile, a faintly mocking smile.

Somehow she got through the evening. Three boys called; Marjorie disappeared with one of them, and Bernice made a listless unsuccessful attempt to entertain the two others – sighed thankfully as she climbed the stairs to her room at half-past ten. What a day!

When she had undressed for the night, the door opened and Marjorie came in.

"Bernice," she said, "I'm awfully sorry about the Deyo dance. I'll give you my word of honour I'd forgotten all about it."

"'Sall right," said Bernice shortly. Standing before the mirror, she passed her comb slowly through her short hair.

"I'll take you downtown tomorrow," continued Marjorie, "and the hairdresser'll fix it so you'll look slick. I didn't imagine you'd go through with it. I'm really mighty sorry."

"Oh, 'sall right!"

"Still it's your last night, so I suppose it won't matter much."

Then Bernice winced as Marjorie tossed her own hair over her shoulders and began to twist it slowly into two long blond braids until in her cream-coloured negligee she looked like a delicate painting of some Saxon princess. Fascinated, Bernice watched the braids grow. Heavy and luxurious they were, moving under the supple fingers like restive snakes – and to Bernice remained this relic and the curling iron and a tomorrow full of eyes. She could see G. Reece Stoddard, who liked her, assuming his Harvard manner and telling his dinner partner that Bernice shouldn't have been allowed to go to the movies so much; she could see Draycott Deyo exchanging glances with his mother and then being conscientiously charitable to her. But then perhaps by tomorrow Mrs Deyo would have heard the news; would send round an icy little note requesting that she fail to appear – and behind her back they would all laugh and know that Marjorie had made a fool of her; that her change at beauty had been sacrificed to the jealous whim of a selfish girl. She sat down suddenly before the mirror, biting the inside of her cheek.

"I like it," she said with an effort. "I think it'll be becoming."

Marjorie smiled.

"It looks all right. For Heaven's sake, don't let it worry you!"

"I won't."

"Goodnight, Bernice."

But as the door closed, something snapped within Bernice. She sprang dynamically to her feet, clenching her hands, then swiftly and noiselessly crossed over to her bed and from underneath it dragged out her suitcase. Into it she tossed toilet articles and a change of clothing. Then she turned to her trunk and quickly dumped in two drawerfuls of lingerie and summer dresses. She moved quietly, but with deadly efficiency, and in three quarters of an hour her trunk was locked and strapped and she was fully dressed in a becoming new travelling suit that Marjorie had helped her pick out.

Sitting down at her desk, she wrote a short note to Mrs Harvey, in which she briefly outlined her reasons for going. She sealed it, addressed it and laid it on her pillow. She glanced at her watch. The train left at one, and she knew that if she walked down to the Marborough Hotel two blocks away she could easily get a taxicab.

Suddenly she drew in her breath sharply and an expression flashed into her eyes that a practised character reader might have connected vaguely with the set look she had worn in the barber's chair – somehow a development of it. It was quite a new look for Bernice – and it carried consequences.

She went stealthily to the bureau, picked up an article that lay there and, turning out all the lights, stood quietly until her eyes became accustomed to the darkness. Softly she pushed open the door to Marjorie's room. She heard the quiet, even breathing of an untroubled conscience asleep.

She was by the bedside now, very deliberate and calm. She acted swiftly. Bending over she found one of the braids of Marjorie's hair, followed it up with her hand to the point nearest the head, and then, holding it a little slack so that the sleeper would feel no pull, she reached down with the shears and severed it. With the pigtail in her hand she held her breath. Marjorie had muttered something in her sleep. Bernice deftly amputated the other braid, paused for an instant, and then flitted swiftly and silently back to her own room.

Downstairs she opened the big front door, closed it carefully behind her and, feeling oddly happy and exuberant, stepped off the porch into the moonlight, swinging her heavy grip like a shopping bag. After a minute's brisk walk she discovered that her left hand still held the two blond braids. She laughed unexpectedly – had to shut her mouth hard to keep from emitting an absolute peal. She was passing Warren's house now, and on the impulse she set down her baggage and, swinging the braids like pieces of rope, flung them at the wooden porch, where they landed with a slight thud. She laughed again, no longer restraining herself.

"Huh!" she giggled wildly. "Scalp the selfish thing!"

Then picking up her suitcase she set off at a half-run down the moonlit street.

Benediction

1

THE BALTIMORE STATION WAS HOT and crowded, so Lois was forced to stand by the telegraph desk for interminable, sticky seconds while a clerk with big front teeth counted and recounted a large lady's day message, to determine whether it contained the innocuous forty-nine words or the fatal fifty-one.

Lois, waiting, decided she wasn't quite sure of the address, so she took the letter out of her bag and ran over it again.

> *Darling* – it began – *I understand and I'm happier than life ever meant me to be. If I could give you the things you've always been in tune with – but I can't, Lois; we can't marry and we can't lose each other and let all this glorious love end in nothing.*
>
> *Until your letter came, dear, I'd been sitting here in the half-dark thinking and thinking where I could go and ever forget you; abroad, perhaps, to drift through Italy or Spain and dream away the pain of having lost you where the crumbling ruins of older, mellower civilizations would mirror only the desolation of my heart – and then your letter came.*
>
> *Sweetest, bravest girl, if you'll wire me I'll meet you in Wilmington – till then I'll be here just waiting and hoping for every long dream of you to come true.*
>
> HOWARD

She had read the letter so many times that she knew it word by word, yet it still startled her. In it she found many faint reflections of the man who wrote it – the mingled sweetness and sadness in his dark eyes, the furtive, restless excitement she felt sometimes when he talked to her, his dreamy sensuousness that lulled her mind to sleep. Lois was nineteen and very romantic and curious and courageous.

The large lady and the clerk having compromised on fifty words, Lois took a blank and wrote her telegram. And there were no overtones to the finality of her decision.

It's just destiny – she thought – it's just the way things work out in this damn world. If cowardice is all that's been holding me back, there won't be any holding back. So we'll just let things take their course and never be sorry.

The clerk scanned her telegram:

Arrived Baltimore today spend day with my brother meet me Wilmington three p.m. Wednesday Love
  Lois

"Fifty-four cents," said the clerk admiringly.

And never be sorry – thought Lois – and never be sorry...

2

TREES FILTERING LIGHT onto dappled grass. Trees like tall, languid ladies with feather fans coquetting airily with the ugly roof of the monastery. Trees like butlers, bending courteously over placid walks and paths. Trees, trees over the hills on either side and scattering out in clumps and lines and woods all through eastern Maryland, delicate lace on the hems of many yellow fields, dark opaque backgrounds for flowered bushes or wild climbing gardens.

Some of the trees were very gay and young, but the monastery trees were older than the monastery, which, by true monastic standards, wasn't very old at all. And, as a matter of fact, it wasn't technically called a monastery, but only a seminary; nevertheless it shall be a monastery here, despite its Victorian architecture or its Edward VII additions, or even its Woodrow Wilsonian, patented, last-a-century roofing.

Out behind was the farm where half a dozen lay brothers were sweating lustily as they moved with deadly efficiency around the vegetable gardens. To the left, behind a row of elms, was an informal baseball diamond where three novices were being batted out by a fourth, amid great chasings and puffings and blowings. And in front, as a great mellow bell boomed the half-hour, a swarm of black, human leaves were blown over the chequerboard of paths under the courteous trees.

Some of these black leaves were very old with cheeks furrowed like the first ripples of a splashed pool. Then there was a scattering of middle-aged leaves, whose forms when viewed in profile in their revealing gowns were beginning to be faintly unsymmetrical. These carried thick volumes of Thomas Aquinas and Henry James and Cardinal Mercier and Immanuel Kant, and many bulging notebooks filled with lecture data.

But most numerous were the young leaves; blond boys of nineteen with very stern, conscientious expressions; men in the late twenties with a keen self-assurance from having taught out in the world for five years – several hundreds of them, from city and town and country in Maryland and Pennsylvania and Virginia and West Virginia and Delaware.

There were many Americans and some Irish and some tough Irish and a few French, and several Italians and Poles, and they walked informally arm in arm with each other in twos and threes or in long rows, almost universally distinguished by the straight mouth and the considerable chin – for this was the Society of Jesus, founded in Spain five hundred years before by a tough-minded soldier who trained men to hold a breach or a salon, preach a sermon or write a treaty, and do it and not argue...

Lois got out of a bus into the sunshine down by the outer gate. She was nineteen with yellow hair and eyes that people were tactful enough not to call green. When men of talent saw her in a streetcar, they often furtively produced little stub pencils and backs of envelopes and tried to sum up that profile or the thing that the eyebrows did to her eyes. Later they looked at their results and usually tore them up with wondering sighs.

Though Lois was very jauntily attired in an expensively appropriate travelling affair, she did not linger to pat out the dust which covered her clothes, but started up the central walk with curious glances at either side. Her face was very eager and expectant, yet she hadn't at all that glorified expression that girls wear when they arrive for a senior prom at Princeton or New Haven; still, as there were no senior proms here, perhaps it didn't matter.

She was wondering what he would look like, whether she'd possibly know him from his picture. In the picture, which hung over her mother's bureau at home, he seemed very young and hollow-cheeked and rather pitiful, with only a well-developed mouth and an ill-fitting probationer's gown to show that he had already made a momentous decision about his life. Of course he had been only nineteen then and now he was thirty-six – didn't look like that at all; in recent snapshots he was much broader and his hair had grown a little thin – but the impression of her brother she had always retained was that of the big picture. And so she had always been a little sorry for him. What a life for a man! Seventeen years of preparation and he wasn't even a priest yet – wouldn't be for another year.

Lois had an idea that this was all going to be rather solemn if she let it be. But she was going to give her very best imitation of undiluted sunshine, the imitation she could give even when her head was splitting or when her mother had a nervous breakdown or when she was particularly romantic and curious and courageous. This brother of hers undoubtedly needed cheering up, and he was going to be cheered up, whether he liked it or not.

As she drew near the great, homely front door, she saw a man break suddenly away from a group and, pulling up the skirts of his gown, run towards her. He was smiling, she noticed, and he looked very big and… and reliable. She stopped and waited, knew that her heart was beating unusually fast.

"Lois!" he cried, and in a second she was in his arms. She was suddenly trembling.

"Lois!" he cried again. "Why, this is wonderful! I can't tell you, Lois, how *much* I've looked forward to this. Why, Lois, you're beautiful!"

Lois gasped.

His voice, though restrained, was vibrant with energy and that odd sort of enveloping personality she had thought that she only of the family possessed.

"I'm mighty glad, too – Keith."

She flushed, but not unhappily, at this first use of his name.

"Lois... Lois... Lois," he repeated in wonder. "Child, we'll go in here a minute, because I want you to meet the rector, and then we'll walk around. I have a thousand things to talk to you about."

His voice became graver. "How's Mother?"

She looked at him for a moment and then said something that she had not intended to say at all, the very sort of thing she had resolved to avoid.

"Oh, Keith... she's... she's getting worse all the time, every way."

He nodded slowly as if he understood.

"Nervous, well... you can tell me about that later. Now..."

She was in a small study with a large desk, saying something to a little, jovial, white-haired priest who retained her hand for some seconds.

"So this is Lois!"

He said it as if he had heard of her for years.

He entreated her to sit down.

Two other priests arrived enthusiastically and shook hands with her and addressed her as "Keith's little sister", which she found she didn't mind a bit.

How assured they seemed; she had expected a certain shyness, reserve at least. There were several jokes unintelligible to her, which seemed to delight everyone, and the little Father Rector referred to the trio of them as "dim old monks", which she appreciated, because of course they weren't monks at all. She had a lightning impression that they were especially fond of Keith – the Father Rector had called him "Keith" and one of the others had kept a hand on his shoulder all through the conversation. Then she was shaking hands again and promising to come back a little later for some ice cream, and smiling and smiling and being rather absurdly happy... she told herself that it was because Keith was so delighted in showing her off.

Then she and Keith were strolling along a path, arm in arm, and he was informing her what an absolute jewel the Father Rector was.

"Lois," he broke off suddenly, "I want to tell you before we go any farther how much it means to me to have you come up here. I think it was... mighty sweet of you. I know what a gay time you've been having."

Lois gasped. She was not prepared for this. At first, when she had conceived the plan of taking the hot journey down to Baltimore, staying the night with a friend and then coming out to see her brother, she had felt rather consciously virtuous, hoped he wouldn't be priggish or resentful about her not having come before – but walking here with him under the trees seemed such a little thing, and surprisingly a happy thing.

"Why, Keith," she said quickly, "you know I couldn't have waited a day longer. I saw you when I was five, but of course I didn't remember, and how could I have gone on without practically ever having seen my only brother?"

"It was mighty sweet of you, Lois," he repeated.

Lois blushed – he *did* have personality.

"I want you to tell me all about yourself," he said after a pause. "Of course I have a general idea what you and Mother did in Europe those fourteen years, and then we were all so worried, Lois, when you had pneumonia and couldn't come down with Mother – let's see, that was two years ago – and then, well, I've seen your name in the papers, but it's all been so unsatisfactory. I haven't known you, Lois."

She found herself analysing his personality as she analysed the personality of every man she met. She wondered if the effect of... of intimacy that he gave was bred by his constant repetition of her name. He said it as if he loved the word, as if it had an inherent meaning to him.

"Then you were at school," he continued.

"Yes, at Farmington. Mother wanted me to go to a convent – but I didn't want to."

She cast a side glance at him to see if he would resent this.

But he only nodded slowly.

"Had enough convents abroad, eh?"

"Yes – and Keith, convents are different there anyway. Here even in the nicest ones there are so many *common* girls."

He nodded again.

"Yes," he agreed, "I suppose there are, and I know how you feel about it. It grated on me here, at first, Lois, though I wouldn't say that to anyone but you; we're rather sensitive, you and I, to things like this."

"You mean the men here?"

"Yes, some of them of course were fine, the sort of men I'd always been thrown with, but there were others; a man named Regan, for instance – I hated the fellow, and now he's about the best friend I have. A wonderful character, Lois; you'll meet him later. Sort of man you'd like to have with you in a fight."

Lois was thinking that Keith was the sort of man she'd like to have with *her* in a fight.

"How did you... how did you first happen to do it?" she asked, rather shyly, "to come here, I mean. Of course Mother told me the story about the Pullman car."

"Oh, that..." He looked rather annoyed.

"Tell me that. I'd like to hear you tell it."

"Oh, it's nothing, except what you probably know. It was evening and I'd been riding all day and thinking about... about a hundred things, Lois, and then suddenly I had a sense that someone was sitting across from me, felt that he'd been there for some time, and had a vague idea that he was another traveller. All at once he leant over towards me and I heard a voice say: 'I want you to be a priest, that's what I want.' Well, I jumped up and cried out, 'Oh, my God, not that!' – made an idiot of myself before about twenty people; you see there wasn't anyone sitting there at all. A week after that I went to the Jesuit College in Philadelphia and crawled up the last flight of stairs to the rector's office on my hands and knees."

There was another silence and Lois saw that her brother's eyes wore a faraway look, that he was staring unseeingly out over the sunny fields. She was stirred by the modulations of his voice and the sudden silence that seemed to flow about him when he finished speaking.

She noticed now that his eyes were of the same fibre as hers, with the green left out, and that his mouth was much gentler, really, than in the picture – or was it that the face had grown up to it lately? He was getting a little bald just on top of his head. She wondered if that was from wearing a hat so much. It seemed awful for a man to grow bald and no one to care about it.

"Were you... pious when you were young, Keith?" she asked. "You know what I mean. Were you religious? If you don't mind these personal questions."

"Yes," he said with his eyes still far away – and she felt that his intense abstraction was as much a part of his personality as his attention. "Yes, I suppose I was, when I was... sober."

Lois thrilled slightly.

"Did you drink?"

He nodded.

"I was on the way to making a bad hash of things." He smiled and, turning his grey eyes on her, changed the subject.

"Child, tell me about Mother. I know it's been awfully hard for you there, lately. I know you've had to sacrifice a lot and put up with a great deal, and I want you to know how fine of you I think it is. I feel, Lois, that you're sort of taking the place of both of us there."

Lois thought quickly how little she had sacrificed; how lately she had constantly avoided her nervous, half-invalid mother.

"Youth shouldn't be sacrificed to age, Keith," she said steadily.

"I know," he sighed, "and you oughtn't to have the weight on your shoulders, child. I wish I were there to help you."

She saw how quickly he had turned her remark and instantly she knew what this quality was that he gave off. He was *sweet*. Her thoughts went off on a sidetrack and then she broke the silence with an odd remark.

"Sweetness is hard," she said suddenly.

"What?"

"Nothing," she denied in confusion. "I didn't mean to speak aloud. I was thinking of something – of a conversation with a man named Freddy Kebble."

"Maury Kebble's brother?"

"Yes," she said, rather surprised to think of him having known Maury Kebble. Still there was nothing strange about it. "Well, he and I were talking about sweetness a few weeks ago. Oh, I don't know – I said that a man named Howard... that a man I knew was sweet, and he didn't agree with me, and we began talking about what sweetness in a man was. He kept telling me I meant a sort of soppy softness, but I knew I didn't – yet I didn't know exactly how to put it. I see now. I meant just the opposite. I suppose real sweetness is a sort of hardness – and strength."

Keith nodded.

"I see what you mean. I've known old priests who had it."

"I'm talking about young men," she said, rather defiantly.

"Oh!"

They had reached the now deserted baseball diamond and, pointing her to a wooden bench, he sprawled full length on the grass.

"Are these *young* men happy here, Keith?"

"Don't they look happy, Lois?"

"I suppose so, but those *young* ones, those two we just passed – have they... are they..."

"Are they signed up?" he laughed. "No, but they will be next month."

"Permanently?"

"Yes – unless they break down mentally or physically. Of course in a discipline like ours a lot drop out."

"But those *boys*. Are they giving up fine chances outside – like you did?"

He nodded.

"Some of them."

"But, Keith, they don't know what they're doing. They haven't had any experience of what they're missing."

"No, I suppose not."

"It doesn't seem fair. Life has just sort of scared them at first. Do they all come in so *young*?"

"No, some of them have knocked around, led pretty wild lives – Regan, for instance."

"I should think that sort would be better," she said meditatively, "men that had *seen* life."

"No," said Keith earnestly, "I'm not sure that knocking about gives a man the sort of experience he can communicate to others. Some of the broadest men I've known have been absolutely rigid about themselves. And reformed libertines are a notoriously intolerant class. Don't you think so, Lois?"

She nodded, still meditative, and he continued:

"It seems to me that when one weak person goes to another, it isn't help they want; it's a sort of companionship in guilt, Lois. After you were born, when Mother began to get nervous she used to go and weep with a certain Mrs Comstock. Lord, it used to make me shiver. She said it comforted her, poor old mother. No, I don't think that to help others you've got to show yourself at all. Real help comes from a stronger person whom you respect. And their sympathy is all the bigger because it's impersonal."

"But people want human sympathy," objected Lois. "They want to feel the other person's been tempted."

"Lois, in their hearts they want to feel that the other person's been weak. That's what they mean by human.

"Here in this old monkery, Lois," he continued with a smile, "they try to get all that self-pity and pride in our own wills out of us right at the first. They put us to scrubbing floors – and other things. It's like that idea of saving your life by losing it. You see we sort of feel that the less human a man is, in your sense of human, the better servant he can be to humanity. We carry it out to the end too. When one of us dies, his family can't even have him then. He's buried here under a plain wooden cross with a thousand others."

His tone changed suddenly and he looked at her with a great brightness in his grey eyes.

"But way back in a man's heart there are some things he can't get rid of – and one of them is that I'm awfully in love with my little sister."

With a sudden impulse she knelt beside him in the grass and, leaning over, kissed his forehead.

"You're hard, Keith," she said, "and I love you for it – and you're sweet."

3

BACK IN THE RECEPTION ROOM Lois met a half-dozen more of Keith's particular friends; there was a young man named Jarvis, rather pale and delicate-looking, who, she knew, must be a grandson of old Mrs Jarvis at home, and she mentally compared this ascetic with a brace of his riotous uncles.

And there was Regan with a scarred face and piercing intent eyes that followed her about the room and often rested on Keith with something very like worship. She knew then what Keith had meant about "a good man to have with you in a fight".

He's the missionary type – she thought vaguely – China or something.

"I want Keith's sister to show us what the shimmy is," demanded one young man with a broad grin.

Lois laughed.

"I'm afraid the Father Rector would send me shimmying out the gate. Besides, I'm not an expert."

"I'm sure it wouldn't be best for Jimmy's soul anyway," said Keith solemnly. "He's inclined to brood about things like shimmies. They were just starting to do the... maxixe, wasn't it, Jimmy? – when he became a monk, and it haunted him his whole first year. You'd see him when he was peeling potatoes, putting his arm around the bucket and making irreligious motions with his feet."

There was a general laugh in which Lois joined.

"An old lady who comes here to Mass sent Keith this ice cream," whispered Jarvis under cover of the laugh, "because she'd heard you were coming. It's pretty good, isn't it?"

There were tears trembling in Lois's eyes.

4

THEN HALF AN HOUR LATER over in the chapel things suddenly went all wrong. It was several years since Lois had been at Benediction, and at first she was thrilled by the gleaming monstrance with its central spot of white, the air rich and heavy with incense, and the sun shining through the stained-glass window of St Francis Xavier overhead and falling in warm red tracery on the cassock of the man in front of her, but at the first notes of the 'O Salutaris Hostia'* a heavy weight seemed to descend upon her soul. Keith was on her right and young Jarvis on her left, and she stole uneasy glances at both of them.

What's the matter with me? she thought impatiently.

She looked again. Was there a certain coldness in both their profiles that she had not noticed before – a pallor about the mouth and a curious set expression in their eyes? She shivered slightly: they were like dead men.

She felt her soul recede suddenly from Keith's. This was her brother – this, this unnatural person. She caught herself in the act of a little laugh.

"What is the matter with me?"

She passed her hand over her eyes and the weight increased. The incense sickened her and a stray, ragged note from one of the tenors in the choir grated on her ear like the shriek of a slate pencil. She fidgeted and, raising her hand to her hair, touched her forehead, found moisture on it.

"It's hot in here, hot as the deuce."

Again she repressed a faint laugh, and then in an instant the weight upon her heart suddenly diffused into cold fear... It was that candle on the altar. It was all wrong – wrong. Why didn't somebody see it? There was something *in* it. There was something coming out of it, taking form and shape above it.

She tried to fight down her rising panic, told herself it was the wick. If the wick wasn't straight, candles did something – but they didn't do this! With incalculable rapidity a force was gathering within her, a tremendous, assimilative force, drawing from every sense, every corner of her brain, and as it surged up inside her she felt an enormous, terrified repulsion. She drew her arms in close to her side, away from Keith and Jarvis.

Something in that candle... she was leaning forward – in another moment she felt she would go forward towards it – didn't anyone see it?... Anyone?

"Ugh!"

She felt a space beside her and something told her that Jarvis had gasped and sat down very suddenly... then she was kneeling and, as the flaming monstrance slowly left the altar in the hands of the priest, she heard a great rushing noise in her ears – the crash of the bells was like hammer blows... and then in a moment that seemed eternal a great torrent rolled over her heart – there was a shouting there and a lashing as of waves...

...She was calling, felt herself calling for Keith, her lips mouthing the words that would not come:

"Keith! Oh, my God! *Keith!*"

Suddenly she became aware of a new presence, something external, in front of her, consummated and expressed in warm red tracery. Then she knew. It was the window of St Francis Xavier. Her mind gripped at it, clung to it finally, and she felt herself calling again endlessly, impotently – Keith – Keith!

Then out of a great stillness came a voice:

"Blessed be God."

With a gradual rumble sounded the response rolling heavily through the chapel:

"Blessed be God."

The words sang instantly in her heart; the incense lay mystically and sweetly peaceful upon the air, and *the candle on the altar went out.*

"Blessed be His Holy Name."

"Blessed be His Holy Name."

Everything blurred into a swinging mist. With a sound half-gasp, half-cry, she rocked on her feet and reeled backward into Keith's suddenly outstretched arms.

5

"LIE STILL, CHILD."

She closed her eyes again. She was on the grass outside, pillowed on Keith's arm, and Regan was dabbing her head with a cold towel.

"I'm all right," she said quietly.

"I know, but just lie still a minute longer. It was too hot in there. Jarvis felt it too."

She laughed as Regan again touched her gingerly with the towel.

"I'm all right," she repeated.

But though a warm peace was filling her mind and heart, she felt oddly broken and chastened, as if someone had held her stripped soul up and laughed.

6

HALF AN HOUR LATER she walked, leaning on Keith's arm, down the long central path towards the gate.

"It's been such a short afternoon," he sighed, "and I'm so sorry you were sick, Lois."

"Keith, I'm feeling fine now, really; I wish you wouldn't worry."

"Poor old child. I didn't realize that Benediction'd be a long service for you after your hot trip out here and all."

She laughed cheerfully.

"I guess the truth is I'm not much used to Benediction. Mass is the limit of my religious exertions."

She paused and then continued quickly:

"I don't want to shock you, Keith, but I can't tell you how... how *inconvenient* being a Catholic is. It really doesn't seem to apply any more. As far as morals go, some of the wildest boys I know are Catholics. And the brightest boys – I mean the ones who think and read a lot – don't seem to believe in much of anything any more."

"Tell me about it. The bus won't be here for another half-hour."

They sat down on a bench by the path.

"For instance, Gerald Carter, he's published a novel. He absolutely roars when people mention immortality. And then Howa... well, another man I've known well, lately, who was Phi Beta Kappa at Harvard, says that no intelligent person can believe in Supernatural Christianity. He says Christ was a great socialist, though. Am I shocking you?"

She broke off suddenly.

Keith smiled.

"You can't shock a monk. He's a professional shock-absorber."

"Well," she continued, "that's about all. It seems so... so *narrow*. Church schools, for instance. There's more freedom about things that Catholic people can't see – like birth control."

Keith winced, almost imperceptibly, but Lois saw it.

"Oh," she said quickly, "everybody talks about everything now."

"It's probably better that way."

"Oh, yes, much better. Well, that's all, Keith. I just wanted to tell you why I'm a little... lukewarm, at present."

"I'm not shocked, Lois. I understand better than you think. We all go through those times. But I know it'll come out all right, child. There's that gift of faith that we have, you and I, that'll carry us past the bad spots."

He rose as he spoke and they started again down the path.

"I want you to pray for me sometimes, Lois. I think your prayers would be about what I need. Because we've come very close in these few hours, I think."

Her eyes were suddenly shining.

"Oh, we have, we have!" she cried. "I feel closer to you now than to anyone in the world."

He stopped suddenly and indicated the side of the path.

"We might… just a minute…"

It was a *pietà*, a life-size statue of the Blessed Virgin set within a semicircle of rocks.

Feeling a little self-conscious, she dropped on her knees beside him and made an unsuccessful attempt at prayer.

She was only half through when he rose. He took her arm again.

"I wanted to thank Her for letting us have this day together," he said simply.

Lois felt a sudden lump in her throat and she wanted to say something that would tell him how much it had meant to her too. But she found no words.

"I'll always remember this," he continued, his voice trembling a little – "this summer day with you. It's been just what I expected. You're just what I expected, Lois."

"I'm awfully glad, Keith."

"You see, when you were little, they kept sending me snapshots of you, first as a baby and then as a child in socks playing on the beach with a pail and shovel, and then suddenly as a wistful little girl with wondering, pure eyes – and I used to build dreams about you. A man has to have something living to cling to. I think, Lois, it was your little white soul I tried to keep near me – even when life was at its loudest and every intellectual idea of God seemed the sheerest mockery, and desire and love and a million things came up to me and said: 'Look here at me! See, I'm Life. You're turning your back on it!' All the way through that shadow, Lois, I could always see your baby soul flitting on ahead of me, very frail and clear and wonderful."

Lois was crying softly. They had reached the gate and she rested her elbow on it and dabbed furiously at her eyes.

"And then later, child, when you were sick I knelt all one night and asked God to spare you for me – for I knew then that I wanted more; He had taught me to want more. I wanted to know you moved and breathed in the same world with me. I saw you growing up, that white innocence of yours changing to a flame and burning to give light to other weaker souls. And then I wanted some day to take your children on my knee and hear them call the crabbed old monk Uncle Keith."

He seemed to be laughing now as he talked.

"Oh, Lois, Lois, I was asking God for more then. I wanted the letters you'd write me and the place I'd have at your table. I wanted an awful lot, Lois, dear."

"You've got me, Keith," she sobbed, "you know it, say you know it. Oh, I'm acting like a baby but I didn't think you'd be this way, and I… oh, Keith… Keith…"

He took her hand and patted it softly.

"Here's the bus. You'll come again, won't you?"

She put her hands on his cheeks and, drawing his head down, pressed her tear-wet face against his.

"Oh, Keith, brother, some day I'll tell you something…"

He helped her in, saw her take down her handkerchief and smile bravely at him, as the driver flicked his whip and the bus rolled off. Then a thick cloud of dust rose around it and she was gone.

For a few minutes he stood there on the road, his hand on the gatepost, his lips half parted in a smile.

"Lois," he said aloud in a sort of wonder, "Lois, Lois."

Later, some probationers passing noticed him kneeling before the *pietà*, and coming back after a time found him still there. And he was there until twilight came down and the courteous trees grew garrulous overhead and the crickets took up their burden of song in the dusky grass.

7

T HE FIRST CLERK in the telegraph booth in the Baltimore Station whistled through his buck teeth at the second clerk.

"S'matter?"

"See that girl – no, the pretty one with the big black dots on her veil. Too late – she's gone. You missed somep'n."

"What about her?"

"Nothing. 'Cept she's damn good-looking. Came in here yesterday and sent a wire to some guy to meet her somewhere. Then a minute ago she came in with a telegram all written out and was standin' there goin' to give it to me when she changed her mind or somep'n and all of a sudden tore it up."

"Hm."

The first clerk came around the counter and, picking up the two pieces of paper from the floor, put them together idly. The second clerk read them over his shoulder and subconsciously counted the words as he read. There were just thirteen.

This is in the way of a permanent goodbye. I should suggest Italy.

Lois

"Tore it up, eh?" said the second clerk.

Dalyrimple Goes Wrong

1

IN THE MILLENNIUM an educational genius will write a book to be given to every young man on the date of his disillusion. This work will have the flavour of Montaigne's essays and Samuel Butler's notebooks – and a little of Tolstoy and Marcus Aurelius. It will be neither cheerful nor pleasant, but will contain numerous passages of striking humour. Since first-class minds never believe anything very strongly until they've experienced it, its value will be purely relative... all people over thirty will refer to it as "depressing".

This prelude belongs to the story of a young man who lived, as you and I do, before the book.

2

THE GENERATION WHICH NUMBERED Bryan Dalyrimple drifted out of adolescence to a mighty fanfare of trumpets. Bryan played the star in an affair which included a Lewis gun and a nine-day romp behind the retreating German lines, so luck triumphant or sentiment rampant awarded him a row of medals and on his arrival in the States he was told that he was second in importance only to General Pershing and Sergeant York.* This was a lot of fun. The governor of his state, a stray congressman and a citizens' committee gave him enormous smiles and "By God, Sirs" on the dock at Hoboken; there were newspaper reporters and photographers who said "would you mind" and "if you could just"; and back in his home town there were old ladies the rims of whose eyes grew red as they talked to him, and girls who

158

hadn't remembered him so well since his father's business went blah! in Nineteen-twelve.

But when the shouting died, he realized that for a month he had been the house guest of the mayor, that he had only fourteen dollars in the world, and that "the name that will live for ever in the annals and legends of this State" was already living there very quietly and obscurely.

One morning he lay late in bed and, just outside his door, he heard the upstairs maid talking to the cook. The upstairs maid said that Mrs Hawkins, the mayor's wife, had been trying for a week to hint Dalyrimple out of the house. He left at eleven o'clock in intolerable confusion, asking that his trunk be sent to Mrs Beebe's boarding house.

Dalyrimple was twenty-three and he had never worked. His father had given him two years at the State University and passed away about the time of his son's nine-day romp, leaving behind him some mid-Victorian furniture and a thin packet of folded papers that turned out to be grocery bills. Young Dalyrimple had very keen grey eyes, a mind that delighted the army psychological examiners, a trick of having read it – whatever it was – some time before, and a cool hand in a hot situation. But these things did not save him a final unresigned sigh when he realized that he had to go to work – right away.

It was early afternoon when he walked into the office of Theron G. Macy, who owned the largest wholesale grocery house in town. Plump, prosperous, wearing a pleasant but quite unhumorous smile, Theron G. Macy greeted him warmly.

"Well... how do, Bryan? What's on your mind?"

To Dalyrimple, straining with his admission, his own words, when they came, sounded like an Arab beggar's whine for alms.

"Why... this question of a job." ("This question of a job" seemed somehow more clothed than just "a job".)

"A job?" An almost imperceptible breeze blew across Mr Macy's expression.

"You see, Mr Macy," continued Dalyrimple, "I feel I'm wasting time. I want to get started at something. I had several chances about a month ago but they all seem to have… gone—"

"Let's see," interrupted Mr Macy. "What were they?"

"Well, just at the first the governor said something about a vacancy on his staff. I was sort of counting on that for a while, but I hear he's given it to Allen Gregg, you know, son of G.P. Gregg. He sort of forgot what he said to me – just talking, I guess."

"You ought to push those things."

"Then there was that engineering expedition, but they decided they'd have to have a man who knew hydraulics, so they couldn't use me unless I paid my own way."

"You had just a year at the university?"

"Two. But I didn't take any science or mathematics. Well, the day the battalion paraded, Mr Peter Jordan said something about a vacancy in his store. I went around there today and I found he meant a sort of floorwalker – and then you said something one day" – he paused and waited for the older man to take him up, but noting only a minute wince continued – "about a position, so I thought I'd come and see you."

"There was a position," confessed Mr Macy reluctantly, "but since then we've filled it." He cleared his throat again. "You've waited quite a while."

"Yes, I suppose I did. Everybody told me there was no hurry – and I'd had these various offers."

Mr Macy delivered a paragraph on present-day opportunities which Dalyrimple's mind completely skipped.

"Have you had any business experience?"

"I worked on a ranch two summers as a rider."

"Oh, well," Mr Macy disparaged this neatly, and then continued: "What do you think you're worth?"

"I don't know."

"Well, Bryan, I tell you, I'm willing to strain a point and give you a chance."

Dalyrimple nodded.

"Your salary won't be much. You'll start by learning the stock. Then you'll come in the office for a while. Then you'll go on the road. When could you begin?"

"How about tomorrow?"

"All right. Report to Mr Hanson in the stockroom. He'll start you off."

He continued to regard Dalyrimple steadily until the latter, realizing that the interview was over, rose awkwardly.

"Well, Mr Macy, I'm certainly much obliged."

"That's all right. Glad to help you, Bryan."

After an irresolute moment, Dalyrimple found himself in the hall. His forehead was covered with perspiration, and the room had not been hot.

"Why the devil did I thank the son of a gun?" he muttered.

3

NEXT MORNING MR HANSON informed him coldly of the necessity of punching the time clock at seven every morning, and delivered him for instruction into the hands of a fellow worker, one Charley Moore.

Charley was twenty-six, with that faint musk of weakness hanging about him that is often mistaken for the scent of evil. It took no psychological examiner to decide that he had drifted into indulgence and laziness as casually as he had drifted into life, and was to drift out. He was pale and his clothes stank of smoke; he enjoyed burlesque shows, billiards and Robert Service,* and was always looking back upon his last intrigue or forward to his next one. In his youth his taste had run to loud ties, but now it seemed to have faded, like his vitality, and was expressed in pale-lilac four-in-hands and indeterminate grey collars. Charley was listlessly struggling that losing struggle against mental, moral and physical anaemia that takes place ceaselessly on the lower fringe of the middle classes.

The first morning he stretched himself on a row of cereal cartons and carefully went over the limitations of the Theron G. Macy Company.

"It's a piker organization. My Gosh! Lookit what they give me. I'm quittin' in a coupla months. Hell! Me stay with this bunch!"

The Charley Moores are always going to change jobs next month. They do, once or twice in their careers, after which they sit around comparing their last job with the present one, to the infinite disparagement of the latter.

"What do you get?" asked Dalyrimple curiously.

"Me? I get sixty." This rather defiantly.

"Did you start at sixty?"

"Me? No, I started at thirty-five. He told me he'd put me on the road after I learnt the stock. That's what he tells 'em all!"

"How long've you been here?" asked Dalyrimple with a sinking sensation.

"Me? Four years. My last year too, you bet your boots."

Dalyrimple rather resented the presence of the store detective as he resented the time clock, and he came into contact with him almost immediately through the rule against smoking. This rule was a thorn in his side. He was accustomed to his three or four cigarettes in a morning, and after three days without it he followed Charley Moore by a circuitous route up a flight of back stairs to a little balcony where they indulged in peace. But this was not for long. One day in his second week the detective met him in a nook of the stairs, on his descent, and told him sternly that next time he'd be reported to Mr Macy. Dalyrimple felt like an errant schoolboy.

Unpleasant facts came to his knowledge. There were "cave-dwellers" in the basement who had worked there for ten or fifteen years at sixty dollars a month, rolling barrels and carrying boxes through damp, cement-walled corridors, lost in that echoing half-darkness between seven and five thirty and, like himself, compelled several times a month to work until nine at night.

At the end of a month he stood in line and received forty dollars. He pawned a cigarette case and a pair of field glasses and managed to live – to eat, sleep and smoke. It was, however, a narrow scrape; as the ways and means of economy were a closed book to him and the second month brought no increase, he voiced his alarm.

"If you've got a drag with old Macy, maybe he'll raise you," was Charley's disheartening reply. "But he didn't raise *me* till I'd been here nearly two years."

"I've got to live," said Dalyrimple simply. "I could get more pay as a labourer on the railroad but, golly, I want to feel I'm where there's a chance to get ahead."

Charles shook his head sceptically, and Mr Macy's answer next day was equally unsatisfactory.

Dalyrimple had gone to the office just before closing time.

"Mr Macy, I'd like to speak to you."

"Why... yes." The unhumorous smile appeared. The voice was faintly resentful.

"I want to speak to you in regard to more salary."

Mr Macy nodded.

"Well," he said doubtfully, "I don't know exactly what you're doing. I'll speak to Mr Hanson."

He knew exactly what Dalyrimple was doing, and Dalyrimple knew he knew.

"I'm in the stockroom – and, sir, while I'm here, I'd like to ask you how much longer I'll have to stay there."

"Why... I'm not sure exactly. Of course it takes some time to learn the stock."

"You told me two months when I started."

"Yes. Well, I'll speak to Mr Hanson."

Dalyrimple paused, irresolute.

"Thank you, sir."

Two days later he again appeared in the office with the result of a count that had been asked for by Mr Hesse, the bookkeeper. Mr Hesse was engaged and Dalyrimple, waiting, began idly fingering a ledger on the stenographer's desk.

Half-unconsciously he turned a page – he caught sight of his name – it was a salary list:

     Dalyrimple
     Demming
     Donahoe
     Everett

His eyes stopped:

     Everett...$60

So Tom Everett, Macy's weak-chinned nephew, had started at sixty – and in three weeks he had been out of the packing room and into the office.

So that was it! He was to sit and see man after man pushed over him: sons, cousins, sons of friends, irrespective of their capabilities, while *he* was cast for a pawn, with "going on the road" dangled before his eyes – put off with the stock remark: "I'll see; I'll look into it." At forty, perhaps, he would be a bookkeeper like old Hesse, tired, listless Hesse with dull routine for his stint and a dull background of boarding-house conversation.

This was a moment when a genie should have pressed into his hand the book for disillusioned young men. But the book has not been written.

A great protest swelling into revolt surged up in him. Ideas half-forgotten, chaotically perceived and assimilated, filled his mind. Get on – that was the rule of life – and that was all. How he did it, didn't matter – but to be Hesse or Charley Moore.

"I won't!" he cried aloud.

The bookkeeper and the stenographers looked up in surprise.

"What?"

For a second Dalyrimple stared – then walked up to the desk.

"Here's that data," he said brusquely. "I can't wait any longer."

Mr Hesse's face expressed surprise.

It didn't matter what he did – just so he got out of this rut. In a dream he stepped from the elevator into the stockroom and, walking to an unused aisle, sat down on a box, covering his face with his hands.

His brain was whirring with the frightful jar of discovering a platitude for himself.

"I've got to get out of this," he said aloud and then repeated, "I've got to get out" – and he didn't mean only out of Macy's wholesale house.

When he left at five thirty, it was pouring rain, but he struck off in the opposite direction from his boarding house, feeling, in the first cool moisture that oozed soggily through his old suit, an odd exultation and freshness. He wanted a world that was like walking through rain, even though he could not see far ahead of him, but fate had put him in the world of Mr Macy's fetid storerooms and corridors. At first merely the overwhelming need of change took him, then half-plans began to formulate in his imagination.

"I'll go East – to a big city – meet people – bigger people – people who'll help me. Interesting work somewhere. My God, there *must* be."

With sickening truth it occurred to him that his facility for meeting people was limited. Of all places it was here in his own town that he should be known, was known – famous – before the waters of oblivion had rolled over him.

You had to cut corners, that was all. Pull – relationship – wealthy marriages...

For several miles the continued reiteration of this preoccupied him, and then he perceived that the rain had become thicker and more opaque in the heavy grey of twilight and that the houses were falling away. The district of full blocks, then of big houses, then of scattering little ones, passed, and great sweeps of misty country opened out on both sides. It was hard walking here. The sidewalk had given place to a dirt road, streaked with furious brown rivulets that splashed and squashed around his shoes.

Cutting corners – the words began to fall apart, forming curious phrasings – little illuminated pieces of themselves. They resolved into sentences, each of which had a strangely familiar ring.

Cutting corners meant rejecting the old childhood principles that success came from faithfulness to duty, that evil was necessarily punished or virtue necessarily rewarded – that honest poverty was happier than corrupt riches.

It meant being hard.

This phrase appealed to him and he repeated it over and over. It had to do somehow with Mr Macy and Charley Moore – the attitudes, the methods of each of them.

He stopped and felt his clothes. He was drenched to the skin. He looked about him and, selecting a place in the fence where a tree sheltered it, perched himself there.

In my credulous years – he thought – they told me that evil was a sort of dirty hue, just as definite as a soiled collar, but it seems to me that evil is only a manner of hard luck, or heredity-and-environment, or "being found out". It hides in the vacillations of dubs like Charley Moore as certainly as it does in the intolerance of Macy, and if it ever gets much more tangible it becomes merely an arbitrary label to paste on the unpleasant things in other people's lives.

In fact – he concluded – it isn't worth worrying over what's evil and what isn't. Good and evil aren't any standard to me – and they can be a devil of a bad hindrance when I want something. When I want something bad enough, common sense tells me to go and take it – and not get caught.

And then suddenly Dalyrimple knew what he wanted first. He wanted fifteen dollars to pay his overdue board bill.

With a furious energy he jumped from the fence, whipped off his coat, and from its black lining cut with his knife a piece about five inches square. He made two holes near its edge and then fixed it on his face, pulling his hat down to hold it in place. It flapped grotesquely and then dampened and clung to his forehead and cheeks.

Now... The twilight had merged to dripping dusk... black as pitch. He began to walk quickly back towards town, not waiting to remove the mask but watching the road with difficulty through the jagged eyeholes. He was not conscious of any nervousness... the only tension was caused by a desire to do the thing as soon as possible.

He reached the first sidewalk, continued on until he saw a hedge far from any lamp-post, and turned in behind it. Within a minute he heard several series of footsteps – he waited – it was a woman and he held his breath until she passed... and then a man, a labourer. The next passer, he felt, would be what he wanted... the labourer's footfalls died far up the drenched street... other steps grew near, grew suddenly louder.

Dalyrimple braced himself.

"Put up your hands!"

The man stopped, uttered an absurd little grunt, and thrust pudgy arms skyward.

Dalyrimple went through the waistcoat.

"Now, you shrimp," he said, setting his hand suggestively to his own hip pocket, "you run, and stamp – loud! If I hear your feet stop I'll put a shot after you!"

Then he stood there in sudden uncontrollable laughter as audibly frightened footsteps scurried away into the night.

After a moment he thrust the roll of bills into his pocket, snatched off his mask and, running quickly across the street, darted down an alley.

4

YET, HOWEVER DALYRIMPLE justified himself intellectually, he had many bad moments in the weeks immediately following his decision. The tremendous pressure of sentiment and inherited tradition kept raising riot with his attitude. He felt morally lonely.

The noon after his first venture he ate in a little lunchroom with Charley Moore and, watching him unspread the paper, waited for a remark about the hold-up of the day before. But either the hold-up was not mentioned or Charley wasn't interested. He turned listlessly to the sporting sheet, read Doctor Crane's crop of seasoned bromides, took in an editorial on ambition with his mouth slightly ajar, and then skipped to Mutt and Jeff.

Poor Charley – with his faint aura of evil and his mind that refused to focus, playing a lifeless solitaire with cast-off mischief.

Yet Charley belonged on the other side of the fence. In him could be stirred up all the flamings and denunciations of righteousness; he would weep at a stage heroine's lost virtue, he could become lofty and contemptuous at the idea of dishonour.

On my side, thought Dalyrimple, there aren't any resting places; a man who's a strong criminal is after the weak criminals as well, so it's all guerrilla warfare over here.

What will it all do to me? he thought, with a persistent weariness. Will it take the colour out of life with the honour? Will it scatter my courage and dull my mind? Despiritualize me completely – does it mean eventual barrenness, eventual remorse, failure?

With a great surge of anger, he would fling his mind upon the barrier – and stand there with the flashing bayonet of his pride. Other men who broke the laws of justice and charity lied to all the world. He at any rate would not lie to himself. He was more than Byronic now: not the spiritual rebel, Don Juan; not the philosophical rebel, Faust; but a new psychological rebel of his own century – defying the sentimental a-priori forms of his own mind...

Happiness was what he wanted – a slowly rising scale of gratifications of the normal appetites – and he had a strong conviction that the materials, if not the inspiration of happiness, could be bought with money.

5

THE NIGHT CAME THAT DREW HIM out upon his second venture, and as he walked the dark street he felt in himself a great resemblance to a cat – a certain supple, swinging litheness. His muscles were rippling smoothly and sleekly under his spare, healthy flesh – he had an absurd desire to bound along the street, to run dodging among trees, to turn "cartwheels" over soft grass.

It was not crisp, but in the air lay a faint suggestion of acerbity, inspirational rather than chilling.

"The moon is down – I have not heard the clock!"

He laughed in delight at the line which an early memory had endowed with a hushed, awesome beauty.

He passed a man, and then another a quarter of a mile afterwards.

He was on Philmore Street now and it was very dark. He blessed the city council for not having put in new lamp-posts as a recent budget had recommended. Here was the red-brick Sterner residence which marked the beginning of the avenue; here was the Jordon house, the Eisenhaurs', the Dents', the Markhams', the Frasers'; the Hawkins', where he had been a guest; the Willoughbys', the Everetts', colonial and ornate; the little cottage where lived the Watts old maids between the imposing fronts of the Macys' and the Krupstadts'; the Craigs'...

Ah... *there!* He paused, wavered violently – far up the street was a blot, a man walking, possibly a policeman. After an eternal second he found himself following the vague, ragged shadow of a lamp-post across a lawn, running bent very low. Then he was standing tense, without breath or need of it, in the shadow of his limestone prey.

Interminably he listened – a mile off a cat howled, a hundred yards away another took up the hymn in a demoniacal snarl, and he felt his heart dip and swoop, acting as shock-absorber for his mind. There were other sounds; the faintest fragment of song far away; strident, gossiping laughter from a back porch diagonally across the alley; and crickets, crickets singing in the patched, patterned, moonlit grass of the yard. Within the house there seemed to lie an ominous silence. He was glad he did not know who lived here.

His slight shiver hardened to steel; the steel softened and his nerves became pliable as leather; gripping his hands, he gratefully found them supple and, taking out knife and pliers, he went to work on the screen.

So sure was he that he was unobserved that, from the dining room where in a minute he found himself, he leant out and carefully pulled the screen up into position, balancing it so it would neither fall by chance nor be a serious obstacle to a sudden exit.

Then he put the open knife in his coat pocket, took out his pocket flash and tiptoed around the room.

There was nothing here he could use – the dining room had never been included in his plans, for the town was too small to permit disposing of silver.

As a matter of fact his plans were of the vaguest. He had found that with a mind like his, lucrative in intelligence, intuition and lightning decision, it was best to have but the skeleton of a campaign. The machine-gun episode had taught him that. And he was afraid that a method preconceived would give him two points of view in a crisis – and two points of view meant wavering.

He stumbled slightly on a chair, held his breath, listened, went on, found the hall, found the stairs, started up; the seventh stair creaked at his step, the ninth, the fourteenth. He was counting them automatically. At the third creak he paused again for over a minute – and in that minute he felt more alone than he had ever felt before. Between the lines on patrol, even when alone, he had had behind him the moral support of half a billion people; now he was alone, pitted against that same moral pressure – a bandit. He had never felt this fear, yet he had never felt this exultation.

The stairs came to an end, a doorway approached; he went in and listened to regular breathing. His feet were economical of steps and his body swayed sometimes at stretching as he felt over the bureau, pocketing all articles which held promise – he could not have enumerated them ten seconds afterwards. He felt on a chair for possible trousers, found soft garments, women's lingerie. The corners of his mouth smiled mechanically.

Another room... the same breathing, enlivened by one ghastly snort that sent his heart again on its tour of his breast. Round object – watch; chain; roll of bills; stickpins; two rings – he remembered that he had got rings from the other bureau. He started out, winced as a faint glow flashed in front of him, facing him. God! – it was the glow of his own wristwatch on his outstretched arm.

Down the stairs. He skipped two creaking steps but found another. He was all right now, practically safe; as he neared the bottom, he felt a slight boredom. He reached the dining room – considered the silver – again decided against it.

Back in his room at the boarding house he examined the additions to his personal property:

Sixty-five dollars in bills.

A platinum ring with three medium diamonds, worth, probably, about seven hundred dollars. Diamonds were going up.

A cheap gold-plated ring with the initials O.S. and the date inside – '03 – probably a class ring from school. Worth a few dollars. Unsaleable.

A red-cloth case containing a set of false teeth.

A silver watch.

A gold chain worth more than the watch.

An empty ring box.

A little ivory Chinese god – probably a desk ornament.

A dollar and sixty-two cents in small change.

He put the money under his pillow and the other things in the toe of an infantry boot, stuffing a stocking in on top of them. Then for two hours his mind raced like a high-power engine here and there through his life, past and future, through fear and laughter. With a vague, inopportune wish that he were married, he fell into a deep sleep about half-past five.

6

THOUGH THE NEWSPAPER ACCOUNT of the burglary failed to mention the false teeth, they worried him considerably. The picture of a human waking in the cool dawn and groping for them in vain, of a soft, toothless breakfast, of a strange, hollow, lisping voice calling the police station, of weary, dispirited visits to the dentist, roused a great fatherly pity in him.

Trying to ascertain whether they belonged to a man or a woman, he took them carefully out of the case and held them up near his mouth. He moved his own jaws experimentally; he measured with his fingers; but he failed to decide: they might belong either to a large-mouthed woman or a small-mouthed man.

On a warm impulse he wrapped them in brown paper from the bottom of his army trunk, and printed FALSE TEETH on the package in clumsy pencil letters. Then, the next night, he walked down Philmore Street, and shied the package onto the lawn so that it would be near the door. Next day the paper announced that the police had a clue – they knew that the burglar was in town. However, they didn't mention what the clue was.

7

AT THE END OF A MONTH, "Burglar Bill of the Silver District" was the nurse girl's standby for frightening children. Five burglaries were attributed to him, but though Dalyrimple had only committed three, he considered that majority had it and appropriated the title to himself. He had once been seen – "a large bloated creature with the meanest face you ever laid eyes on". Mrs Henry Coleman, awaking at two o'clock at the beam of an electric torch flashed in her eye, could not have been expected to recognize Bryan Dalyrimple, at whom she had waved flags last Fourth of July, and whom she had described as "not at all the daredevil type, do you think?"

When Dalyrimple kept his imagination at white heat, he managed to glorify his own attitude, his emancipation from petty scruples and remorses – but let him once allow his thought to rove unarmoured, great unexpected horrors and depressions would overtake him. Then for reassurance he had to go back to think out the whole thing over again. He found that it was on the whole better to give up considering himself as a rebel. It was more consoling to think of everyone else as a fool.

His attitude towards Mr Macy underwent a change. He no longer felt a dim animosity and inferiority in his presence. As his fourth month in the store ended, he found himself regarding his employer in a manner that was almost fraternal. He had a vague but very assured conviction that Mr Macy's innermost soul would have abetted and approved. He no longer worried about his future. He had the intention of accumulating several thousand dollars and then clearing out – going east, back to France, down to South America. Half a dozen times in the last two months he had been about to stop work, but a fear of attracting attention to his being in funds prevented him. So he worked on, no longer in listlessness, but with contemptuous amusement.

8

THEN WITH ASTOUNDING SUDDENNESS something happened that changed his plans and put an end to his burglaries.

Mr Macy sent for him one afternoon, and with a great show of jovial mystery asked him if he had an engagement that night. If he hadn't, would he please call on Mr Alfred J. Fraser at eight o'clock. Dalyrimple's wonder was mingled with uncertainty. He debated with himself whether it were not his cue to take the first train out of town. But an hour's consideration decided him that his fears were unfounded, and at eight o'clock he arrived at the big Fraser house in Philmore Avenue.

Mr Fraser was commonly supposed to be the biggest political influence in the city. His brother was Senator Fraser, his son-in-law was Congressman Demming, and his influence, though not wielded in such a way as to make him an objectionable boss, was strong nevertheless.

He had a great, huge face, deep-set eyes and a barn door of an upper lip, the melange approaching a worthy climax in a long professional jaw.

During his conversation with Dalyrimple, his expression kept starting towards a smile, reached a cheerful optimism, and then receded back to imperturbability.

"How do you do, sir?" he said, holding out his hand. "Sit down. I suppose you're wondering why I wanted you. Sit down."

Dalyrimple sat down.

"Mr Dalyrimple, how old are you?"

"I'm twenty-three."

"You're young. But that doesn't mean you're foolish. Mr Dalyrimple, what I've got to say won't take long. I'm going to make you a proposition. To begin at the beginning, I've been watching you ever since last Fourth of July, when you made that speech in response to the loving cup."

Dalyrimple murmured disparagingly, but Fraser waved him to silence.

"It was a speech I've remembered. It was a brainy speech, straight from the shoulder, and it got to everybody in that crowd. I know. I've watched crowds for years." He cleared his throat, as if tempted to digress on his knowledge of crowds – then continued. "But, Mr Dalyrimple, I've seen too many young men who promised brilliantly go to pieces, fail through want of steadiness, too many high-power ideas and not enough willingness to work. So I waited. I wanted to see what you'd do. I wanted to see if you'd go to work, and if you'd stick to what you started."

Dalyrimple felt a glow settle over him.

"So," continued Fraser, "when Theron Macy told me you'd started down at his place, I kept watching you, and I followed your record through him. The first month I was afraid for a while. He told me you were getting restless, too good for your job, hinting around for a raise…"

Dalyrimple started.

"…But he said after that you evidently made up your mind to shut up and stick to it. That's the stuff I like in a young man! That's the stuff that wins out. And don't think I don't understand. I know how much harder it was for you, after all that silly flattery a lot of old women had been giving you. I know what a fight it must have been…"

Dalyrimple's face was burning brightly. He felt young and strangely ingenuous.

"Dalyrimple, you've got brains and you've got the stuff in you – and that's what I want. I'm going to put you into the State Senate."

"The *what*?"

"The State Senate. We want a young man who has got brains, but is solid and not a loafer. And when I say State Senate I don't stop there. We're up against it here, Dalyrimple. We've got to get some young men into politics – you know the old blood that's been running on the party ticket year in and year out."

Dalyrimple licked his lips.

"You'll run me for the State Senate?"

"I'll *put* you in the State Senate."

Mr Fraser's expression had now reached the point nearest a smile, and Dalyrimple, in a happy frivolity, felt himself urging it mentally on – but it stopped, locked and slid from him. The barn door and the jaw were separated by a line straight as a nail. Dalyrimple remembered with an effort that it was a mouth, and talked to it.

"But I'm through," he said. "My notoriety's dead. People are fed up with me."

"Those things," answered Mr Fraser, "are mechanical. Linotype is a resuscitator of reputations. Wait till you see the *Herald*, beginning next week – that is if you're with us – that is," and his voice hardened slightly, "if you haven't got too many ideas yourself about how things ought to be run."

"No," said Dalyrimple, looking him frankly in the eyes. "You'll have to give me a lot of advice at first."

"Very well. I'll take care of your reputation then. Just keep yourself on the right side of the fence."

Dalyrimple started at this repetition of a phrase he had thought of so much lately. There was a sudden ring of the doorbell.

"That's Macy now," observed Fraser, rising. "I'll go let him in. The servants have gone to bed."

He left Dalyrimple there in a dream. The world was opening up suddenly... The State Senate, the United States Senate... so life was this after all... cutting corners... cutting corners... common sense, that was the rule. No more foolish risks now unless necessity called – but it was being hard that counted… Never to let remorse or self-reproach lose him a night's sleep… let his life be a sword of courage… there was no payment… all that was drivel… drivel. He sprang to his feet with clenched hands in a sort of triumph.

"Well, Bryan," said Mr Macy stepping through the portières.

The two older men smiled their half-smiles at him.

"Well, Bryan," said Mr Macy again.

Dalyrimple smiled also.

"How do, Mr Macy?"

He wondered if some telepathy between them had made this new appreciation possible – some invisible realization…

Mr Macy held out his hand.

"I'm glad we're to be associated in this scheme – I've been for you all along – especially lately. I'm glad we're to be on the same side of the fence."

"I want to thank you, sir," said Dalyrimple simply. He felt a whimsical moisture gathering back of his eyes.

The Four Fists

1

A T THE PRESENT TIME no one I know has the slightest desire to hit Samuel Meredith; possibly this is because a man over fifty is liable to be rather severely cracked at the impact of a hostile fist, but, for my part, I am inclined to think that all his hittable qualities have quite vanished. But it is certain that at various times in his life hittable qualities were in his face, as surely as kissable qualities have ever lurked in a girl's lips.

I'm sure everyone has met a man like that, been casually introduced, even made a friend of him, yet felt he was the sort who aroused passionate dislike – expressed by some in the involuntary clenching of fists, and in others by mutterings about "takin' a poke" and "landin' a swift smash in ee eye". In the juxtaposition of Samuel Meredith's features this quality was so strong that it influenced his entire life.

What was it? Not the shape, certainly, for he was a pleasant-looking man from earliest youth: broad-browed, with grey eyes that were frank and friendly. Yet I've heard him tell a room full of reporters angling for a "success" story that he'd be ashamed to tell them the truth, that they wouldn't believe it, that it wasn't one story but four, that the public would not want to read about a man who had been walloped into prominence.

It all started at Phillips Andover Academy when he was fourteen. He had been brought up on a diet of caviar and bellboys' legs in half the capitals of Europe, and it was pure luck that his mother had nervous prostration and had to delegate his education to less tender, less biased hands.

At Andover he was given a room-mate named Gilly Hood. Gilly was thirteen, undersized and rather the school pet. From the September day when Mr Meredith's valet stowed Samuel's clothing in the best bureau and asked, on departing, "hif there was hanything helse, Master Samuel?" Gilly cried out that the faculty had played him false. He felt like an irate frog in whose bowl has been put a goldfish.

"Good gosh!" he complained to his sympathetic contemporaries. "He's a damn stuck-up Willie. He said, 'Are the crowd here gentlemen?' and I said, 'No, they're boys,' and he said age didn't matter, and I said, 'Who said it did?' Let him get fresh with me, the ole pieface!"

For three weeks Gilly endured in silence young Samuel's comments on the clothes and habits of Gilly's personal friends, endured French phrases in conversation, endured a hundred half-feminine meannesses that show what a nervous mother can do to a boy, if she keeps close enough to him – then a storm broke in the aquarium.

Samuel was out. A crowd had gathered to hear Gilly be wrathful about his room-mate's latest sins.

"He said, 'Oh, I don't like the windows open at night,' he said, 'except only a little bit,'" complained Gilly.

"Don't let him boss you."

"Boss me? You bet he won't. I open those windows, I guess, but the darn fool won't take turns shuttin' 'em in the morning."

"Make him, Gilly, why don't you?"

"I'm going to." Gilly nodded his head in fierce agreement. "Don't you worry. He needn't think I'm any ole butler."

"Le's see you make him."

At this point the darn fool entered in person and included the crowd in one of his irritating smiles. Two boys said, "'Lo, Mer'dith"; the others gave him a chilly glance and went on talking to Gilly. But Samuel seemed unsatisfied.

"Would you mind not sitting on my bed?" he suggested politely to two of Gilly's particulars who were perched very much at ease.

"Huh?"

"My bed. Can't you understand English?"

This was adding insult to injury. There were several comments on the bed's sanitary condition and the evidence within it of animal life.

"S'matter with your old bed?" demanded Gilly truculently.

"The bed's all right, but—"

Gilly interrupted this sentence by rising and walking up to Samuel. He paused several inches away and eyed him fiercely.

"You an' your crazy ole bed," he began. "You an' your crazy—"

"Go to it, Gilly," murmured someone.

"Show the darn fool—"

Samuel returned the gaze coolly.

"Well," he said finally, "it's my bed—"

He got no further, for Gilly hauled off and hit him succinctly in the nose.

"Yea! Gilly!"

"Show the big bully!"

"Just let him touch you – he'll see!"

The group closed in on them and for the first time in his life Samuel realized the insuperable inconvenience of being passionately detested. He gazed around helplessly at the glowering, violently hostile faces. He towered a head taller than his room-mate, so if he hit back he'd be called a bully and have half a dozen more fights on his hands within five minutes; yet if he didn't he was a coward. For a moment he stood there facing Gilly's blazing eyes, and then, with a sudden choking sound, he forced his way through the ring and rushed from the room.

The month following bracketed the thirty most miserable days of his life. Every waking moment he was under the lashing tongues of his contemporaries; his habits and mannerisms became butts for intolerable witticisms and, of course, the sensitiveness of adolescence was a further thorn. He considered that he was a natural pariah; that the unpopularity at school would follow him through life. When he went home for the Christmas holidays, he was so despondent that his father sent him to a nerve specialist. When he returned to Andover, he arranged to arrive late so that he could be alone in the bus during the drive from station to school.

Of course, when he had learnt to keep his mouth shut, everyone promptly forgot all about him. The next autumn, with his realization that consideration for others was the discreet attitude, he made good use of the clean start given him by the shortness of boyhood memory. By the beginning of his senior year Samuel Meredith was one of the best-liked boys of his class – and no one was any stronger for him than his first friend and constant companion, Gilly Hood.

2

SAMUEL BECAME the sort of college student who in the early Nineties drove tandems and coaches and tallyhos between Princeton and Yale and New York City to show that they appreciated the social importance of football games. He believed passionately in good form – his choosing of gloves, his tying of ties, his holding of reins were imitated by impressionable freshmen. Outside of his own set he was considered rather a snob, but as his set was *the* set, it never worried him. He played football in the autumn, drank highballs in the winter and rowed in the spring. Samuel despised all those who were merely sportsmen without being gentlemen, or merely gentlemen without being sportsmen.

He lived in New York and often brought home several of his friends for the weekend. Those were the days of the horse car, and in case of a crush it was, of course, the proper thing for any one of Samuel's set to rise and deliver his seat to a standing lady with a formal bow. One night in Samuel's junior year he boarded a car with two of his intimates. There were three vacant seats. When Samuel sat down, he noticed a heavy-eyed labouring man sitting next to him who smelt objectionably of garlic, sagged slightly against Samuel and, spreading a little as a tired man will, took up quite too much room.

The car had gone several blocks when it stopped for a quartet of young girls, and, of course, the three men of the world sprang to their feet and proffered their seats with due observance of form. Unfortunately, the labourer, being unacquainted with the code of neckties and tally-hos, failed to follow their example, and one young lady was left at an embarrassed stance. Fourteen eyes glared reproachfully at the barbarian; seven lips curled slightly; but the object of scorn stared stolidly into the foreground in sturdy unconsciousness of his despicable conduct. Samuel was the most violently affected. He was humiliated that any male should so conduct himself. He spoke aloud.

"There's a lady standing," he said sternly.

That should have been quite enough, but the object of scorn only looked up blankly. The standing girl tittered and exchanged nervous glances with her companions. But Samuel was aroused.

"There's a lady standing," he repeated, rather raspingly. The man seemed to comprehend.

"I pay my fare," he said quietly.

Samuel turned red and his hands clenched, but the conductor was looking their way, so at a warning nod from his friends he subsided into sullen gloom.

They reached their destination and left the car, but so did the labourer, who followed them, swinging his little pail. Seeing his chance, Samuel no longer resisted his aristocratic inclination. He turned around and, launching a full-featured, dime-novel sneer, made a loud remark about the right of the lower animals to ride with human beings.

In a half-second the workman had dropped his pail and let fly at him. Unprepared, Samuel took the blow neatly on the jaw and sprawled full length into the cobblestone gutter.

"Don't laugh at me!" cried his assailant. "I been workin' all day. I'm tired as hell!"

As he spoke the sudden anger died out of his eyes and the mask of weariness dropped again over his face. He turned and picked up his pail. Samuel's friends took a quick step in his direction.

"Wait!" Samuel had risen slowly and was motioning them back. Some time, somewhere, he had been struck like that before. Then he remembered – Gilly Hood. In the silence, as he dusted himself off, the whole scene in the room at Andover was before his eyes – and he knew intuitively that he had been wrong again. This man's strength, his rest, was the protection of his family. He had more use for his seat in the streetcar than any young girl.

"It's all right," said Samuel gruffly. "Don't touch him. I've been a damn fool."

Of course it took more than an hour, or a week, for Samuel to rearrange his ideas on the essential importance of good form. At first he simply admitted that his wrongness had made him powerless – as it had made him powerless against Gilly – but eventually his mistake about the workman influenced his entire attitude. Snobbishness is, after all, merely good breeding grown dictatorial; so Samuel's code remained, but the necessity of imposing it upon others had faded out in a certain gutter. Within that year his class had somehow stopped referring to him as a snob.

3

AFTER A FEW YEARS SAMUEL'S UNIVERSITY decided that it had shone long enough in the reflected glory of his neckties, so they declaimed to him in Latin, charged him ten dollars for the paper which proved him irretrievably educated, and sent him into the turmoil with much self-confidence, a few friends and the proper assortment of harmless bad habits.

His family had by that time started back to shirtsleeves, through a sudden decline in the sugar market, and it had already unbuttoned its vest, so to speak, when Samuel went to work. His mind was that exquisite tabula rasa that a university education sometimes leaves, but he had both energy and influence, so he used his former ability as a dodging half-back in twisting through Wall Street crowds as runner for a bank.

His diversion was – women. There were half a dozen: two or three debutantes, an actress (in a minor way), a grass widow and one sentimental little brunette who was married and lived in a little house in Jersey City.

They had met on a ferry boat. Samuel was crossing from New York on business (he had been working several years by this time) and he helped her look for a package that she had dropped in the crush.

"Do you come over often?" he enquired casually.

"Just to shop," she said shyly. She had great brown eyes and the pathetic kind of little mouth. "I've only been married three months, and we find it cheaper to live over here."

"Does he… does your husband like your being alone like this?"

She laughed, a cheery young laugh.

"Oh, dear me, no. We were to meet for dinner, but I must have misunderstood the place. He'll be awfully worried."

"Well," said Samuel disapprovingly, "he ought to be. If you'll allow me, I'll see you home."

She accepted his offer thankfully, so they took the cable car together. When they walked up the path to her little house, they saw a light there; her husband had arrived before her.

"He's frightfully jealous," she announced, laughingly apologetic.

"Very well," answered Samuel, rather stiffly. "I'd better leave you here."

She thanked him and, waving a goodnight, he left her.

That would have been quite all if they hadn't met on Fifth Avenue one morning a week later. She started and blushed and seemed so glad to see him that they chatted like old friends. She was going to her dressmaker's, eat lunch alone at Taine's, shop all afternoon and meet her husband on the ferry at five. Samuel told her that her husband was a very lucky man. She blushed again and scurried off.

Samuel whistled all the way back to his office, but about twelve o'clock he began to see that pathetic, appealing little mouth everywhere – and those brown eyes. He fidgeted when he looked at the clock; he thought of the grill downstairs where he lunched and the heavy male conversation thereof, and opposed to that picture appeared another: a little table at Taine's with the brown eyes and the mouth a few feet away. A few minutes before twelve thirty he dashed on his hat and rushed for the cable car.

She was quite surprised to see him.

"Why... hello," she said. Samuel could tell that she was just pleasantly frightened.

"I thought we might lunch together. It's so dull eating with a lot of men."

She hesitated.

"Why, I suppose there's no harm in it. How could there be!"

It occurred to her that her husband should have taken lunch with her – but he was generally so hurried at noon. She told Samuel all about him: he was a little smaller than Samuel, but oh, *much* better-looking. He was a bookkeeper and not making a lot of money, but they were very happy and expected to be rich within three or four years.

Samuel's grass widow had been in a quarrelsome mood for three or four weeks, and, through contrast, he took an accentuated pleasure in this meeting; so fresh was she, and earnest, and faintly adventurous. Her name was Marjorie.

They made another engagement; in fact, for a month they lunched together two or three times a week. When she was sure that her husband would work late, Samuel took her over to New Jersey on the ferry, leaving her always on the tiny front porch, after she had gone in and lit the gas to use the security of his masculine presence outside. This grew to be a ceremony – and it annoyed him. Whenever the comfortable glow fell out through the front windows, that was his *congé*; yet he never suggested coming in and Marjorie didn't invite him.

Then, when Samuel and Marjorie had reached a stage in which they sometimes touched each other's arms gently, just to show that they were very good friends, Marjorie and her husband had one of those ultra-sensitive, super-critical quarrels that couples never indulge in unless they care a great deal about each other. It started with a cold mutton chop or a leak in the gas jet – and one day Samuel found her in Taine's, with dark shadows under her brown eyes and a terrifying pout.

By this time Samuel thought he was in love with Marjorie – so he played up the quarrel for all it was worth. He was her best friend and patted her hand – and leant down close to her brown curls while she whispered in little sobs what her husband had said that morning; and he was a little more than her best friend when he took her over to the ferry in a hansom.

"Marjorie," he said gently, when he left her, as usual, on the porch, "if at any time you want to call on me, remember that I am always waiting, always waiting."

She nodded gravely and put both her hands in his.

"I know," she said. "I know you're my friend, by best friend."

Then she ran into the house and he watched there until the gas went on.

For the next week Samuel was in a nervous turmoil. Some persistently rational strain warned him that at bottom he and Marjorie had little in common, but in such cases there is usually so much mud in the water that one can seldom see to the bottom. Every dream and desire told him that he loved Marjorie, wanted her, had to have her.

The quarrel developed. Marjorie's husband took to staying in New York until late at night, came home several times disagreeably overstimulated and made her generally miserable. They must have had too much pride to talk it out – for Marjorie's husband was, after all, pretty decent – so it drifted on from one misunderstanding to another. Marjorie kept coming more and more to Samuel; when a woman can accept masculine sympathy it is much more satisfactory to her than crying to another girl. But Marjorie didn't realize how much she had begun to rely on him, how much he was part of her little cosmos.

One night, instead of turning away when Marjorie went in and lit the gas, Samuel went in too, and they sat together on the sofa in the little parlour. He was very happy. He envied their home, and he felt that the man who neglected such a possession out of stubborn pride was a fool and unworthy of his wife. But when he kissed Marjorie for the first time, she cried softly and told him to go. He sailed home on the wings of desperate excitement, quite resolved to fan this spark of romance, no matter how big the blaze or who was burnt. At the time he considered that his thoughts were unselfishly of her; in a later perspective he knew that she had meant no more than the white screen in a motion picture: it was just Samuel – blind, desirous.

Next day at Taine's, when they met for lunch, Samuel dropped all pretence and made frank love to her. He had no plans, no definite intentions, except to kiss her lips again, to hold her in his arms and feel that she was very little and pathetic and lovable... He took her home, and this time they kissed until both their hearts beat high – words and phrases formed on his lips.

And then suddenly there were steps on the porch – a hand tried the outside door. Marjorie turned dead-white.

"Wait!" she whispered to Samuel in a frightened voice, but in angry impatience at the interruption he walked to the front door and threw it open.

Everyone has seen such scenes on the stage – seen them so often that when they actually happen people behave very much like actors. Samuel felt that he was playing a part and the lines came quite naturally: he announced that all had a right to lead their own lives and looked at Marjorie's husband menacingly, as if daring him to doubt it. Marjorie's husband spoke of the sanctity of the home, forgetting that it hadn't seemed very holy to him lately; Samuel continued along the line of "the right to happiness"; Marjorie's husband mentioned firearms and the divorce court. Then suddenly he stopped and scrutinized both of them – Marjorie in pitiful collapse on the sofa, Samuel haranguing the furniture in a consciously heroic pose.

"Go upstairs, Marjorie," he said, in a different tone.

"Stay where you are!" Samuel countered quickly.

Marjorie rose, wavered and sat down, rose again and moved hesitatingly towards the stairs.

"Come outside," said her husband to Samuel. "I want to talk to you."

Samuel glanced at Marjorie, tried to get some message from her eyes; then he shut his lips and went out.

There was a bright moon, and when Marjorie's husband came down the steps Samuel could see plainly that he was suffering – but he felt no pity for him.

They stood and looked at each other, a few feet apart, and the husband cleared his throat as though it were a bit husky.

"That's my wife," he said quietly, and then a wild anger surged up inside him. "Damn you!" he cried – and hit Samuel in the face with all his strength.

In that second, as Samuel slumped to the ground, it flashed to him that he had been hit like that twice before, and simultaneously the incident altered like a dream – he felt suddenly awake. Mechanically he sprang to his feet and squared off. The other man was waiting, fists up, a yard away, but Samuel knew that, though physically he had him by several inches and many pounds, he wouldn't hit him. The situation had miraculously and entirely changed – a moment before Samuel had seemed to himself heroic; now he seemed the cad, the outsider, and Marjorie's husband, silhouetted against the lights of the little house, the eternal heroic figure, the defender of his home.

There was a pause and then Samuel turned quickly away and went down the path for the last time.

4

OF COURSE, AFTER THE THIRD BLOW Samuel put in several weeks at conscientious introspection. The blow years before at Andover had landed on his personal unpleasantness; the workman of his college days had jarred the snobbishness out of his system; and Marjorie's husband had given a severe jolt to his greedy selfishness. It threw women out of his ken until a year later, when he met his future wife; for the only sort of woman worthwhile seemed to be the one who could be protected as Marjorie's husband had protected her. Samuel could not imagine his grass widow, Mrs De Ferriac, causing any very righteous blows on her own account.

His early thirties found him well on his feet. He was associated with old Peter Carhart, who was in those days a national figure. Carhart's physique was like a rough model for a statue of Hercules, and his record was just as solid – a pile made for the pure joy of it, without cheap extortion or shady scandal. He had been a great friend of Samuel's father, but he watched the son for six years before taking him into his own office. Heaven knows how many things he controlled at that time – mines, railroads, banks, whole cities. Samuel was very close to him, knew his likes and dislikes, his prejudices, weaknesses and many strengths.

One day Carhart sent for Samuel and, closing the door of his inner office, offered him a chair and a cigar.

"Everything OK, Samuel?" he asked.

"Why, yes."

"I've been afraid you're getting a bit stale."

"Stale?" Samuel was puzzled.

"You've done no work outside the office for nearly ten years?"

"But I've had vacations, in the Adiron—"

Carhart waved this aside.

"I mean outside work. Seeing the things move that we've always pulled the strings of here."

"No," admitted Samuel, "I haven't."

"So," he said abruptly, "I'm going to give you an outside job that'll take about a month."

Samuel didn't argue. He rather liked the idea, and he made up his mind that, whatever it was, he would put it through just as Carhart wanted it. That was his employer's greatest hobby, and the men around him were as dumb under direct orders as infantry subalterns.

"You'll go to San Antonia and see Hamil," continued Carhart. "He's got a job on hand and he wants a man to take charge."

Hamil was in charge of the Carhart interests in the South-west, a man who had grown up in the shadow of his employer, and with whom, though they had never met, Samuel had had much official correspondence.

"When do I leave?"

"You'd better go tomorrow," answered Carhart, glancing at the calendar. "That's the first of May. I'll expect your report here on the first of June."

Next morning Samuel left for Chicago, and two days later he was facing Hamil across a table in the office of the Merchants' Trust in San Antonio. It didn't take long to get the gist of the thing. It was a big deal in oil which concerned the buying-up of seventeen huge adjoining ranches. This buying-up had to be done in one week, and it was a pure squeeze. Forces had been set in motion that put the seventeen owners between the devil and the deep sea, and Samuel's part was simply to "handle" the matter from a little village near Pueblo. With tact and efficiency the right man could bring it off without any friction, for it was merely a question of sitting at the wheel and keeping a firm hold. Hamil, with an astuteness many times valuable to his chief, had arranged a situation that would give a much greater clear gain than any dealing in the open market. Samuel shook hands with Hamil, arranged to return in two weeks and left for San Felipe, New Mexico.

It occurred to him, of course, that Carhart was trying him out. Hamil's report on his handling of this might be a factor in something big for him, but even without that he would have done his best to put the thing through. Ten years in New York hadn't made him sentimental, and he was quite accustomed to finish everything he began – and a little bit more.

All went well at first. There was no enthusiasm, but each one of the seventeen ranchers concerned knew Samuel's business, knew what he had behind him, and that they had as little chance of holding out as flies on a window pane. Some of them were resigned – some of them cared like the devil, but they'd talked it over, argued it with lawyers and couldn't see any possible loophole. Five of the ranches had oil, the other twelve were part of the chance, but quite as necessary to Hamil's purpose, in any event.

Samuel soon saw that the real leader was an early settler named McIntyre, a man of perhaps fifty, grey-haired, clean-shaven, bronzed by forty New Mexico summers, and with those clear, steady eyes that Texas and New Mexico weather are apt to give. His ranch had not as yet shown oil, but it was in the pool, and if any man hated to lose his land, McIntyre did. Everyone had rather looked to him at first to avert the big calamity, and he had hunted all over the territory for the legal means with which to do it, but he had failed and he knew it. He avoided Samuel assiduously, but Samuel was sure that when the day came for the signatures he would appear.

It came – a baking May day, with hot waves rising off the parched land as far as eyes could see, and as Samuel sat stewing in his little improvised office – a few chairs, a bench and a wooden table – he was glad the thing was almost over. He wanted to get back East the worst way, and join his wife and children for a week at the seashore.

The meeting was set for four o'clock, and he was rather surprised at three thirty when the door opened and McIntyre came in. Samuel could not help respecting the man's attitude and feeling a bit sorry for him. McIntyre seemed closely related to the prairies, and Samuel had the little flicker of envy that city people feel towards men who live in the open.

"Afternoon," said McIntyre, standing in the open doorway, with his feet apart and his hands on his hips.

"Hello, Mr McIntyre." Samuel rose, but omitted the formality of offering his hand. He imagined the rancher cordially loathed him, and he hardly blamed him. McIntyre came in and sat down leisurely.

"You got us," he said suddenly.

This didn't seem to require any answer.

"When I heard Carhart was back of this," he continued, "I gave up."

"Mr Carhart is—" began Samuel, but McIntyre waved him silent.

"Don't talk about the dirty sneak thief!"

"Mr McIntyre," said Samuel briskly, "if this half-hour is to be devoted to that sort of talk—"

"Oh, dry up, young man," McIntyre interrupted, "you can't abuse a man who'd do a thing like this."

Samuel made no answer.

"It's simply a dirty filch. There just *are* skunks like him too big to handle."

"You're being paid liberally," offered Samuel.

"Shut up!" roared McIntyre suddenly. "I want the privilege of talking." He walked to the door and looked out across the land, the sunny, steaming pasturage that began almost at his feet and ended with the grey-green of the distant mountains. When he turned around, his mouth was trembling.

"Do you fellows love Wall Street?" he said hoarsely. "Or wherever you do your dirty scheming…" He paused. "I suppose you do. No critter gets so low that he doesn't sort of love the place he's worked, where he's sweated out the best he's had in him."

Samuel watched him awkwardly. McIntyre wiped his forehead with a huge blue handkerchief, and continued:

"I reckon this rotten old devil had to have another million. I reckon we're just a few of the poor beggars he's blotted out to buy a couple more carriages or something." He waved his hand towards the door. "I built a house out there when I was seventeen, with these two hands. I took a wife there at twenty-one, added two wings and, with four mangy steers, I started out. Forty summers I've saw the sun come up over those mountains and drop down red as blood in the evening, before the heat drifted off and the stars came out. I been happy in that house. My boy was born there and he died there, late one spring, in the hottest part of an afternoon like this. Then the wife and I lived there alone like we'd lived before, and sort of tried to have a home, after all, not a real home but nigh it – cause the boy always seemed around close, somehow, and we expected a lot of nights to see him runnin' up the path to supper." His voice was shaking so he could hardly speak, and he turned again to the door, his grey eyes contracted.

"That's my land out there," he said, stretching out his arm, "my land, by God… It's all I got in the world – and ever wanted." He dashed his sleeve across his face, and his tone changed as he turned slowly and faced Samuel. "But I suppose it's got to go when they want it… it's got to go."

Samuel had to talk. He felt that in a minute more he would lose his head. So he began, as level-voiced as he could – in the sort of tone he saved for disagreeable duties.

"It's business, Mr McIntyre," he said. "It's inside the law. Perhaps we couldn't have bought out two or three of you at any price, but most of you did have a price. Progress demands some things…"

Never had he felt so inadequate, and it was with the greatest relief that he heard hoof beats a few hundred yards away.

But at his words the grief in McIntyre's eyes had changed to fury.

"You and your dirty gang of crooks!" he cried. "Not one of you has got an honest love for anything on God's earth! You're a herd of money swine!"

Samuel rose and McIntyre took a step towards him.

"You long-winded dude. You got our land – take that for Peter Carhart!"

He swung from the shoulder quick as lightning and down went Samuel in a heap. Dimly he heard steps in the doorway and knew that someone was holding McIntyre, but there was no need. The rancher had sunk down in his chair, and dropped his head in his hands.

Samuel's brain was whirring. He realized that the fourth fist had hit him, and a great flood of emotion cried out that the law that had inexorably ruled his life was in motion again. In a half-daze he got up and strode from the room.

The next ten minutes were perhaps the hardest of his life. People talk of the courage of convictions, but in actual life a man's duty to his family may make a rigid course seem a selfish indulgence of his own righteousness. Samuel thought mostly of his family, yet he never really wavered. That jolt had brought him to.

When he came back in the room there were a lot of worried faces waiting for him, but he didn't waste any time explaining.

"Gentlemen," he said, "Mr McIntyre has been kind enough to convince me that in this matter you are absolutely right, and the Peter Carhart interests absolutely wrong. As far as I am concerned, you can keep your ranches to the rest of your days."

He pushed his way through an astounded gathering, and within a half-hour he had sent two telegrams that staggered the operator into complete unfitness for business; one was to Hamil in San Antonio; one was to Peter Carhart in New York.

Samuel didn't sleep much that night. He knew that for the first time in his business career he had made a dismal, miserable failure. But some instinct in him, stronger than will, deeper than training, had forced him to do what would probably end his ambitions and his happiness. But it was done, and it never occurred to him that he could have acted otherwise.

Next morning two telegrams were waiting for him. The first was from Hamil. It contained three words:

"You blamed idiot!"

The second was from New York:

"Deal off come to New York immediately Carhart."

Within a week things had happened. Hamil quarrelled furiously and violently defended his scheme. He was summoned to New York, and spent a bad half-hour on the carpet in Peter Carhart's office. He broke with the Carhart interests in July, and in August Samuel Meredith, at thirty-five years old, was, to all intents, made Carhart's partner. The fourth fist had done its work.

I suppose that there's a caddish streak in every man that runs crosswise across his character and disposition and general outlook. With some men it's secret and we never know it's there until they strike us in the dark one night. But Samuel's showed when it was in action, and the sight of it made people see red. He was rather lucky in that, because every time his little devil came up it met a reception that sent it scurrying down below in a sickly, feeble condition. It was the same devil, the same streak that made him order Gilly's friends off the bed, that made him go inside Marjorie's house.

If you could run your hand along Samuel Meredith's jaw, you'd feel a lump. He admits he's never been sure which fist left it there, but he wouldn't lose it for anything. He says there's no cad like an old cad, and that sometimes, just before making a decision, it's a great help to stroke his chin. The reporters call it a nervous characteristic, but it's not that. It's so he can feel again the gorgeous clarity, the lightning sanity of those four fists.

Note on the Text

The text in the present edition is based on the fourth printing of the first edition of *Flappers and Philosophers* (1920). The spelling and punctuation have been anglicized, standardized, modernized and made consistent throughout.

Notes

p. 3, *The Revolt of the Angels, by Anatole France*: A novel (1914) by the Nobel Prize-winning French author Anatole France (1844–1924).

p. 7, *the statue of France Aroused*: A statue by the American sculptor Jo Davidson (1883–1952) commissioned as a war memorial for the village of Senlis.

p. 10, *Stonewall Jackson claimed that lemon juice cleared his head*: A reference to the popular belief that the Confederate general Thomas Jonathan "Stonewall" Jackson (1824–63) regularly sucked on lemons on the battlefield.

p. 20, *Booker T. Washington*: Booker T. Washington (1856–1915) was a prominent African-American activist, orator and writer.

p. 25, *Pollyanna*: The protagonist of the eponymous 1913 best-seller by Eleanor H. Porter (1868–1920), a character who became a byword for optimism.

p. 45, *Then blow... I will go*: From a famous traditional English folk song.

p. 49, *Dangerous Dan McGrew*: A reference to *The Shooting of Dan McGrew*, a 1907 narrative poem by Robert W. Service (1874–1958).

p. 53, *Peer Gynt*: An 1876 play by Henrik Ibsen (1828–1906), for which Edvard Grieg (1843–1907) famously composed the music.

p. 53, *the Serbia in the case*: A reference to the Bosnian Serb Gavrilo Princip's (1894–18) assassination of the Archduke Franz Ferdinand of Austria (1875–1914), which precipitated the First World War.

p. 55, *'Dixie'*: A popular mid-nineteenth century American song of uncertain origin.

p. 57, *Kubla Khan... caves of ice*: Ll. 33–34 from 'Kubla Khan' (1816) by Samuel Taylor Coleridge (1772–1834).

p. 58, *'Hail, Hail, the Gang's All Here!'*: A popular 1917 song written by Arthur Sullivan (1842–1900), with words by Theodora Morse (1883–1953).

p. 63, *George M. Cohan was composing 'Over There'*: George M. Cohan (1878–1942) composed this song, very popular with soldiers during the First World War, in 1917.

p. 63, *the battle Château-Thierry*: A famous Allied victory against the Germans in June 1918 near Paris.

p. 65, *Omar Khayyam*: Omar Khayyam (1048–1131) was a Persian polymath who became most famous to English-speaking audiences for his *rubaiyat* poems.

p. 66, *ten-twenty-thirty*: A cheap and popular theatre production.

p. 66, *I just call you Omar because you remind me of a smoked cigarette*: Omar was a brand of cigarettes at the time inspired by Omar Khayyam.

p. 66, *the Florodora Sextet*: A reference to the cast of the popular 1899 musical *Florodora*.

p. 66, *Mrs Sol Smith's Juliet*: A reference to a performance as Shakespeare's Juliet by Elizabeth Smith (*c.*1912–87), the wife of the theatre impresario Sol Smith.

p. 68, *Uncle Remus*: The fictional African-American narrator of folk tales written and compiled by Joel Chandler Harris (1848–1908).

p. 69, *Bergsonian*: Pertaining to the philosophy of Henri Bergson (1859–1941).

p. 69, *The Bohemian Girl*: An 1843 opera composed by Michael William Balfe (1808–70), with a libretto by Alfred Bunn (1796–1860).

p. 81, *Mens sana in corpore sano*: "A healthy mind in a healthy body" (Latin), a famous adage originally found in Juvenal, Satires x, 356.

p. 82, *quod erat demonstrandum*: "That which was to be proved" (Latin).

p. 86, *as Schopenhauer had popularized pessimism and William James pragmatism*: Arthur Schopenhauer (1788–1860) was a leading exponent of philosophical pessimism, while William James (1842–1910) is the most famous philosopher associated with the American school of pragmatism.

p. 114, *Hiram Johnson or Ty Cobb*: Hiram Warren Johnson (1866–1945) was governor of California and one of the leading figures of the Progressive Party. Ty Cobb (1886–1961) was one of the most successful baseball players of his time.

p. 117, *Annie Fellows Johnston*: Annie Fellows Johnston (1863–1931) was the author of the series of popular children's novels *The Little Colonel*.

p. 122, *Don't you think common kindness... quote Little Women*: Although Bernice does not quote directly from *Little Women* (1868–69) by Louisa May Alcott (1832–88), Marjorie seems to be dismissing the conventional sentiments the novel was seen to espouse.

p. 151, '*O Salutaris Hostia*': "O Saving Host" (Latin), from a hymn written by St Thomas Aquinas for the feast of Corpus Christi.

p. 158, *General Pershing and Sergeant York*: General John J. Pershing (1860–1948) led the American forces during the First World War. Sergeant Alvin C. York (1887–1964) was an American soldier who distinguished himself for bravery in the First World War and was awarded the Medal of Honor.

p. 161, *Robert Service*: See note to p. 49.

Extra Material

on

F. Scott Fitzgerald's

Flappers and Philosophers

F. Scott Fitzgerald's Life

Francis Scott Key Fitzgerald was born on 24th September 1896 at 481 Laurel Avenue in St Paul, Minnesota. Fitzgerald, who would always be known as "Scott", was named after Francis Scott Key, the author of 'The Star-Spangled Banner' and his father's second cousin three times removed. His mother, Mary "Mollie" McQuillan, was born in 1860 in one of St Paul's wealthier streets, and would come into a modest inheritance at the death of her father in 1877. His father, Edward Fitzgerald, was born in 1853 near Rockville, Maryland. A wicker-furniture manufacturer at the time of Fitzgerald's birth, his business would collapse in 1898 and he would then take to the road as a wholesale grocery salesman for Procter & Gamble. This change of job necessitated various moves of home and the family initially shifted east to Buffalo, New York, in 1898, and then on to Syracuse, New York, in 1901. By 1903 they were back in Buffalo and in March 1908 they were in St Paul again after Edward lost his job at Procter & Gamble. The *déclassé* Fitzgeralds would initially live with the McQuillans and then moved into a series of rented houses, settling down at 599 Summit Avenue.

Early Life

This itinerancy would disrupt Fitzgerald's early schooling, isolating him and making it difficult to make many friends at his various schools in Buffalo, Syracuse and St Paul. The first one at which Fitzgerald would settle for a prolonged period was the St Paul Academy, which he entered in September 1908. It was here that Fitzgerald would achieve his first appearance in print, 'The Mystery of the Raymond Mortgage', which appeared in the St Paul Academy school magazine *Now and Then* in October 1909. 'Reade, Substitute Right Half' and 'A Debt of Honor' would follow in the February and March 1910 numbers, and 'The Room with the Green Blinds' in the June 1911 number. His reading at this time was dominated by adventure stories and the other typical literary interests of a turn-of-the-century American teen, with the novels of G.A. Henty, Walter Scott's *Ivanhoe* and Jane Porter's *The Scottish Chiefs* among his favourites; their influence was apparent in the floridly melodramatic tone of his early pieces, though themes that would recur throughout

Schooling and Early Writings

Fitzgerald's mature fiction, such as the social difficulties of the outsider, would be introduced in these stories. An interest in the theatre also surfaced at this time, with Fitzgerald writing and taking the lead role in *The Girl from Lazy J*, a play that would be performed with a local amateur-dramatic group, the Elizabethan Drama Club, in August 1911. The group would also produce *The Captured Shadow* in 1912, *The Coward* in 1913 and *Assorted Spirits* in 1914.

At the end of the summer of 1911, Fitzgerald was once again uprooted (in response to poor academic achievements) and moved to the Newman School, a private Catholic school in Hackensack, New Jersey. He was singularly unpopular with the other boys, who considered him aloof and overbearing. This period as a social pariah at Newman was a defining time for Fitzgerald, one that would be echoed repeatedly in his fiction, most straightforwardly in the "Basil" stories, the most famous of which, 'The Freshest Boy', would appear in *The Saturday Evening Post* in July 1928 and is clearly autobiographical in its depiction of a boastful schoolboy's social exclusion.

Hackensack had, however, the advantage of proximity to New York City, and Fitzgerald began to get to know Manhattan, visiting a series of shows, including *The Quaker Girl* and *Little Boy Blue*. His first publication in Newman's school magazine, *The Newman News*, was 'Football', a poem written in an attempt to appease his peers following a traumatic incident on the football field that led to widespread accusation of cowardice, compounding the young writer's isolation. In his last year at Newman he would publish three stories in *The Newman News*.

Father Fay and the Catholic Influence

Also in that last academic year Fitzgerald would encounter the prominent Catholic priest Father Cyril Sigourney Webster Fay, a lasting and formative connection that would influence the author's character, oeuvre and career. Father Fay introduced Fitzgerald to such figures as Henry Adams and encouraged the young writer towards the aesthetic and moral understanding that underpins all of his work. In spite of the licence and debauchery for which Fitzgerald's life and work are often read, a strong moral sense informs all of his fiction – a sense that can be readily traced to Fay and the author's Catholic schooling at Newman. Fay would later appear in thinly disguised form as Amory Blaine's spiritual mentor, and man of the world, Monsignor Darcy, in *This Side of Paradise*.

Princeton

Fitzgerald's academic performance was little improved at Newman, and he would fail four courses in his two years there. In spite of this, in May 1913 Fitzgerald took the entrance exams for Princeton, the preferred destination for Catholic undergraduates in New Jersey. He would go up in September 1913, his fees paid for through a legacy left by his grandmother Louisa McQuillan, who had died in August.

At Princeton Fitzgerald would begin to work in earnest on the process of turning himself into an author: in his first year he met confrères and future collaborators John Peale Bishop and Edmund Wilson. During his freshman year Fitzgerald won a competition to write the book and lyrics for the 1914–15 Triangle Club (the Princeton dramatic society) production *Fie! Fie! Fi-Fi!* He would also co-author, with Wilson, the 1915–16 production, *The Evil Eye*, and the lyrics for *Safety First*, the 1916–17 offering. He also quickly began to contribute to the Princeton humour magazine *The Princeton Tiger*, while his reading tastes had moved on to the social concerns of George Bernard Shaw, Compton Mackenzie and H.G. Wells. His social progress at Princeton also seemed assured as Fitzgerald was approached by the Cottage Club (one of Princeton's exclusive eating clubs) and prominence in the Triangle Club seemed inevitable.

September 1914 and the beginning of Fitzgerald's sophomore year would mark the great calamity of his Princeton education, causing a trauma that Fitzgerald would approach variously in his writing (notably in *This Side of Paradise* and Gatsby's abortive "Oxford" career in *The Great Gatsby*). Poor academic performance meant that Fitzgerald was barred from extra-curricular activities; he was therefore unable to perform in *Fie! Fie! Fi-Fi!*, and took to the road with the production in an attendant capacity. Fitzgerald's progress at the Triangle and Cottage clubs stagnated (he made Secretary at Triangle nonetheless, but did not reach the heights he had imagined for himself), and his hopes of social dominance on campus were dashed.

The second half of the 1914–15 academic year saw a brief improvement and subsequent slipping of Fitzgerald's performance in classes, perhaps in response to a budding romance with Ginevra King, a sixteen-year-old socialite from Lake Forest, Illinois. Their courtship would continue until January 1917. King would become the model for a series of Fitzgerald's characters, including Judy Jones in the 1922 short story 'Winter Dreams', Isabelle Borgé in *This Side of Paradise* and, most famously, Daisy Miller in *The Great Gatsby*. In November 1915 Fitzgerald's academic career was once again held up when he was diagnosed with malaria (though it is likely that this was in fact the first appearance of the tuberculosis that would sporadically disrupt his health for the rest of his life) and left Princeton for the rest of the semester to recuperate. At the same time as all of this disruption, however, Fitzgerald was building a head of steam in terms of his literary production. Publications during this period included stories, reviews and poems for Princeton's *Nassau Literary Magazine*.

Ginevra King and Ill Health

Army
Commission

The USA entered the Great War in May 1917 and a week later Fitzgerald joined up, at least partly motivated by the fact that his uncompleted courses at Princeton would automatically receive credits as he signed up. Three weeks of intensive training and the infantry commission exam soon followed, though a commission itself did not immediately materialize. Through the summer he stayed in St Paul, undertaking important readings in William James, Henri Bergson and others, and in the autumn he returned to Princeton (though not to study) and took lodgings with John Biggs Jr, the editor of the *Tiger*. More contributions appeared in both the *Nassau Literary Magazine* and the *Tiger*, but the commission finally came and in November Fitzgerald was off to Fort Leavenworth, Kansas, where he was to report as a second lieutenant in the infantry. Convinced that he would die in the war, Fitzgerald began intense work on his first novel, *The Romantic Egoist*, the first draft of which would be finished while on leave from Kansas in February 1918. The publishing house Charles Scribner's Sons, despite offering an encouraging appreciation of the novel, rejected successive drafts in August and October 1918.

Zelda Sayre

As his military training progressed and the army readied Fitzgerald and his men for the fighting in Europe, he was relocated, first to Camp Gordon in Georgia, and then on to Camp Sheridan, near Montgomery, Alabama. There, at a dance at the Montgomery Country Club in July, he met Zelda Sayre, a beautiful eighteen-year-old socialite and daughter of a justice of the Alabama Supreme Court. An intense courtship began and Fitzgerald soon proposed marriage, though Zelda was nervous about marrying a man with so few apparent prospects.

As the armistice that ended the Great War was signed on 11th November 1918, Fitzgerald was waiting to embark for Europe, and had already been issued with his overseas uniform. The closeness by which he avoided action in the Great War stayed with Fitzgerald, and gave him another trope for his fiction, with many of his characters, Amory Blaine from *This Side of Paradise* and Jay Gatsby among them, attributed with abortive or ambiguous military careers. Father Fay, who had been involved, and had tried to involve Fitzgerald, in a series of mysterious intelligence operations during the war, died in January 1919, leaving Fitzgerald without a moral guide just as he entered the world free from the restrictions of Princeton and the army. Fay would be the dedicatee of *This Side of Paradise*.

Literary
Endeavours

Fitzgerald's first move after the war was to secure gainful employment at Barron Collier, an advertising agency, producing copy for trolley-car advertisements. At night he continued to work hard at his fiction, collecting 112 rejection slips over this period. Relief was close at hand, however, with *The Smart Set* printing a revised version of 'Babes in the Wood' (a short story that had previous appeared in *Nassau Literary Magazine* and that would soon be cannibalized for *This Side of Paradise*) in their September 1919 issue. *The Smart Set*, edited by this time by H.L. Mencken and George Jean Nathan, who would both become firm supporters of Fitzgerald's talent, was a respected literary magazine, but not a high payer; Fitzgerald received $30 for this first appearance. Buoyed by this, and frustrated by his job, Fitzgerald elected to leave work and New York and return to his parents' house in St Paul, where he would make a concerted effort to finish his novel. As none of the early drafts of *The Romantic Egoist* survive, it is impossible to say with complete certainty how much of that project was preserved in the draft of *This Side of Paradise* that emerged at St Paul. It was, at any rate, more attractive to Scribner in its new form, and the editor Maxwell Perkins, who would come to act as both editor and personal banker for Fitzgerald, wrote on 16th September to say that the novel had been accepted. Soon after he would hire Harold Ober to act as his agent, an arrangement that would continue throughout the greatest years of Fitzgerald's output and that would benefit the author greatly, despite sometimes causing Ober a great deal of difficulty and anxiety. Though Fitzgerald would consider his novels the artistically important part of his work, it would be his short stories, administered by Ober, which would provide the bulk of his income. Throughout his career a regular supply of short stories appeared between his novels, a supply that became more essential and more difficult to maintain as the author grew older.

Newly confident after the acceptance of *This Side of Paradise*, Fitzgerald set about revising a series of his previous stories, securing another four publications in *The Smart Set*, one in *Scribner's Magazine* and one in *The Saturday Evening Post*, an organ that would prove to be one of the author's most dependable sources of income for many years to come. By the end of 1919 Fitzgerald had made $879 from writing: not yet a living, but a start. His receipts would quickly increase. Thanks to Ober's skilful assistance *The Saturday Evening Post* had taken another six stories by February 1920, at $400 each. In March *This Side of Paradise* was published and proved to be a surprising success, selling 3,000 in its first three days and making instant celebrities of Fitzgerald and Zelda, who would marry the author on 3rd April, her earlier concerns about her suitor's solvency apparently eased by his sudden literary success. During the whirl of 1920, the couple's *annus mirabilis*, other miraculous portents of a future of plenty included the sale of a story, 'Head and

Success

Shoulders', to Metro Films for $2,500, the sale of four stories to *Metropolitan Magazine* for $900 each and the rapid appearance of *Flappers and Philosophers*, a volume of stories, published by Scribner in September. By the end of the year Fitzgerald, still in his mid-twenties, had moved into an apartment on New York's West 59th Street and was hard at work on his second novel.

Zelda discovered she was pregnant in February 1921, and in May the couple headed to Europe where they visited various heroes and attractions, including John Galsworthy. They returned in July to St Paul, where a daughter, Scottie, was born on 26th October. Fitzgerald was working consistently and well at this time, producing a prodigious amount of high-quality material. *The Beautiful and Damned*, his second novel, was soon ready and began to appear as a serialization in *Metropolitan Magazine* from September. Its publication in book form would have to wait until March 1922, at which point it received mixed reviews, though Scribner managed to sell 40,000 copies of it in its first year of publication. Once again it would be followed within a few months by a short-story collection, *Tales of the Jazz Age*, which contained such classics of twentieth-century American literature as 'May Day', 'The Diamond as Big as the Ritz' and 'The Curious Case of Benjamin Button'.

1923 saw continued successes and a first failure. Receipts were growing rapidly: the Hearst organization bought first option in Fitzgerald's stories for $1,500, he sold the film rights for *This Side of Paradise* for $10,000 and he began selling stories to *The Saturday Evening Post* for $1,250 each. *The Vegetable*, on the other hand, a play that he had been working on for some time, opened in Atlantic City and closed almost immediately following poor reviews, losing Fitzgerald money. By the end of the year his income had shot up to $28,759.78, but he had spent more than that on the play and fast living, and found himself in debt as a result.

The Fitzgeralds' high living was coming at an even higher price. In an attempt to finish his new project Fitzgerald set out for Europe with Zelda and landed up on the French Riviera, a situation that provided the author with the space and time to make some real progress on his novel. While there, however, Zelda met Édouard Jozan, a French pilot, and began a romantic entanglement that put a heavy strain on her marriage. This scenario has been read by some as influencing the final drafting of *The Great Gatsby*, notably Gatsby's disillusionment with Daisy. It would also provide one of the central threads of *Tender Is the Night*, while Gerald and Sara Murphy, two friends they made on the Riviera, would be models for that novel's central characters. Throughout 1924 their relations became more difficult, their volatility was expressed through increasingly erratic behaviour and by the end of the year Fitzgerald's drinking was developing into alcoholism.

Some progress was made on the novel, however, and a draft was sent to Scribner in October. A period of extensive and crucial revisions followed through January and February 1925, with the novel already at the galley-proof stage. After extensive negotiations with Max Perkins, the new novel also received its final title at about this time. Previous titles had included *Trimalchio* and *Trimalchio in West Egg*, both of which Scribner found too obscure for a mass readership, despite Fitzgerald's preference for them, while *Gold-Hatted Gatsby*, *On the Road to West Egg*, *The High-Bouncing Lover* and *Among Ash Heaps and Millionaires* were also suggestions. Shortly before the novel was due to be published, Fitzgerald telegrammed Scribner with the possible title *Under the Red, White and Blue*, but it was too late, and the work was published as *The Great Gatsby* on 10th April. The reception for the new work was impressive, and it quickly garnered some of Fitzgerald's most enthusiastic reviews, but its sales did not reach the best-seller levels the author and Scribner had hoped for.

Fitzgerald was keen to get on with his work and, rather mis- *Paris* guidedly, set off to Paris with Zelda to begin his next novel. Paris at the heart of the Roaring Twenties was not a locale conducive to careful concentration, and little progress was made on the new project. There was much socializing, however, and Fitzgerald invested quite a lot of his time in cementing his reputation as one of the more prominent drunks of American letters. The couple's time was spent mostly with the American expatriate community, and among those he got to know there were Edith Wharton, Gertrude Stein, Robert McAlmon and Sylvia Beach of Shakespeare & Company. Perhaps the most significant relationship with another writer from this period was with Ernest Hemingway, with whom Fitzgerald spent much time (sparking jealousy in Zelda), and for whom he would become an important early supporter, helping to encourage Scribner to publish *The Torrents of Spring* and *The Sun Also Rises*, for which he also gave extensive editorial advice. The summer of 1925 was again spent on the Riviera, but this time with a rowdier crowd (which included John Dos Passos, Archibald MacLeish and Rudolph Valentino) and little progress was made on the new book. February 1926 saw publication of the inevitable follow-up short-story collection, this time *All the Sad Young Men*, of which the most significant pieces were 'The Rich Boy', 'Winter Dreams' and 'Absolution'. All three are closely associated with *The Great Gatsby*, and can be read as alternative routes into the Gatsby story.

Hollywood

With the new novel still effectively stalled, Fitzgerald decamped to Hollywood at the beginning of 1927, where he was engaged by United Artists to write a flapper comedy that was never produced in the end. These false starts were not, however, adversely affecting Fitzgerald's earnings, and 1927 would represent the highest annual earnings the author had achieved so far: $29,757.87, largely from short-story sales. While in California Fitzgerald began a dalliance with Lois Moran, a seventeen-year-old aspiring actress – putting further strain on his relationship with Zelda. After the couple moved back east (to Delaware) Zelda began taking ballet lessons in an attempt to carve a niche for herself that might offer her a role beyond that of the wife of a famous author. She would also make various attempts to become an author in her own right. The lessons would continue under the tutelage of Lubov Egorova when the Fitzgeralds moved to Paris in the summer of 1928, with Zelda's obsessive commitment to dance practice worrying those around her and offering the signs of the mental illness that was soon to envelop her.

Looking for a steady income stream (in spite of very high earnings expenditure was still outstripping them), Fitzgerald set to work on the "Basil" stories in 1928, earning $31,500 for nine that appeared in *The Saturday Evening Post*, forcing novel-writing into the background. The next year his *Post* fee would rise to $4,000 a story. Throughout the next few years he would move between the USA and Europe, desperate to resuscitate that project, but make little inroads.

Zelda's Mental
Illness

By 1930 Zelda's behaviour was becoming more and more erratic, and on 23rd April she was checked into the Malmaison clinic near Paris for rest and assistance with her mental problems. Deeply obsessed with her dancing lessons, and infatuated with Egorova, she discharged herself from the clinic on 11th May and attempted suicide a few days later. After this she was admitted to the care of Dr Oscar Forel in Switzerland, who diagnosed her as schizophrenic. Such care was expensive and placed a new financial strain on Fitzgerald, who responded by selling another series of stories to the *Post* and earning $32,000 for the year. The most significant story of this period was 'Babylon Revisited'. Zelda improved and moved back to Montgomery, Alabama, and the care of the Sayre family in September 1931. That autumn Fitzgerald would make another abortive attempt to break into Hollywood screenwriting.

At the beginning of 1932 Zelda suffered a relapse during a trip to Florida and was admitted to the Henry Phipps Psychiatric Clinic in Baltimore. While there she would finish work on a novel, *Save Me the Waltz*, that covered some of the same material her husband was using in his novel about the Riviera. Upon completion she sent the manuscript to Perkins at Scribner, without passing it to her husband, which caused much distress. Fitzgerald helped her to edit the book nonetheless, removing much of the material he intended to use, and Scribner accepted it and published it on 7th October. It received poor reviews and did not sell. Finally accepting that she had missed her chance to become a professional dancer, Zelda now poured her energies into painting. Fitzgerald would organize a show of these in New York in 1934, and a play, *Scandalabra*, that would be performed by the Junior Vagabonds, an amateur Baltimore drama group, in the spring of 1933.

His own health now beginning to fail, Fitzgerald returned to his own novel and rewrote extensively through 1933, finally submitting it in October. *Tender Is the Night* would appear in serialized form in *Scribner's Magazine* from January to April 1934 and would then be published, in amended form, on 12th April. It was generally received positively and sold well, though again not to the blockbusting extent that Fitzgerald had hoped for. This would be Fitzgerald's final completed novel. He was thirty-seven.

Final Novel

With the receipts for *Tender Is the Night* lower than had been hoped for and Zelda still erratic and requiring expensive medical supervision, Fitzgerald's finances were tight. From this point on he found it increasingly difficult to produce the kind of high-quality, extended pieces that could earn thousands of dollars in glossies like *The Saturday Evening Post*. From 1934 many of his stories were shorter and brought less money, while some of them were simply sub-standard. Of the outlets for this new kind of work, *Esquire* proved the most reliable, though it only paid $250 a piece, a large drop from his salad days at the *Post*.

Financial Problems and Artistic Decline

March 1935 saw the publication of *Taps at Reveille*, another collection of short stories from Scribner. It was a patchy collection, but included the important 'Babylon Revisited', while 'Crazy Sunday' saw his first sustained attempt at writing about Hollywood, a prediction of the tendency of much of his work to come. His next significant writing came, however, with three articles that appeared in the February, March and April 1936 numbers of *Esquire*: 'The Crack-up', 'Pasting It Together' and 'Handle with Care'. These essays were brutally confessional, and irritated many of those around Fitzgerald, who felt that he was airing his dirty laundry in public. His agent Harold Ober was concerned that by publicizing his own battles with depression and alcoholism he would give the high-paying glossies the impression that he was unreliable, making future magazine work harder to come by. The pieces have, however, come to be regarded as Fitzgerald's greatest non-fiction work and are an essential document in both the construction of his own legend and in the mythologizing of the Jazz Age.

Suicide Attempt and Worsening Health

Later in 1936, on the author's fortieth birthday in September, he gave an interview in *The New York Post* to Michael Mok. The article was a sensationalist hatchet job entitled 'Scott Fitzgerald, 40, Engulfed in Despair' and showed him as a depressed dipsomaniac. The publication of the article wounded Fitzgerald further and he tried to take his own life through an overdose of morphine. After this his health continued to deteriorate and various spates in institutions followed, for influenza, for tuberculosis and, repeatedly, in attempts to treat his alcoholism.

His inability to rely on his own physical and literary powers meant a significant drop in his earning capabilities; by 1937 his debts exceeded $40,000, much of which was owed to his agent Ober and his editor Perkins, while Fitzgerald still had to pay Zelda's medical fees and support his daughter and himself. A solution to this desperate situation appeared in July: MGM would hire him as a screenwriter at $1,000 a week for six months. He went west, hired an apartment and set about his work. He contributed to various films, usually in collaboration with other writers, a system that irked him. Among these were *A Yank at Oxford* and various stillborn projects, including *Infidelity*, which was to have starred Joan Crawford, and an adaptation of 'Babylon Revisited'. He only received one screen credit from this time, for an adaptation of Erich Maria Remarque's novel *Three Comrades*, produced by Joseph Mankiewicz. His work on this picture led to a renewal of his contract, but no more credits followed.

Sheila Graham

While in Hollywood Fitzgerald met Sheila Graham, a twenty-eight-year-old English gossip columnist, with whom he began an affair. Graham, who initially attracted Fitzgerald because of her physical similarity to the youthful Zelda, became Fitzgerald's partner during the last years of his life, cohabiting with the author quite openly in Los Angeles. It seems unlikely that Zelda, still in medical care, ever knew about her. Graham had risen up from a rather murky background in England and Fitzgerald set about improving her with his "College of One", aiming to introduce her to his favoured writers and thinkers. She would be the model for Kathleen Moore in *The Last Tycoon*.

Among the film projects he worked on at this time were *Madame Curie* and *Gone with the Wind*, neither of which earned him a credit. The contract with MGM was terminated in 1939 and Fitzgerald became a freelance screenwriter. While engaged on the screenplay for *Winter Carnival* for United

Artists, Fitzgerald went on a drinking spree at Dartmouth College, resulting in his getting fired. A final period of alcoholic excess followed, marring a trip to Cuba with Zelda in April and worsening his financial straits. At this time Ober finally pulled the plug and refused to lend Fitzgerald any more money, though he would continue to support Scottie, Fitzgerald's daughter, whom the Obers had effectively brought up. The writer, now his own agent, began working on a Hollywood novel based on the life of the famous Hollywood producer Irving Thalberg. Hollywood would also be the theme of the last fiction Fitzgerald would see published; the Pat Hobby stories. These appeared in *Esquire* beginning in January 1940 and continued till after the author's death, ending in July 1941 and appearing in each monthly number between those dates.

In November 1940 Fitzgerald suffered a heart attack and was told to rest, which he did at Graham's apartment. On 21st December he had another heart attack and died, aged just forty-four. Permission was refused to bury him in St Mary's Church in Rockville, Maryland, where his father had been buried, because Fitzgerald was not a practising Catholic. Instead he was buried at Rockville Union Cemetery on 27th December 1940. In 1975 Scottie Fitzgerald would successfully petition to have her mother and father moved to the family plot at St Mary's. *Death*

Following Fitzgerald's death his old college friend Edmund Wilson would edit Fitzgerald's incomplete final novel, shaping his drafts and notes into *The Last Tycoon*, which was published in 1941 by Scribner. Wilson also collected Fitzgerald's confessional *Esquire* pieces and published them with a selection of related short stories and essays as *The Crack-up and Other Pieces and Stories* in 1945.

Zelda lived on until 1948, in and out of mental hospitals. After reading *The Last Tycoon* she began work on *Caesar's Things*, a novel that was not finished when the Highland hospital caught fire and she died, locked in her room in preparation for electro-shock therapy.

F. Scott Fitzgerald's Works

Fitzgerald's first novel, *This Side of Paradise*, set the tone for his later classic works. The novel was published in 1920 and was a remarkable success, impressing critics and readers alike. Amory Blaine, the directionless and guilelessly dissolute protagonist, is an artistically semi-engaged innocent, and perilously, though charmingly unconsciously, déclassé. His long drift towards destruction (and implicit reincarnation as Fitzgerald himself) *This Side of Paradise* sees Blaine's various arrogances challenged one by one as he moves from a well-heeled life in the Midwest through private school and middling social successes at Princeton towards a life of vague and unrewarding artistic involvement. Beneath Fitzgerald's precise observations of American high society in the late 1910s can be witnessed the creation of a wholly new American type, and Blaine would become a somewhat seedy role model for his generation. Fast-living and nihilist tendencies would become the character traits of Fitzgerald's set and the Lost Generation more generally. Indeed, by the novel's end, it has become clear that Blaine's experiences of lost love, a hostile society and the deaths of his mother and friends have imparted important life lessons upon him. Blaine, having returned to a Princeton that he has outgrown and poised before an unknowable future, ends the novel with his Jazz Age *cogito*: "'I know myself,' he cried, 'but that is all.'"

Flappers and Philosophers

Fitzgerald's next publication would continue this disquisition on his era and peers: *Flappers and Philosophers* (1920) is a collection of short stories, including such famous pieces as 'Bernice Bobs Her Hair' and 'The Ice Palace'. The first of these tells the tale of Bernice, who visits her cousin Marjorie only to find herself rejected for being a stop on Marjorie's social activities. Realizing that she can't rid herself of Bernice, Marjorie decides to coach her to become a young femme fatale like herself – and Bernice is quickly a hit with the town boys. Too much of a hit though, and Marjorie takes her revenge by persuading Bernice that it would be to her social advantage to bob her hair. It turns out not to be and Bernice leaves the town embarrassed, but not before cutting off Marjorie's pigtails in her sleep and taking them with her to the station.

The Beautiful and Damned

The Beautiful and Damned (1922) would follow, another novel that featured a thinly disguised portrait of Fitzgerald in the figure of the main character, Anthony Patch. He was joined by a fictionalized version of Fitzgerald's new wife Zelda, whom the author married as *This Side of Paradise* went to press. The couple are here depicted on a rapidly downward course that both mirrored and predicted the Fitzgeralds' own trajectory. Patch is the heir apparent of his reforming grandfather's sizable fortune but lives a life of dissolution in the city, promising that he'll find gainful employment. He marries Gloria Gilbert, a great but turbulent beauty, and they gradually descend into alcoholism, wasting what little capital Anthony has on high living and escapades. When his grandfather walks in on a scene of debauchery, Anthony is disinherited and the Patches' decline quickens. When the grandfather dies,

Anthony embarks on a legal case to reclaim the money from the good causes to which it has been donated and wins their case, although not before Anthony has lost his mind and Gloria her beauty.

Another volume of short stories, *Tales of the Jazz Age*, was published later in the same year, in accordance with Scribner's policy of quickly following successful novels with moneymaking collections of short stories. Throughout this period Fitzgerald was gaining for himself a reputation as America's premier short-story writer, producing fiction for a selection of high-profile "glossy" magazines and earning unparalleled fees for his efforts. The opportunities and the pressures of this commercial work, coupled with Fitzgerald's continued profligacy, led to a certain unevenness in his short fiction. This unevenness is clearly present in *Tales of the Jazz Age*, with some of Fitzgerald's very best work appearing beside some fairly average pieces. Among the great works were 'The Diamond as Big as the Ritz' and the novella 'May Day'. The first of these tells the story of the Washingtons, a family that live in seclusion in the wilds of Montana on top of a mountain made of solid diamond. The necessity of keeping the source of their wealth hidden from all makes the Washingtons' lives a singular mixture of great privilege and isolation; friends that visit the children are briefly treated to luxury beyond their imagining and are then executed to secure the secrecy of the Washington diamond. When young Percy's friend John T. Unger makes a visit during the summer vacation their unusual lifestyle and their diamond are lost for ever.

Tales of the Jazz Age

The novella 'May Day' is very different in style and execution, but deals with some of the same issues, in particular the exigencies of American capitalism in the aftermath of the Great War. It offers a panorama of Manhattan's post-war social order as the anti-communist May Day Riots of 1919 unfold. A group of privileged Yale alumni enjoy the May Day ball and bicker about their love interests, while ex-soldiers drift around the edges of their world.

In spite of the apparent success that Fitzgerald was experiencing by this time, his next novel came with greater difficulty than his first four volumes. *The Great Gatsby* is the story of Jay Gatsby, born poor as James Gatz, an *arriviste* of mysterious origins who sets himself up in high style on Long Island's north shore only to find disappointment and his demise there. Like Fitzgerald, and some of his other characters, including Anthony Patch, Gatsby falls in love during the war, this time with Daisy Miller. Following Gatsby's departure, however, Daisy marries the greatly wealthy Tom Buchanan,

The Great Gatsby

which convinces Gatsby that he lost her only because of his penuriousness. Following this, Gatsby builds himself a fortune comparable to Buchanan's through mysterious and proscribed means and, five years after Daisy broke off their relations, uses his newfound wealth to throw a series of parties from an enormous house across the water from Buchanan's Long Island pile. His intention is to impress his near neighbour Daisy with the lavishness of his entertainments, but he miscalculates and the "old money" Buchanans stay away, not attracted by Gatsby's *parvenu* antics. Instead Gatsby approaches Nick Carraway, the novel's narrator (who took that role in one of the masterstrokes of the late stages of the novel's revision), Daisy's cousin and Gatsby's neighbour. Daisy is initially affected by Gatsby's devotion, to the extent that she agrees to leave Buchanan, but once Buchanan reveals Gatsby's criminal source of income she has second thoughts. Daisy, shocked by this revelation, accidentally kills Buchanan's mistress Myrtle in a hit-and-run accident with Gatsby in the car and returns to Buchanan, leaving Gatsby waiting for her answer. Buchanan then lets Myrtle's husband believe that Gatsby was driving the car and the husband shoots him, leaving him floating in the unused swimming pool of his great estate.

All the Sad Young Men

Of *All the Sad Young Men* (1926) the most well-known pieces are 'The Rich Boy', 'Winter Dreams' and 'Absolution'. All three have much in common with *The Great Gatsby*, in terms of the themes dealt with and the characters developed. 'The Rich Boy' centres on the rich young bachelor Anson Hunter, who has romantic dalliances with women, but never marries and grows increasingly lonely. 'Winter Dreams' tells the tale of Dexter Green and Judy Jones, similar characters to Jay Gatsby and Daisy Miller. Much like Gatsby, Green raises himself from nothing with the intention of winning Jones's affections. And, like Gatsby, he finds the past lost. 'Absolution' is a rejected false start on *The Great Gatsby* and deals with a young boy's difficulties around the confessional and an encounter with a deranged priest.

'Babylon Revisited' is probably the greatest and most read story of the apparently fallow period between *The Great Gatsby* and *Tender Is the Night*. It deals with Charlie Wales, an American businessman who enacts some of Fitzgerald's guilt for his apparent abandonment of his daughter Scottie and wife Zelda. Wales returns to a Paris unknown to him since he gave up drinking. There he fights his dead wife's family for custody of his daughter, only to find that friends from his past undo his careful efforts.

The next, and last completed, novel came even harder, and it would not be until 1934 that *Tender Is the Night* would appear. This novel was met by mixed reviews and low, but not disastrous sales. It has remained controversial among readers of Fitzgerald and is hailed by some as his masterpiece and others as an aesthetic failure. The plotting is less finely wrought than the far leaner *The Great Gatsby*, and apparent chronological inconsistencies and longueurs have put off some readers. The unremitting detail of Dick Diver's descent, however, is unmatched in Fitzgerald's oeuvre.

Tender Is the Night

It begins with an impressive set-piece description of life on the Riviera during the summer of 1925. There Rosemary Hoyt, modelled on the real-life actress Lois Moran, meets Dick and Nicole Driver, and becomes infatuated with Dick. It is then revealed that Dick had been a successful psychiatrist and had met Nicole when she was his patient, being treated in the aftermath of being raped by her father. Now Dick is finding it difficult to maintain his research interests in the social whirl that Nicole's money has thrust him into. Dick is forced out of a Swiss clinic for his unreliability and incipient alcoholism. Later Dick consummates his relationship with Rosemary on a trip to Rome, and gets beaten by police after drunkenly involving himself in a fight. When the Divers return to the Riviera Dick drinks more and Nicole leaves him for Tommy Barban, a French-American mercenary soldier (based on Zelda's Riviera beau Édouard Jozan). Dick returns to America, where he becomes a provincial doctor and disappears.

The "Pat Hobby" stories are the most remarkable product of Fitzgerald's time in Hollywood to see publication during the author's lifetime. Seventeen stories appeared in all, in consecutive issues of *Esquire* through 1940 and 1941. Hobby is a squalid Hollywood hack fallen upon hard times and with the days of his great success, measured by on-screen credits, some years behind him. He is a generally unsympathetic character and most of the stories depict him in unflattering situations, saving his own skin at the expense of those around him. It speaks to the hardiness of Fitzgerald's talent that even at this late stage he was able to make a character as amoral as Hobby vivid and engaging on the page. The Hobby stories are all short, evidencing Fitzgerald's skill in his later career at compressing storylines that would previously have been extrapolated far further.

Pat Hobby Stories

Fitzgerald's final project was *The Last Tycoon*, a work which, in the partial and provisional version that was published after the author's death, has all the hallmarks of a quite remarkable work. The written portion of the novel, which it seems likely would have been rewritten extensively before publication (in accordance with Fitzgerald's previous practice), is a classic conjuring of the

The Last Tycoon

golden age of Hollywood through an ambiguous and suspenseful story of love and money. The notes that follow the completed portion of *The Last Tycoon* suggest that the story would have developed in a much more melodramatic direction, with Stahr embarking on transcontinental business trips, losing his edge, ordering a series of murders and dying in an aeroplane crash. If the rewrites around *Tender Is the Night* are anything to go by, it seems likely that Fitzgerald would have toned down Stahr's adventures before finishing the story: in the earlier novel stories of matricide and other violent moments had survived a number of early drafts, only to be cut before the book took its final form.

– Richard Parker

Select Bibliography

Standard Edition:
The Cambridge University Press edition (2012) of *Flappers and Philosophers*, with extensive annotations, variants and background material, is the most authoritative edition to date.

Biographies:
Bruccoli, Matthew J., *Some Sort of Epic Grandeur: The Life of F. Scott Fitzgerald*, 2nd edn. (Columbia, SC: University of South Carolina Press, 2002)
Mizener, Arthur, *The Far Side of Paradise: A Biography of F. Scott Fitzgerald*, (Boston, MS: Houghton Mifflin, 1951)
Turnbull, Andrew, *Scott Fitzgerald* (Harmondsworth: Penguin, 1970)

Additional Recommended Background Material:
Curnutt, Kirk, ed., *A Historical Guide to F. Scott Fitzgerald* (Oxford: Oxford University Press, 2004)
Prigozy, Ruth, ed., *The Cambridge Companion to F. Scott Fitzgerald* (Cambridge: Cambridge University Press, 2002)